SKYWATCHERS

Also by Carrie Arcos

Crazy Messy Beautiful
We Are All That's Left

SKYWATCHERS

CARRIE ARCOS

PHILOMEL BOOKS

PHILOMEL BOOKS
An imprint of Penguin Random House LLC, New York

First published in the United States of America by Philomel,
an imprint of Penguin Random House LLC, 2020.

Philomel Books is a registered trademark of Penguin Random House LLC.

Visit us online at penguinrandomhouse.com

Library of Congress Cataloging-in-Publication Data is available.

Printed in the United States of America

ISBN 9781984812292

1 3 5 7 9 10 8 6 4 2

Edited by Liza Kaplan.
Design by Ellice M. Lee.
Text set in Goudy Modern MT Pro.

TO MY FAVORITE STUDENTS

(YOU KNOW WHO YOU ARE)

However, in this new age in which hostile forces are known to possess long-range bombers and atomic weapons, we cannot risk being caught unprepared to defend ourselves. We must have a trained force of skywatchers. If an enemy should try to attack us, we will need every minute and every second of warning that our skywatchers can give us.

—HARRY S. TRUMAN, JULY 12, 1952

What do you want to be *if* you grow up?

—J‎OKE TOLD IN THE 1950s

PROLOGUE

THE BOYS ALWAYS BROUGHT THE CIGARETTES, MATCHES, CARDS, and magazines. The matches served two purposes: fire for the smokes and currency for the games they played, mainly five card stud. In the winter, they would have lit the small stove in the corner. But it was late summer of 1952. And summer along the central coast of California meant warm days and nights, with a cool coastal breeze playing softly in the background like a Cole Porter song.

For the most part, the magazines remained stacked in a small pile during card games, perused later, at leisure, in between lookout duties. They were a compilation of *Popular Mechanics*, *Popular Science*, *Life*, *Amazing Stories*, and the *Saturday Evening Post*—the latter being left over from the older couple, Mabel and Jim, whose shift was right before the high school club.

The girls brought the snacks: usually chips and cookies, gum, sometimes small tuna sandwiches with pickles made by Eleanor's mom, and a portable radio. They kept the music on low. Not that they would have gotten in trouble. No official ever came to their tower. But the red phone on the small desk by the window and the sign with the rules posted over it was

• • • 1

enough to hint at the possibility of a swift reprimand from their supervisor.

They were good kids. Rule followers.

For the most part.

While the boys played poker, the girls talked or practiced dance moves they learned from watching television. It was still swing, but low and smooth, with steps different from their parents' swing. Caroline was the best, but she didn't flaunt it. She went slow so Eleanor could follow, while the boys pretended not to watch out of the corner of their eyes. But they always watched.

Growing up during World War II and now living with the reality of the Cold War between the United States and the Soviet Union, they were aware of how everything could end in a moment. In between shows like *I Love Lucy* and *What's My Line*, they sat next to their parents on the couch and watched Senator McCarthy grill government officials, artists, and entertainers about their salacious personal lives, exposing communists among the elite. Communists, they were warned, lurked everywhere—a cancer to the American way of life.

After the programs ended and the TVs glowed in the dark, their minds processed the world they lived in: unsafe and unpredictable. They balanced on the precarious edge of fear and paranoia, wondering if they'd even have a future of their own.

For Teddy, John, Caroline, Eleanor, Bunny, Frank, and Oscar, the Skywatch club was their answer.

The club was their chance to make a difference.

Twice a week, at six in the evening, for a couple of hours during their shift, they tilted their eyes toward the open sky— watching, waiting for the future to drop.

1

TEDDY

TEDDY STOOD AT THE OPEN WINDOW, HIS BINOCULARS SCANNING the sky—a hazy blue gray with a hint of orange. It would be evening soon. He moved his binoculars down toward the ocean. The water was still, but, having lived his whole life in and out of the sea, he knew it was deceiving. Teddy's dad was a fisherman, and so he spent most of his free hours working with his father, fishing the dwindling sardine population that was common to their area.

Every day his father followed the same routine, like traveling a well-worn wooded path. Up before light. Down to the docks. Coffee and a pastry bought at the water's edge from Harold's. A prayer to the Virgin or to Saint Peter, the patron saint of fishermen. The casting of boats—half-ringers more common now than the large purse seines they used back when his dad was young—into the sea just as the sun cracks open one eye. Hours later returning with the day's catch. In the evening, prepping everything to begin the work again.

Today Teddy was tired, having stayed up late worrying about his future. He had one more year of school left before graduation. The worry wasn't about what he was going to do, it was about how he was going to tell his father. His father, who wasn't very forthcoming with his affections and feelings, and who never spoke about his own time fighting in Europe almost ten years ago. There was an expectation always hovering over Teddy, a net that had been cast and threatened to snag him. A life on the water wasn't so terrible, but Teddy had his sights on the skies. His plan was to graduate and enter the Air Force, with or without his father's blessing. Joining the Skywatch club was his first step. Next month, when school started back up again, he would speak with a recruiter. He'd be eighteen by then anyway. He wouldn't need his father's permission, but still, he hoped for his blessing.

Teddy hid a yawn, kept his posture straight, his eyes alert. A plane could come at any moment. His body tensed, waiting. It was excruciating, never knowing when the Reds would send the bombs. Teddy knew two things: One, that one day they would send them. The second was that as a Skywatcher, he was most likely the first line of defense, and that was a reality he took very seriously—unlike others in the group.

Teddy turned his ear to the commotion in the room.

"Hit me," Oscar said. He was playing poker with Frank at the small table in the corner, close to the door.

"You sure?" Frank said.

"Do it."

Frank put down another card and Oscar pursed his lips.

"That's what you get when you play with the big boys," Frank said.

From the middle of the room, Caroline coached Eleanor

through a new dance step to the music coming from the portable radio.

"Yep. Just like that. See, you got it."

Eleanor tried to tap her foot and sway her hips at the same time, but she couldn't get the rhythm right.

"Like this, Eleanor," Caroline said, showing her the move.

Frank let out a laugh, making Eleanor stop. She hugged her arms across her chest.

"Knock it off, Frank!" Caroline said.

Teddy wondered if he needed to intervene. If Caroline thought Frank was teasing Eleanor, her best friend, she wouldn't stand for it.

"What?" Frank leaned back in his chair. "Oscar just made a joke. I can't laugh at a joke?"

Caroline walked over to stand above Frank, hands on her hips. "What was so funny?" She looked at Oscar, who stared down at the cards in his hands. "Huh?"

"He was just saying—"

"It's fine, Caroline," said Eleanor, cutting Frank off. She slid down against the wall next to Bunny, who was reading one of her novels.

Eleanor picked up *Life* from the top of the magazine pile. Teddy watched her trace Marilyn Monroe's face on the cover with her fingers, down her neck, over the edges of the white dress. He almost felt sorry for Eleanor. She was always in Caroline's shadow. Caroline was, well, she was the prettiest girl in school. And Eleanor was a nice girl—not a Marilyn like Caroline.

"You know, you don't have to be a jerk," Caroline said to Frank, still hovering over him at the table.

Teddy turned back to the sky. Again his binoculars slowly scanned the horizon. A small speck came in range to the south of the tower. He focused the lens to be sure.

"Got one!" he yelled.

Caroline ran to shut off the radio, while the other two boys jumped to join Teddy at the lookout. Bunny and Eleanor stopped reading, but only Eleanor got up and walked over for a better look.

As the plane came into view, Teddy's shoulders sagged. "It's just a single engine passenger," Teddy said, his voice flat with disappointment. It wasn't that he wanted the Reds to attack, of course. But they'd been watching the skies for months now, and he longed for something to happen. Something more.

Their principal was the one who had started the high school's Ground Observer Corps, which turned into the Operation Skywatch program earlier that summer, answering a civilian call President Truman issued to the country. Their country needed them to act as human radar, to detect the threat of atomic bombs, which would most certainly come from the sky.

But though the club was relatively new to the school, the rickety wooden tower that served as their base was not. It had been thrown together back in '41, right after Pearl Harbor was bombed. A little off the coast, but with a full view of the beautiful rocky coastline and its tide pools, it had been used by the Ground Observer Corps to scout possible Japanese subs or aircraft. A few flaps of old green-and-brown cloth still clung to the wooden legs—remnants of its camouflage days.

Their training hadn't taken long. At school, they had

watched a video put out by the Air Force and practiced looking through the transparent plastic cards with circles of varying sizes to gauge the distance and altitude of observed aircraft. They learned how to identify commercial and military airplanes, how to call them in to filter centers, how to log their direction and speed. They were told they played an important and essential part in the defense against an attack from the Soviet Union. The Russians had detonated their first atomic bomb in '49 and were currently creating a fleet of bombers that could devastate the country. An attack was imminent, the fear palpable. Diligence a matter of civic duty and responsibility.

The club wasn't a tight-knit group.

Outside of the club, the friendships existed in smaller pairings. John and Teddy were friends through their fishermen fathers. Both had a sense of duty and loyalty, which guided their involvement in the club. Caroline and Eleanor were best friends, had been for years. There was also Frank, a science fiction devotee, and his protégé, Oscar, who loved science fiction almost as much as he loved to work on cars. Bunny was the only one not born there. She had moved to Monterey from New York last year. Teddy didn't know much about her, and he suspected Bunny liked it that way.

He lowered the binoculars.

"Probably Mr. Stenoic again," Oscar said, peering up at the small plane.

Teddy held up the transparent template that they used to gauge distance. The plane fit inside the five-mile hole, but he thought it might be closer.

"I'd say about four miles."

Teddy logged the type of aircraft, the direction and the time, 6:54 p.m., in the book. It was the same book that everyone who manned the tower used.

"Mark it very high," Caroline said behind him. She pointed. "See the trail of vapors?"

Teddy tensed his shoulders, but he made the note. He didn't bother telling Caroline he already knew that. He also knew to pick his battles when it came to her or else he'd be there forever arguing about vapors. That was the thing about Caroline. She didn't like to be wrong about anything. It's why he never went for her. They'd be arguing every minute.

Because he was the one who spotted the plane, Teddy walked over to the red phone and called the filter center.

"Aircraft flash, Elliot 1234," he said into the receiver.

After about thirty seconds, a woman's voice responded. "Air defense, go ahead."

"Aircraft flash. One multi high. No delay. Bravo Kitty 10 Black. West. Flying South." Teddy read the information off the log that he had filled out.

"Check," the female voice said. "Thank you."

Teddy hung up the phone. Even though it wasn't a threat, he felt sweat running down his back. So far, the most exciting thing that had happened since joining was when he got to report a single bomber—five weeks ago now. He had known by the noise that it wasn't an ordinary plane—a small passenger or cargo plane. Teddy and Frank had been the only ones on duty that day, and Teddy's hand had shaken as he called it in. Frank had to hold the log steady.

It had ended up being a false alarm. A simple training

exercise. Not the enemy coming to bomb them. Not a nuclear attack. But Teddy knew an attack was coming. The whole country did, and it felt like each day was a step closer to this inevitability. Just this past April he'd been glued to the small TV in his living room, like everyone else he knew, watching the atomic explosion in a test site in Nevada on the network news. Even though the picture was in black and white, Teddy imagined the brilliant orange and red colors the mushroom cloud must have generated in real life. If the US had the ability to test a new atom bomb, what ability did the Russians secretly have? He'd heard from his history teacher at school that the Russians were working with former Nazi scientists. It's why Teddy's grandfather had built them a bomb shelter in the basement last year.

It's why they showed the *Duck and Cover* film with Bert the Turtle in school. The film warned that the atomic bomb could come anytime and anywhere. Teddy doubted that putting his head under his desk would save him from an atomic bomb. Or that covering his body with a newspaper would offer protection. Once the flash hit, they'd all be poisoned with radiation. Or killed.

Their high school principal had been in World War II, so he took the threat very seriously. In the beginning, after starting the club, he even volunteered at the tower. At lunch, sometimes Teddy would see him staring up, searching for what could come at any moment.

Teddy thought his principal should have kept eyes on the teachers. The drama teacher, Mr. Valentino, had been escorted off campus the last month of school after being found a communist. It was illegal in most states to teach if you were one. Teddy wondered how many other commies were hiding in plain sight. Supposedly there were sleeper agents planted in high levels of government and even in small towns across the country, just waiting for the right time to be activated. The human threat was real.

The sky, though, had yet to give a sign of threat. It was always big, blue much of the time, or gray with the slow fog rolling in and out. For Teddy, it carried freedom and possibility. There was nothing he wanted more than to be up there one day, learn to fly. Teddy wanted more than smelly fish and a life on the sea. He wanted another world. The Air Force would give him that.

"Okay. My turn," Caroline said, her eyes sparkling with excitement and the unspoken words that said he'd better hand over the binoculars.

Teddy reluctantly gave them up, but instead of joining Frank and Oscar at the card table, he took Eleanor's place against the wall next to Bunny. She didn't even look up from her book as he sank down next to her. *Strange girl*, Teddy thought. She reminded him a little of the actress Audrey Hepburn with her brown pixie cut and the way she usually dressed in all black. It was probably the style in New York, but here it made her stand out like a sore thumb.

Teddy wondered why the heck she had even joined the club. She barely spoke to them when she was there. Always reading her mystery novels. He could tell she felt above them—especially John and Teddy. But he still checked out her legs, bare because she'd rolled her denim jeans almost all the way to her knees.

He looked up and saw Bunny watching him. She flashed him a strange, knowing smile.

"Hi, Teddy," she said. "See anything interesting?"

"Nope," he said, knowing that she didn't just mean in the sky.

Bunny laughed and returned to her book, *A Murder Is Announced* by Agatha Christie.

Teddy picked up the magazine Eleanor had been reading. His eyes lingered on the cover, on Marilyn's bare shoulders, her cleavage where it dipped into the white dress, before catching the title of an article in the right-hand corner, "There Is a Case for Interplanetary Saucers."

Teddy grunted. He read the date at the bottom, April 7, 1952, a couple months old already. It wouldn't have the story about what happened in Washington, D.C., last month. Teddy only knew about that because Frank and Oscar had come running at him with *The Washington Post* and the headline " 'Saucer' Outran Jet, Pilot Reveals." They insisted this was the start of an invasion from Mars.

Frank and Oscar had joined the Skywatch club because they wanted to be part of something bigger, sure, but also because of their belief in extraterrestrials. They read everything they could get their hands on about them—from *Amazing Stories* to books, like the one they'd brought to the tower the other day, *The Day of the Triffids*. Something about giant human-eating alien plants.

Teddy was too pragmatic for aliens. Whatever objects were in the sky, he doubted they were flying saucers. They were probably military. The only invasion they'd have to worry about would be man-made.

He said as much to the guys, but they wouldn't hear it.

Still, the title of the article and the interplanetary reference made him curious, and with Caroline as the lookout now, there wasn't much else to do. So Teddy opened the magazine to the table of contents, turned to the corresponding page, and began reading.

2

CAROLINE

CAROLINE TRACKED THE VAPORS STILL STAINING THE SKY. THE strands looked to her like worms wiggling across the sky. She wished she had been the one to spot the plane. Teddy wasn't as diligent as her, so she didn't think it was fair. Caroline understood that it only took a second to miss the most important moments. A second and everything could change forever.

It was an easy job. All anyone needed was patience and a good eye. Which is why, if she had her way, it would just be the girls. She would ditch Bunny, though, who was nothing more than a stuck-up, spoiled East Coast girl. Caroline didn't know why she stayed in the group. Most of the time she rolled her eyes and acted aloof. Caroline almost told their advisor Mr. Smith about it, but she didn't want to cause trouble. So she ignored Bunny right back.

When Caroline first heard about Operation Skywatch, she joined right away. Her father had been a pilot in World War II and had died in a battle on Anzio Beach. There were two pictures of him on her nightstand. One of him in his uniform, handsome with his dark hair and eyes. The other was of him smiling with his thumbs up in the cockpit of his plane. She didn't remember much about her father, only small images and feelings. The most vivid was when she was three years old, sitting on his lap in a truck and holding the steering wheel. His hands rested on top of hers at ten and two. She remembered how heavy and strong they felt.

Caroline was a patriot, like her father before her. Joining the club was not just a chance for her to feel like she was doing something in the fight against the Reds, but a way for her to connect to her dad. She didn't tell that to her stepdad, Charlie, who was a good man and, truthfully, the only father she had ever really known. He married her mother when Caroline was eight. Caroline didn't talk about her dad a whole lot. Her mother already had enough ghosts to contend with; she didn't want to give her anything more concrete. Plus, she felt like she owed Charlie the courtesy, too.

Charlie pastored the small Methodist church in town, which meant that Caroline was a pastor's kid, or PK for short. She didn't mind it really, except for the teasing that sometimes followed. The "oh, you're such a good girl" pressure she felt from the weight of a title she hadn't chosen. The pressure to perform the role got to her every now and then, especially recently. It's probably why she lied and said she was staying over at a friend's, but in reality, snuck out and went down by the water to drink cheap beer with some of the other kids on Saturday nights.

When she wasn't with friends or on shift at the Skywatch club, Caroline cleaned the pews, floor, and bathroom of the church. She saved every bit of money Charlie paid her. When she graduated, she wanted to leave, to take a bus somewhere—maybe all the way to Los Angeles. People always said how pretty she was. As pretty as Marilyn Monroe, they said, though Caroline didn't have the same curves. But at least Caroline was a natural blonde. She'd read somewhere that Ms. Monroe dyed her hair. She could have been crowned Miss Butterfly too, if they'd still had the pageant this year during the beautiful Festival of Lanterns. Her favorite part was when they put the lights in the water and she watched them float away. She could be like one of those little lights, just wading and slowly backing away from the shore until she was gone.

Caroline was smart. Her calculus teacher, who was from Boston, wanted her to pursue a field in mathematics, calling it the only pure discipline. Besides, he'd say, they needed more female mathematicians. Math came easy for her, but Caroline didn't stare into the long corridor of her future and see herself with numbers and equations. And as far as jobs went, all she saw for women and mathematics were the ads in the paper for computer programmers. She didn't want to become a human calculator stuck in a small office space all day.

It wasn't that Monterey was a bad place to grow up, but she felt that if she didn't leave, she would suffocate. She needed to get out of the house and away from her mother. Her mother, who had become so wracked with grief over the death of her little brother Jack last year, that she didn't even go outside anymore.

At first, the women in the neighborhood had come by and brought meals. They sat with her mother, speaking in soft, encouraging tones. They listened. They prayed with her. But as the weeks became months, her mother retreated to some-where deep inside herself. The neighbors stopped visiting. Only

Caroline and Charlie were left. They were trapped inside the house with a woman who no longer resembled the person she'd been. She moved about like a small moth, hovering and fluttering with no purpose. Her light had gone.

Jack was only three when he drowned. Their family was having a picnic with a couple other families after church over at Lovers Point Beach. Caroline's parents were talking to friends while she sat on another blanket closer to the water. She remembered Jack playing in the sand right in front of her. She took a bottle of light pink nail polish out of her bag, shook it, opened it, and began painting her toenails the color of a baby's tongue.

When she finished and looked up, Jack was no longer in front of her.

One moment he was there. The next moment he wasn't. It happened so quickly. One second of not paying attention, and Jack had wandered off. And that second became a couple more, until it had been who knew how many minutes. By the time they realized that Jack wasn't with anyone, he had already sunk to the floor of the ocean. His body tossed up on the shore the next day—bloated and gray like a dead fish.

And it was all Caroline's fault.

After Jack died, Caroline felt adrift, her feet stumbling to find their footing. Then she heard about the Skywatch club. She joined the club also as a kind of penance, even though she wasn't Catholic. Her stepfather didn't believe in the concept. No—he believed in a terrible, ocean-size grace. The kind you could lose yourself in.

But she found a part of herself again in the club. A part that she could control. If she couldn't protect Jack, she could at least try her best to protect her country. She found a place to stand. And with Eleanor by her side, she wasn't alone.

Eleanor placed her hand on Caroline's shoulder. "I think I'm gonna go."

"Why?" Caroline asked.

"One plane in"—she looked at her watch—"almost two hours already?"

"But," Caroline lowered her voice. "You're going to leave me alone with them?"

"Mom wants to teach me how to make a meringue," Eleanor said.

"Didn't we already learn that in Home Ec last week?" Caroline asked, distracted, her eyes still on the horizon.

"Yeah, but mine didn't pass."

"How is making a meringue going to be useful in our lives?" Though, even as Caroline said this, she suddenly thought of how she would love to make a meringue with her mother. In fact, she couldn't remember the last time her mother had cooked. No, she did. It was that day. The day Jack died. She had made fried chicken and a potato salad for the picnic.

Eleanor shrugged. "You know how my mom is."

"Yeah, I'm sorry."

But Caroline wasn't thinking of Eleanor's mom. She was thinking of her own, of how she was probably sitting in the rocking chair in the living room, holding a small T-shirt that hadn't been washed in more than a year. A shirt that would never be washed because her mother clung to the smell. At night, when her mother was finally asleep, sometimes Caroline would take the shirt, hold it up, and try to find Jack. But it only smelled of salt and dust. And sometimes guilt.

"Miss Pie Queen can't understand why I wouldn't want to make a meringue. *Doesn't everyone love meringue?*" Eleanor imitated the soft southwestern tone of her mother's voice. According to Eleanor, her mother had been a beauty queen in San Antonio before she had married Eleanor's dad and come to California.

"You may miss out on something," Caroline said, trying to get Eleanor to stay, teasing her for her belief in alien life-forms. But Caroline didn't believe her own words. It would be dark soon. Their shift would end. Curfew would be in place. Though not that much would happen other than being given a warning if an officer were to pick them up. The country would still be safe. Caroline would go home to a quiet, lonely house where the world had already ended.

"Really?" Eleanor said.

Caroline lowered the binoculars and followed Eleanor's gaze around the room. Oscar and Frank had their heads down, staring at the cards in their hands. Frank's cigarette hung from the corner of his mouth. Teddy and Bunny were reading. Caroline noted how close Teddy was to her and smirked.

"Doubtful," Eleanor said. "Look, come over to my house tomorrow morning."

"I have to work." Caroline didn't want to miss out on the money her stepfather would pay her.

"Okay, then after," Eleanor continued. "I'll let you taste my pie."

Caroline smiled. "All right."

Eleanor had been Caroline's best friend through everything that happened with Jack. She was the only one Caroline felt comfortable letting inside the house. She'd seen Caroline's mother in the rocker and just held Caroline's hand. Caroline loved Eleanor like a sister.

At the table, Frank threw down his deck. "I'm out of here too. Come on, Oscar." He stood.

Oscar reached across the table and looked at Frank's discarded cards.

"I knew it! I would have won."

"So what." Frank looked at his watch. "Our shift is over in twenty minutes anyway."

"Twenty-five," Caroline said.

"You coming, Teddy?" Frank asked, ignoring her.

But Teddy was too engrossed in the article he was reading, and shook his head. "No. I'll stay. You guys can cut out."

Caroline hugged Eleanor, and then Eleanor followed Frank and Oscar down the narrow wooden stairs, skipping over the broken step, third from the bottom. It was only a matter of time before someone stepped clear through it and got hurt.

Down below, Caroline heard Frank offer to give Eleanor a ride home. She heard him say something about alien pods and Eleanor laugh in agreement. Caroline rolled her eyes. She didn't understand that guy. Most of the time he annoyed her, but every now and then he could do something decent.

"I'm okay. I've got my bike," Eleanor said.

"Suit yourself," said Frank. He and Oscar hopped into the small blue Ford that Oscar had fixed up earlier this year. Oscar was a whiz with cars, would probably own his own shop one day. Caroline noted the crooked display of the rear license plate as Frank peeled out of the dirt and onto the road.

Eleanor got on her bike and glanced up at the tower.

"Call me later?" Caroline said.

Eleanor nodded. "Bye!"

Caroline watched as her friend pedaled away, suddenly sad to see her go. And Eleanor, riding quickly, didn't think to look back. Caroline stood there, eyes on Eleanor, until she turned right and out of view. Then she picked up the binoculars and returned her attention to the skies.

3

JOHN

JOHN SLOWED DOWN TO TURN RIGHT ONTO THE ROAD THAT LED TO
the tower just as Frank's car stopped at the intersection. Frank
hung his head out the window and yelled, "See you, Kawai!"

John honked twice in response and continued past them. He
was late to the group, too late, and for that, Caroline would give
him a lecture about commitment. He didn't need a lecture. His
dad gave him the same one each week. Work hard. Make money.
Go to school. Become something other than a man who reeks of
fish.

John didn't mind the work with his dad. He liked listening
to the older men and their stories of Japan. One day he hoped to
see it. His mother told him that the coastline, from Big Sur up to
Monterey, reminded her of her home when she was little. That's
why they'd settled there. That and the abalone.

John started diving three years ago. It was dangerous work.
To get the really big marine snails, you had to go deep. You could
drown if you weren't careful. John learned by watching his dad,
who always did everything with a slow, measured patience, and
tried his best to do things in the same careful way.

Except when he was on the baseball field. There, John was explosive. The fastest on the team, known for making the most steals into home plate.

The only thing John wanted to do—more than anything—was play baseball. His plan was to play in college, and afterward, maybe join a team in Hawaii or one of the Nisei teams like the Fresno All-Stars—made up of players whose parents had emigrated here from Japan. John's eyes were on Satoshi "Fibber" Hirayama who had just signed with the St. Louis Browns. If Jackie Robinson could break the color barrier, why couldn't the Japanese be next? John knew it was only a matter of time. And he was poised to be one of the pioneers.

Eleanor came around the corner on her bike. This time John stopped and Eleanor rode up to his window. She placed her hand on the frame, remained on the bike, and smiled at him.

"Hey, Eleanor."

"Hey," she said, a little out of breath.

"You leaving?" he asked.

"Yeah. Gotta get home early today."

"See anything in the tower?" he asked.

"One small plane. But we got him." She gave a little salute. "Nothing gets past these eyes. Caroline, Bunny, and Teddy are still there, finishing out the shift." She cocked her head to the side. "Why're you so late?"

He shrugged. "Just stuff." He didn't want to get into the details of how he'd had to help his dad.

"Stuff, hmm. Well, see you," she said.

"All right," he said. "Be safe."

She laughed. "You're the one who needs safety."

"Ha, Caroline's in a mood?"

"Maybe." She grinned. "Bye!"

She pedaled away. John watched as she stood up to get some momentum for the slight hill, then rounded to the right and out of his sight. He got the odd feeling like he should go after her, follow her, just to make sure she'd get home all right. But the thought passed just as quickly as it came, replaced by Caroline waiting for him up in the tower. She'd be angry, but that was okay. Any feeling from her beyond indifference was okay with him.

When he got to the tower, he parked the truck on the side of the road, looked up, and saw Caroline. She didn't look down at him, even though he knew she knew he was there.

Girls.

He shook his head. He didn't have time for them. They were also bad luck in baseball. Once Antonio Casalero got a girlfriend last year, his pitches were all off. Coach benched him for most of the second half of the season. And Caroline, well, her family probably wouldn't be too keen on her being with him anyway. He was Nisei, second-generation Japanese, and she was . . . he didn't know exactly—maybe a little Irish, English, some kind of European mix—but definitely not Japanese. He also knew that his parents wouldn't approve either. They wanted him to marry a Japanese girl. Teddy, even though he was Italian, and Sicilian at that, would have better luck with Caroline.

Teddy had all the luck. Always. John was grateful that Teddy stuck to basketball and didn't join the baseball team. At least there, John didn't have to compete with his best friend like he felt he had to in everything else. Teddy had an ease with people. He was liked, respected. No one expected him to make himself smaller or move out of the way when he entered a room. Even though their fathers shared the same blue-collar work, Teddy fared much better out in the real world. He looked like the perfect All-American guy with his good looks, light skin, Caucasian features, and loads of confidence. John felt like he lived in Teddy's shadow, and not by choice. Somehow he'd been placed there. And now it had been so long, he didn't know how to get out.

Just last week they'd been walking past a couple of guys waiting at the bus stop. One of them said something under his breath. *Jap*. It wasn't the first time John had heard the slur, nor would it be the last. It wasn't that it didn't bother John, but he knew that if he threw away his time and anger on every prejudiced person out there, all he would ever do is fight. But Teddy, Teddy stepped in and called the man out, walked up to him, got in his face. They were about to come to blows, but one of the others at the bus stop convinced his friend to back off. John had just stood there, his hands clenched in fists at his sides.

"Why'd you let him talk to you that way?" Teddy had asked when they were walking away.

John tried to unstick his mouth. How could he tell Teddy he'd been embarrassed by his friend's actions? That all he did was draw more attention. What did that solve? It wasn't going to change the man's mind about Japanese people. John's father taught him that violence was never the solution. Violence only guaranteed more violence. It took a stronger man to create peace. John could have pinned the guy if he would have taken a swing at him; he'd taken judo for years. But even the translation of judo—"the gentle way"—implied nonviolence. A keeping the peace. Not the first move in a conflict.

There were those at school whose prejudice leaked from time to time, spilling out through comments about his eyes or the food he brought for lunch—visible signs that he was different than them. There were other Japanese residents in town, had been for many years, but they were in the minority. And even more so now because not all the Japanese had moved back to their California homes after the camps were closed.

John knew he wasn't fully American in the eyes of some. Those who equated "American" with a white European ancestry. For them, John would never be American enough no matter how he dressed, spoke, or prayed to their God.

But there were many who accepted him and his family just as they were. And for that, John was grateful. Teddy's family was one.

Teddy's family, the Messinas, and John's family, the Kawais, had an understanding between them because of what Mr. Messina did for John's father during the war. After the attack on Pearl Harbor, when anyone Japanese on the West Coast was rounded up and forced into one of those internment camps, Mr. Messina agreed to take care of John's family's home and abalone and fishing gear until they could return. Legally, the house wasn't even John's father's; the Californian Alien Land Law prevented Japanese immigrants from becoming citizens. They were unable to own the land or even rent it for longer than three years at a time. John's father had been "renting" the home they lived in for over twenty years.

John was only eight when they were sent to the tents in

Arizona. His mother didn't fare well there, not being used to the dry heat. She missed the ocean. The landscape was so barren, John felt he could walk forever and no one would find him. Of course, that wasn't true. He was penned in like the others. Instead of the boundaries of the ocean and the forest, now there were barbed wire and military towers, guns pointed in their direction.

At first John's family slept in an expansive room, like a town hall or a gym, with many strangers. His father had hung a large red blanket to section off their space and to give them some privacy. Other families did the same. Oftentimes John woke up early, peeked out of the blanket, and thought it looked like a bunch of multicolored flags waving. That was before more permanent structures were built. The ones that told them this was going to be a longer stay than originally promised.

If there was one thing that made his time in the camp easier, though, it was that John learned how to play baseball. The camp had a field and a couple of coaches from various high schools. Most days after the morning school, run by volunteers, John booked it to the field, no matter how hot it was—oftentimes not coming back until after the dinner bells rang. He learned to hold the glove out in front of him when another was at bat, how to stand for a pitch, how to catch. He learned by watching and emulating others.

When the war ended, John's family returned home, and except for the thick layer of dust that covered the counters, they found their house exactly as they had left it, thanks to the Messinas. Other Japanese weren't so fortunate. Many lost everything and never came back, or, at best, moved to different parts of the country. For those in communities like John's, though, folks had signed a petition welcoming the Japanese families home that ran in the local paper.

They had developed a conscience, his father had said, especially the Methodists. Some of the church ladies even brought them groceries for a week when they moved back. It never did get John's dad to their Christian church, but sometimes John's mom took him and his brother Gary to the Buddhist temple.

His father legally owned the home now. The law that discriminated against Japanese changed; the McCarran-Walter Act had passed just two months ago, allowing Japanese to become citizens. John was already a citizen, being born here, but now his parents had been naturalized, too.

His father was a model citizen who paid his taxes and worked hard. Who displayed his deed to the house and naturalization papers on the wall of the kitchen, right underneath the photo of his parents from Japan.

What people didn't know was that John's father preferred his own kind in most things—religion, family, even business. He would often mutter about the American ways and how they were lacking compared to the Japanese. But he was a walking contradiction. Though proud of his Japanese heritage, he wanted his sons to be as American as possible. He wanted them to succeed. After all, he told them often, the sign of doing his duty as a father was if they were to surpass him. Become more successful. Become a new American. Become a new Japanese.

John wondered if there was room to be both.

• • •

The feeling of being watched broke him free of his thoughts, and John glanced up at the tower. Caroline had the binoculars pointing down. She waved with one hand, the other still on the binoculars.

He turned away and shook his head, feeling suddenly nauseated. She had that effect on him. He opened the car door with the toe of his boot already pointing in her direction like she was north.

He slammed the door shut and began walking toward the old wooden tower.

John first heard about the Skywatch club through Caroline in homeroom. He showed up at the initial meeting and his spirits sank a little when he saw that Teddy was there, too. Still, he kept his face neutral, pleasant even. Teddy waved him over and John smiled, crossed the room, and sat next to him. Caroline didn't even notice John. But he hoped that would change once they were in the group together.

So far, he'd been closer to her and had spent more time with her than ever before, and yes, they talked about planes and altitude and the weather, but it hadn't panned out like he hoped it would.

"You're late!" Caroline called down to him through the open window.

"Hello to you, too," he said. Even though the sun was beginning to set, he had to shield his eyes to get a good look at her. Caroline O'Sullivan. She was like a dream.

"What's the excuse this time?"

"No excuse. Just work."

"Hmm." She crinkled her nose. "Well, you're here now."

"I'm here now," he said, as he began climbing up. "What'd you spot?"

"Nothing really," she said.

"Sounds right."

A brief smile escaped the corner of her mouth before she went back to watching the sky. He let that smile sit with him for a few seconds. Then he continued up the stairs. When he opened the wooden door to the room at the tower's top, Teddy greeted him first.

"John!"

"Just you and the girls, I see," he said.

Teddy stood from his place on the floor where he was sitting next to the new girl, Bunny.

"Frank and Oscar just left."

"Yeah, I passed them and Eleanor. See anything good?"

"Simple plane," Teddy said, standing with his hands on his hips. "Nothing super exciting."

Nothing super exciting ever happens around here, John thought, which was fine by him. He didn't know what they'd do if there was an actual threat.

John nodded to Bunny on the floor. "Hello, Bunny."

"Hello, John," she said. "How were the abalone?"

"Just fine," he said.

He couldn't figure out if Bunny was friendly or sarcastic. Either way, she made him a little uncomfortable. Maybe it was the city part of her. She always looked at him like she knew something that he didn't. It bothered him. But he just smiled. Kept his true feelings close and buried. Anything to avoid the difficult feelings that threatened to sink him.

Something else he learned from his father.

John turned and admired Caroline's back instead. She was still scanning the sky. He took her all in then: pink tailored shirt with small gingham checks tied at the waist over black capris, white socks with saddle shoes. He should have tried harder with his own clothes. He wore jeans and a plaid shirt. He was missing a belt today, so the pants hung a little too low, which is why, just now, he had to hitch them up a bit before moving to cross to her side.

If Caroline sensed his presence next to her, she didn't show it. Just kept her eyes on the horizon.

John kept his eyes on her.

4

BUNNY

BUNNY GLANCED UP FROM HER BOOK AND GAVE JOHN ONE OF HER slow smiles. One that she knew made him uncomfortable, even though he thought he could hide it with a smile of his own. When he looked away, she was pleased with herself. It was silly, but it made her feel powerful.

She watched John watch Caroline. She sighed. Bunny thought joining the group would make her feel like she was a part of something. But it had just made her miss her friends back home and feel more alone. She would for sure quit the group after today. The people here were so basic, especially Frank and Oscar. They spoke of such childish things—extraterrestrials and all of that. She took one look at the covers of the magazines they read with the half-naked women being carried away by monsters from other planets; that was all she needed to know about them. But at least they read—she had to give them that.

She looked at her watch. Her older brother was late. Will was always late even though he didn't have a job. Bunny had an idea of what he did with his time, but she didn't say anything to their dad. What good would it do? It's not like they'd pack up their things and move back home because Will was gambling. New York had been a worse place for that.

She found where she'd left off on the page and kept reading—a Miss Marple mystery novel from her favorite writer, Agatha Christie. Miss Marple was so funny. She said what she was thinking and didn't sugarcoat it. Sure, she got away with it because she was an old lady, but it didn't matter. Bunny would love to be a private detective one day just like Miss Marple. But she didn't plan to wait until she was as old. You just had to know how to read people and the environment. Bunny could do both.

Take the group she was with now—these people she was stuck with in this dinky town that had no sense of culture. She would never say that, of course—not unless someone asked her. If they did, she'd have no trouble being honest. Bunny valued the truth more than anything. But she knew no one would ever ask; the others had no concept of life outside the Monterey Peninsula.

Teddy was the only one who showed promise, but he'd probably end up fishing the rest of his life, even though she knew he wanted out. It was obvious he wanted to be a pilot. But he was too much of a good guy—the one who does the right thing like stay and work for the family business out of obligation. He'd probably spend his whole life in a five-mile radius and one day go crazy with the weight of it and walk out on his family. She didn't know much about John. She just knew he liked baseball. And Caroline.

Caroline was pretty, though she wore her hair a little too long and in childish ponytails. She was also very smart, but not as smart as Bunny. Of course, Bunny didn't let on how smart she was. She didn't want to alienate people right off the bat, especially boys. Occasionally she scored poorly on an exam so as not to draw too much attention. Her peers didn't need to know she spoke English, Spanish, Italian, and French. She had tried Mandarin, but it had proved much more challenging. Bunny didn't like the feeling of failure, so she'd given up, blaming it on a "terrible instructor." In front of the others in the club she read murder mysteries, which she loved to escape in. The thrill of solving a crime always the motivation. But at home she read books on Boolean logic, computers, and physics. She had a whole bulletin board dedicated to her idol, Ada Lovelace—gifted mathematician and the world's first computer programmer.

Bunny had joined the club for three reasons. The first was that she was bored out of her mind. In the city, there was always something to do and see. She was used to hanging out with friends in cafés, going to hear live music, dancing, seeing plays. All this area had was a drive-in movie theater, a bowling alley, three art galleries, and a few restaurants. The second reason was, for all of her apathy, Bunny was a patriot at heart. She'd watched all the films like the rest of them and couldn't help but get caught up with the whole doing-something-for-the-country attitude. And the third reason, which Bunny kept private, was that, as she looked into the future, she wanted to work with rockets. She kept her eye on the Jet Propulsion Laboratory in Pasadena and all the work they were doing. As a woman, she knew that she could get into their Computing Section, but she was also interested in being a chemist. She figured being part of the human radar chain might get her closer to her goal. She could at least put it on a résumé.

But the club had proved uninspiring. Not enough planes

flew by to keep her attention. The conversation, when there was any, bored her. She missed her friends and the excitement of the city. Bunny spent many evenings on the phone with her best friend Judy hatching a plan. They figured next year Bunny could move in with Judy and finish out her senior year of high school. Her father would be against it, but she would convince him. Just because he had accepted a job at the Defense Language Institute didn't mean she had to be stuck here, too.

The only good thing about where Bunny lived now was the beach and how beautiful it was. Bunny couldn't deny that. When she had first seen the Pacific Ocean and the shoreline, she understood for a moment why people loved California, and why some never wanted to leave. This ocean was a wild, uncontained beauty—something that her city eyes had never seen. But with the beauty came a gray loneliness that seeped over her when she wasn't looking, something she was not used to feeling.

The move had not only uprooted Bunny physically, it had altered her entire sense of self. Back in New York, she was confident; she knew her world and her place in it. She'd had a group of friends. She was liked—well, by some people. No one was liked by everyone. But she knew who she was and where she belonged. Here, she'd had to reinvent herself, and she didn't like who that new person was—a loner who didn't even stand out. She was still the new girl after being there for a year. She hadn't figured out how to get in with these people, and now she didn't even try anymore. So she acted like she didn't care that she was alone every weekend. Acted like she was above the others in the club.

Her whole life felt off-kilter, like she had been knocked out of orbit and now had a new course. The problem was she didn't like the direction, and she didn't know how to get back on track.

"Guys," Caroline said. Her tone was all sharp edges.

Bunny looked up.

"Yeah?" John said, from his position to the left of Caroline.

"Guys, you've got to see this."

Bunny snapped herself out of the little pity party she was having in her head and joined Teddy, John, and Caroline at the window.

"What's that?" Caroline asked, and pointed her finger at something out across the ocean.

Bunny looked and saw what seemed to be a soft, glowing red light. It was small, a good ways away, but it was there. It didn't seem like a plane light, though. They had all been trained to identify every existing aircraft that could possibly be in the sky—both domestic and foreign—and this was not anything Bunny recognized. Since everyone was quiet, she knew the others were thinking the same thing.

This light was something else. As they watched, it changed from red to a greenish silver color. Suddenly, it disappeared.

"Hey. Where'd it go?" John asked.

Bunny watched the spot where the light had been, but nothing was there. A chill moved over her body like the slow-moving fog.

"It's gone," Caroline said.

Bunny was just about to say that was impossible, when Teddy shouted, "Look! There it is."

The light reappeared in a different spot, but following the same trajectory. It was as if it had jumped in the air.

"It's probably some kind of military test again," Teddy said.

"Maybe," John said.

But Bunny felt the electricity and tension radiating off of John's body next to her. All these months of spotting regular aircraft and she never thought they'd actually see anything threatening. She didn't really think they would come under attack. *Was this an attack?*

"See how fast it shifted right?" Teddy's voice was higher than normal.

The light moved quickly again to the right and then seemed to just hover where it was. They all watched as it stayed there, unmoving, like someone had stuck it with a pin up there in the sky. None of it made any sense.

"What aircraft can move side to side like that?" Bunny asked, though she knew the answer, same as the others. None.

No American aircraft anyway. She was almost certain that no foreign power had a plane that could do what she was witnessing, either. She had just read about the B-52 prototype test flight that happened earlier in April. But this was not a B-52.

"Maybe it's just some kind of balloon. You know, like those fire balloons the Japanese launched during the war?" Bunny said. "I read about them somewhere." But Bunny couldn't remember where she had read about them, couldn't remember if they actually blew up. Maybe it was from a book she'd read and not an actual news account.

"Yeah, that really looks like a huge balloon," Teddy said sarcastically. "How many balloons do that?"

The light now moved again—making its way straight

toward them. As it came closer, the green spread to more of a translucent blue-green.

"It looks more like a radium dial watch," Caroline said.

"Or like the kelp beds," John said.

The light streaked across the sky, leaving no fumes trailing. The closer it got, Bunny thought she could see a dark shape that now looked more like the tip of an arrow.

"Get on the phone!" Caroline yelled, waking them all from the spell the light seemed to cast. "The phone! Call it in!"

"It's a missile. Is it a missile?" John asked.

But a missile would leave a trail of vapors behind. *Wouldn't it?* Bunny thought.

"Do missiles just disappear?" Caroline asked.

"We don't know what they do," Teddy said. "This could be all new technology. Some kind of military invasion."

"Um, yes," John said to the person on the other end of the phone, ignoring the protocol for calling in sightings. "I don't know how to report this, but there's some kind of aircraft here. It's kind of like the shape of a triangle or something— a dark triangle—but with a green, well, sort of greenish or bluish, glowing light. And it's moving fast. About two miles out, I'd say."

"Let me see," Bunny said, grabbing the binoculars.

Even with the magnification, she couldn't get a great look at it. It blurred and seemed to move at a terrific speed. One moment it appeared solid, like some kind of plane. The next moment, it was translucent, almost like she could see through it in parts. At one point, it looked like a skinny, singular line. In a matter of seconds, it disappeared and then reappeared in another spot.

It was like nothing she had ever seen. But she could see, clearly now, that it was heading directly toward them.

"It's coming—fast!" Bunny said.

John dropped the receiver and pulled Caroline and Bunny away from the window. Bunny cowered with the others in the center of the room, curled up on the floor. The boys covered both girls, as if their bodies would protect them from whatever was heading their way. Probably the only training they remembered from all those films in school—duck and cover. They waited for something to happen, an explosion.

The seconds ticked by in Bunny's heart.

One . . . two . . . three . . . four . . .

Nothing happened. No boom. No sound at all. But Bunny had an eerie feeling that something had passed overhead.

They waited for the worst to happen.

Minutes passed. Still nothing.

Teddy was the first to untangle himself. He darted to the back window, the one facing away from the ocean and into the forest.

"There," he said and pointed.

Bunny got up and watched as the light appeared to hover close by, unmoving again. Then she followed with her eyes as it went straight down and was lost among the pines.

5

ELEANOR

ELEANOR PEDALED DOWN THE PAVED ROAD SLOWLY, SAVORING THE ride. When she got home, her time would no longer be hers. As soon as she stepped through the door, her mother would sweep her up in some kind of domestic task—beyond the learning of how to make a proper meringue. Her mother's favorite quote, besides "cleanliness is next to godliness," was "idle hands are the devil's tools."

Eleanor wasn't fond of either saying.

She was thinking of what excuse she could give her mother tonight. She could say she wasn't feeling well. But her mother would not be able to find a fever. The back of her hand could diagnose a faked illness better than any doctor's instrument. The best thing to do was oblige. Make the damn meringue. In fact, don't just make it. Become the best meringue maker. Better than her mother. That would show her. Yes, that would be the way to get her mother off her back. Because if there was one thing Rose Marie hated, it was to lose, even to her own children.

Eleanor grinned just thinking about besting her mother's baking endeavors when she caught a glow out of the left side of her peripheral line of sight. She looked and saw a greenish light shaped like a cone hovering over the ocean. It was glowing, kind of like a radium watch.

"What?" She said this out loud, her breath catching.

Was this the beginning of an attack?

It did look a bit like something she'd seen in one of Frank's comic books. . . .

She jerked her head around, back toward the direction of the tower, but it was too far away now, not even in her sight. Better to keep heading toward home. At least maybe she could get to her family in time, or to a neighbor's bomb shelter. The Richardsons up the street had had one installed last year.

Eleanor pedaled faster as the object streaked across the sky from one point to the opposite end, as far as she could see. Traveling at a high speed. Eleanor couldn't know for sure, but it seemed as fast as a jet plane.

Only there was no sound. Nothing except for her heavy breaths and the crunch of gravel beneath her tires. *Strange*, she thought. *Why is it so quiet?* Then the light just disappeared. The fact that it disappeared scared her more than the light itself. She stopped the bike, waited, watched above. The others had to be seeing this too. Didn't they? After a few moments, the light popped up again, like it had made a jump in the dark sky.

Eleanor started pedaling again. She wanted to get home. Now. As she rode, she kept her eyes on the object, wondering what it could be. Was it a missile? Sent all the way from the USSR? The Reds finally delivering on their threats. She pedaled as fast as she could. She needed to get to her parents.

The object in the sky jerked one way and then the other,

like it was caught on a string and some force was pulling it back. Then it just hovered over the trees. Just above the tops of the pines. As if it were going to land.

Eleanor strained to see it. The beautiful, terrifying bluish green. She couldn't wait to tell Caroline about it.

She didn't even see the car coming.

The driver, his eyes also not on the road, was trying to determine what the funny light in the sky was when suddenly he felt a huge thud and jolt against the front of his car. He bounced in his seat as his tires rolled over something. He slammed on the breaks, causing the car to spin 180 degrees and skid to the very edge of the cliff. Something caught underneath the car, scraping across the asphalt, sending the noise across the empty road.

When the car finally came to a stop, he peeled his hands off the steering wheel. Even in the twilight, he recognized blood on the windshield.

Damn deer, he thought.

He got out of the car, walked around to see the damage the animal had done. It would be the second one he had hit that year. Already he was calculating what to tell his wife.

But when he saw what was under the car, he drew his hand to his face in horror. The upper half of a girl's body was still caught in the bike underneath. The lower half was twisted at an unnatural angle. He couldn't see her face. He knew it was a girl, though, because of her flowered skirt. He turned and threw up the roast beef sandwich his wife had packed him for lunch.

Underneath the car, next to the left rear tire, Eleanor's eyes remained open, staring up at, but not seeing, the now empty sky.

6

TEDDY

TEDDY STARED AT THE SPOT WHERE THE LIGHT WENT DOWN. THE others framed him within the doorway of the tower.

"What should we do?" Bunny whispered, close to his ear.

"I'll call them back," Caroline said. She hurried over to the phone and picked up the receiver. Then she swiveled around to face them. "There's no signal."

She held it out for Teddy. He put his ear up and confirmed.

"What does this mean?" she asked.

Teddy slowly panned the room and realized that all three of them were looking at him for answers, even Caroline, as if he had any.

"We don't know anything yet. It could be a practice run like the one before. That's what it probably is." But Teddy's mind raced. The light seemed so different, so not something he'd ever seen before. He remembered the article he'd just been reading. "Or . . ." He strode over to where the *Life* magazine lay, picked it up, and pointed to the cover.

"Marilyn Monroe? What's she got to do with this?" Bunny said.

"No. No. This." He opened the magazine and showed them the title inside. " 'Have We Visitors from Space?' "

"Extraterrestrials?" Caroline said. "You've got to be kidding."

"I know it sounds crazy, but I read it. The government has been investigating reports of sightings all over the country. Lights and spheres, exactly like what we just saw. And the military knows about it. They've got credible witnesses. Look." He flipped to another page in the magazine and opened it to a picture of a drawing of a green fireball over the mountains. He placed it on the small table so they could all get a good look.

"That's not exactly what we saw," John said. "We didn't see a sphere."

"No, but it was a green light. The point is, the Air Force knows about them." He turned the page. "Here, they list ten different UFO sightings, just like what we saw."

"UFO?"

"Unidentified Flying Object," Teddy said. "That's what they're calling them."

The girls and John read over his shoulder, looked at the sketches in the magazine. Teddy already felt like they were wasting time. They needed to do something.

"But who knows if these sources are even credible? They're all anonymous. Doesn't that seem a little odd?" Caroline said.

"Maybe they're afraid of the backlash," said Teddy.

"Or being made fun of. Look, all we saw was a light. Could be a million things. And since when did you start believing in this stuff anyway?" said Caroline. "You sound like Frank and Oscar, right, John?"

John's gaze shifted uncomfortably between her and Teddy. "I don't even know what we saw."

"Which is exactly what a UFO is, something unidentifiable," said Teddy.

The others were not convinced.

"Look," Teddy continued, "I'm not saying we saw a flying saucer, but we don't know. What we *do* know is it landed out there—" He pointed toward the open door with the view of the forest. "And we are on duty, so I'd say it's our responsibility as citizens to investigate. What if it is the Russians?"

"Oh, please." Bunny had remained quiet until now. "You really think the Russians are going to pick our tiny town for the start of their invasion?" she asked.

"It's unexpected. They could set up their whole base here and no one would know. Why do you think the Ground Observer Corps set up a tower in this exact spot?" said Teddy. "It's the perfect infiltration point to access California and the whole West Coast."

"He could be right. There was that Japanese sub during the war," Caroline said.

Teddy knew she was talking about the sub that had tried to sink a US oil tanker, twenty miles off Monterey Bay not too long after Pearl Harbor had been hit. He'd heard the story many times from people who had seen the tanker on fire and zigzagging in the direction of Santa Cruz.

"Well, I think you're all wrong," Bunny said. "It's definitely the start of an alien invasion." Teddy heard the sarcasm in her voice loud and clear. "Come on. You really think we're going to find Klaatu walking around telling us he means peace?"

Teddy caught the reference to *The Day the Earth Stood Still*. He'd seen it when it came to the theater last year along with the others in the room. But that had been fiction.

"This isn't a movie," Teddy said. "This is real."

Bunny laughed—a sharp ring that should have popped the tension in the air, but didn't.

"We have no idea what that light was," Caroline said. "But there's probably a really good explanation. Like maybe it was some kind of gas, or, you know, like those northern lights up in Alaska. Maybe something like that?"

"Lights don't move like that," John said. "They don't have a shape. You saw the shape, right?"

"Yeah, it looked like a flat V, like a big arrowhead," Bunny said.

"Like a bat," Caroline agreed.

"We're wasting time," said Teddy. "Whatever it was, it could be dangerous. We could be the only defense." *Why were they talking? They should be moving.*

"Our training only calls for reporting," Bunny said. "Not getting involved with UFOs. Or whatever that was."

"That's exactly what I'm saying, we need to investigate and report back. John, you coming?"

John took a moment to answer. He nodded to Teddy. "We may be the only ones who saw it. It's our duty to at least try to get closer."

"Technically our shift is over," said Bunny.

The others remained silent.

"Look," she continued. "It's highly doubtful that you're going to find anything real or threatening in the forest. I'm going to wait right here for my brother. Caroline?"

Caroline looked from Teddy and John to Bunny and back again. "I'm going if they are," she said.

"Okay, Bunny, lock the door behind us and set a chair under the handle," Teddy said. "Don't let anyone up here besides your brother."

"Who else would be out there?" Bunny said.

"That's what we're going to find out," said John.

"Grab the flashlights and matches," Teddy said. John grabbed both. Caroline picked up a blanket.

As Teddy closed the door to the tower, he gave Bunny a smile, trying to hide his fear. She just rolled her eyes at him. This felt bigger than fear, like his whole life had been leading to this moment of decision and he had to make the right one. His life would be forever changed because of it. Besides, his dad had taught him that fear was just a feeling. It wasn't real.

"We'll be back as soon as we can," Teddy said. Then he, John, and Caroline climbed down the stairs.

The forest loomed large and menacing in the dark.

"I'd say it went down right about there," John said, pointing to the trees toward the right of them.

The tall, thick pines huddled together like they were cold. And it was a little chilly, Teddy thought, especially for a summer night. As if she knew what he was thinking, Caroline wrapped a blanket around herself. She looked small and sweet just then.

Suddenly there was a crack behind him and he jumped. He turned to see John breaking a stick in two.

"Here." He gave one of the pieces to Caroline.

"What's this for?"

John shrugged. "You never know."

"So," Teddy began, taking in a large breath and exhaling as he spoke. "Let's all stay close. We're just going to take a look."

They began to walk in when they heard a shout behind them.

"Wait!" Bunny was walking down the stairs. "Who knows when Will actually will come. He could be in another all-night card game. I still say this is a waste of time, but I'd rather not be stuck in this tower by myself."

Her foot landed on the faulty step and broke it. As she yanked her leg out, Bunny noticed a large scrape up the side of her ankle that oozed a line of red.

"Damn it," she said.

"You okay?" Caroline asked, moving to help steady her.

"I'm fine."

"Oh." Caroline backed away.

"What?" Bunny said.

"You're bleeding." Caroline held her hand to her mouth as if she were going to throw up right there.

"Only a little," Bunny said, and wiped away the blood with her hand.

"It's just . . . I have a thing with blood."

"Let me see," Teddy said. He looked at her wound and saw

that it wasn't a deep cut. "I doubt you'll need stitches, but it might leave a scar."

"It won't be my first," Bunny said.

Teddy looked into the woods. He and John should go in alone. There was a real threat of danger and he didn't want the liability of having to protect the girls in the face of whatever they might find. He looked at Caroline, who was bent over with her hands on her knees. "Caroline, you should stay here if you don't feel well. You and Bunny."

"Just give me a minute," Caroline said.

Bunny scooted away from her and positioned herself between Teddy and John. A moment later, Caroline joined them.

"All right then," Teddy said, feeling like someone had designated him the leader. He touched the Saint Peter he wore around his neck, said a prayer. "Let's all stay close. We're just going to see. If anything happens and we get separated, head back to the tower. Okay?"

No one said anything, but he caught their nods out of his peripheral vision.

"I'll go first. John, you take up the rear."

Then, one by one by one by one, they entered the dark wood.

7

FRANK

THE LIGHT BURST THROUGH THE NIGHT SKY—A PALE GLOW, LIKE the eyes of a monster emerging from a deep, deep dark.

Frank read back over what he'd written and crossed out *monster*. The word conjured up fear instead of the awe he wanted to transfer to the page. He wrote the words *celestial being* instead. Better, but maybe it was too much? He continued, not wanting to get bogged down on one phrase.

Fear and wonder exploded in his mind. Was this the beginning of an invasion? But why would they send just one ship? Was it a scout? The mother ship being somewhere out of sight but orbiting the Earth nearby. Perhaps it was a rogue ship looking for amnesty. He didn't know what he'd witnessed, but the point was he had seen something. Something that streaked across the sky and then disappeared.

Frank worked the kink in his neck as the sun rose slowly. A pale lavender hue colored the fog like it was cotton candy from a fair. He'd stayed up all night by the telescope, watching the sky, hoping that luck would strike twice. He couldn't have gone to sleep if he wanted to. If he didn't know any better, he might have thought it was a dream, but the blackout that occurred and the scattered pages of a notebook with drawings sprawled on the ground next to his sleeping bag told him otherwise.

They were crude drawings that didn't capture what he'd seen in front of Oscar's house last night, but they were proof that he had seen something. The color was off. He didn't have a crayon or pen the kind of color green that he had seen. But oh how it moved. No one—he didn't care who they'd send from the government, because they would most certainly send someone—no one could tell him that had been a weather balloon or Venus or some trick of the mind. It was definitely something; some dark shape had passed overhead and then jumped—and disappeared.

After the UFO passed and the electricity turned back on, Frank had stood on the curb outside of Oscar's house with his mouth open. He yelled and high-fived him and then jumped back into the car to race home. He wanted to get to his telescope in the backyard. The telescope that his dad had bought him years ago.

He was six the first time his dad showed him the red planet Mars and he was hooked from the first peek. Oftentimes his mom would bring out hot chocolate for him and a cup of coffee for his dad as they sat side by side and stared up and talked about the stars and the sky. In less than a week, Frank learned the names of all the constellations.

After his dad went off to war, Frank kept a nightly vigil at the telescope. He took comfort in knowing that at some point they might be looking to the sky at the same time. Nine months into his service, his dad used his knowledge of the sky to navigate when his platoon was lost. It earned him a Medal of Honor.

Now he worked at Fort Ord just up the coast and trained the infantry divisions in basic combat before they were shipped over to Korea.

What had started as a hobby introduced by his dad became a passion for Frank. He planned on becoming an astronomer. He wanted to study the stars, planets, galaxies. He wanted to discover new planets. What he wouldn't give to be able to look through the high-powered telescope down at Mount Palomar near San Diego. That's where all the astronomers went to get the best look at the universe. What secrets might the sky surrender if he could just spend an hour searching?

Frank believed last night was a sign just for him. One that said he wasn't groping around out there in the cold and the dark. Of course, Frank had no idea what it was he'd seen exactly. But he knew it wasn't any type of aircraft that the US owned. And he was pretty sure it wasn't the Russians or Chinese. He didn't know of any other military in the world that had a plane that could move like that. To Frank, it was the proof he needed that humans weren't alone in the cosmos.

And really, wasn't that what everyone wanted to know? That they weren't alone, drifting in space on a huge rotating rock? That there was some purpose to the drifting?

The universe was constantly expanding, impossible to measure. That much was known. And the current theory was that it had a starting point, a big bang. Frank had read George Gamow's *The Creation of the Universe*. It made sense. Hubble's Law even supported the idea. Galaxies were growing farther and farther apart; they weren't fixed, which suggested that everything has a beginning.

Frank thought the fields of cosmology and astronomy were like the last frontier. The west had been conquered—now, it was time to turn to space. And it was massive. The ancients thought that there was only one galaxy. Now scientists knew that there were multitudes, possibly going on forever.

Lately, Frank had been reading the work of Ralph Alpher, an American cosmologist, who predicted there was cosmic microwave background, leftover radiation from the beginning of time. This hadn't been discovered yet, but that didn't mean the evidence wasn't there. As an astronomer, Frank would look for the photons, the leftovers.

People knew Frank was a fan of science fiction. And sure, he loved a great story, like *When Worlds Collide*—a movie he saw last year where some astronomers had found a rogue star that was on a collision course for Earth and eventually escaped to another planet and found it hospitable for humans. But they had no idea how much real science and news he consumed as well.

Frank knew one day the US would travel to the moon. The Air Force was already in a race against the Soviet Union to be the first ones to launch a spaceship into orbit. Human beings would not only one day walk on the moon, they would even put a colony on it. Then we would go to Mars and then to other galaxies. Astronomers would discover life on other planets. Frank was certain. He just hoped he'd be around to witness some of it.

He wrote a little more in his notebook, wanting to capture everything he remembered seeing on paper while it was still fresh in his mind. Before sending it out, he'd have Oscar look at it; he showed Oscar everything. While being an astronomer was his professional goal, he did have another dream. No one else knew about his short stories, not even his parents. He frequently sent in stories to *Astounding* and *The Magazine of Fantasy & Science Fiction,* wherever he could. Though none had been accepted yet, he saved all of his letters of rejection in the bottom of his desk drawer, knowing that one day, someone would have to say yes.

He was trying to write a conclusion to his latest story when his dad's voice pulled him from his thoughts.

"Frank," his dad said, suddenly standing over him. Even though he hadn't come home last night until close to midnight, he was already dressed in his uniform, shoes polished, coffee in hand.

"Yes, sir?" Frank said, turning over his notebook.

"You stay out here all night?"

"Yes."

His dad took note of the drawings on the ground.

"Seems like the whole county saw what you did. That and the blackout has got people concerned."

"What's the military saying?"

His dad took a sip of his coffee. Frank didn't know if he was avoiding the answer or if he didn't know.

"Whatever it was, it wasn't one of ours."

That admission was all Frank needed.

"Something else happened last night," his dad continued. "There was an accident. A girl was killed while biking home."

"What was her name?"

"Eleanor Hall."

Frank lowered his head. Eleanor was a nice girl, even

though he teased her from time to time. She didn't deserve what happened to her. He should have insisted he drive her home.

"Did you know her?"

"Yeah. She was in the Skywatch group with me."

"I'm sorry, son."

Frank had never known someone his own age to die before. Caroline would take it hard. He wondered if she knew about it yet. Frank usually got any news early because of his dad's position. He also had a police scanner that he monitored. His motto of "always be prepared" taken to an extreme. Danger could come at any time.

"What time did you leave the club last night?"

"I'm not sure, exactly. Close to eight, why?"

His dad nodded. "Do you remember anything unusual?"

"Other than the light, you mean?"

"Not that, I mean before. During your duty?"

He didn't understand what his dad was getting at, but Frank thought back. They had taken turns looking at the sky through the pair of binoculars. Bunny was sitting and reading as she usually did, looking up on occasion to pass judgment. Frank wanted to talk to her, but he was terrified. Something told him she was way out of his league in every way. He'd pissed Caroline off, but he couldn't remember why. Caroline always seemed to be angry at him—or at someone. She had buttons the size of Texas on her anyway. If he just looked at her the wrong way, he could set her off. Frank shook his head. Nothing of note that he could think of.

"Did anyone say anything about going somewhere?"

"What do you mean? Did something else happen?"

"I'm not sure. But Sheriff Jones would like to talk to you. You should clean up, maybe get a shave in. He's coming over in"—he looked at his watch—"thirty-seven minutes."

A tingling began at the back of Frank's brain. He stood up, gathered his sleeping bag and notebook. The light in the sky. It had something to do with the light. He believed that more than anything. He cursed under his breath, angry at himself for leaving the tower early.

He picked up the drawings and stared at one until it began to blur—the black ink shifting into the shape of a sphere. A shape that was metallic and contained a pilot who was not of this world.

8

CAROLINE

CAROLINE RACED THROUGH THE FOREST. ALONE. THE OTHERS should've been with her, but she didn't have time to wonder what had happened to them. She had to get as much distance as she could or else she had the feeling that everything would have been for nothing. She fought the tears that threatened to come and picked up her pace.

The farther she ran, it was as if an unseen hand reached inside her mind and pulled at her memories, her feelings, the guilt and the pain at leaving, like they were nothing more than fragile strands of an intricate web. The wonder at what was happening held on until that feeling was replaced with fear. It almost stopped her, except for the image that flooded her mind.

The tower.

If she could just get to the tower, she would be okay. The thought was primal. Instinctual. Programmed in her brain. Somehow she knew she would be safe there.

She kept going. But she didn't know if she was running in the right direction. The darkness assaulted her on all fronts. The faster she moved, the more it seemed as if the trees closed in, even meeting in their tips above, making it almost impossible to see the sky. A large winged creature swooshed somewhere above her. An owl? The wings beat the air. The sound deafening and terrifying.

A large, octopus-like root tripped her left foot and she went down, scraping her knees and palms on the twigs and leaves of the forest floor. She crawled forward, stumbled to her feet.

Keep moving.

Up ahead, a small shaft of light beamed through the tree-tops. Moonlight. Barely anything. But it was enough for her to get her bearings. She veered to the right. Her body now moving as if by muscle memory. And as she followed the light, all fear and sense of danger fled, as if wiped away. Her mind returned. Her sense of self. She was Caroline O'Sullivan. She was seventeen years old. She lived with her mother and stepfather. Her brother Jack died last year. Her best friend was Eleanor. She was president of the math club, even though she didn't want to be. She and Eleanor were in the glee club. She liked cherry Coke and dancing and—

The tower loomed above as she broke through the tree line.

Just like she knew it would.

She tore through the yellow line of tape wrapped around the outer edges. Odd, she didn't remember seeing that before. She climbed the stairs, noting that the bad one was broken all the way through. She wondered if John or Teddy, no, it would be Oscar who probably busted it. He was big and clumsy.

Inside the tower, she crossed the floor to the red phone on the counter. She picked it up, but didn't speak.

Suddenly, she wasn't sure of something. She knew she had

been in the tower, hadn't she? Her shift should be almost over, but it was so dark outside. What time was it? And why was she alone? She thought back to the last thing she remembered.

She remembered Eleanor had gone home, something about making a pie. Frank and Oscar had left early, but where were John, Teddy, and Bunny? Shouldn't they be with her?

Caroline looked up at the sky over the ocean. There was nothing in it. Nothing for miles. The moon shone bright, making the ocean glisten like a school of silver sardines was gliding along the surface. Normally she'd feel a sense of calm at such a scene. One that she grew up with. But now, suddenly, she felt as though something else was there. And a feeling of great dread came over her. Blanketing her like darkness.

"Hello?" she whispered into the phone.

Silence.

She looked behind her at the closed door. Did she hear footsteps coming from the wood? Up the stairs, waiting now behind the wooden door. The door that could open any minute with something or someone behind it.

"Hello?" Caroline said again.

"Air defense, go ahead," a woman's voice said.

"I don't have a plane to report, but I . . ." Caroline wasn't sure what to say. "I'm sorry, but I think I need help. I—"

"Who is this?"

"Caroline O'Sullivan."

A catch in her throat or maybe a gasp. "Are the others with you?"

"No. No, I'm alone. I . . . I think something's happened."

"Okay. I'm sending someone to you. Just stay where you are. It's going to be okay."

The words offered no comfort.

Caroline didn't know how, but she understood, as clear as she knew her own self, that everything was most certainly not okay.

She doubted it would ever be again.

9

JOHN

JOHN WOKE, HIS BODY ACHY AND HEAVY, AS IF HE HADN'T MOVED in days. His eyes took a minute to adjust to the harsh light of the room. A slow cold spread over him as he realized it wasn't his own. The one he shared with his younger brother Gary. This one was white and barren and reminded him of something, but the memory ran from him.

He sat up in the single bed, slowly and groggily, trying to catch the memory, only grasping the tail, which didn't give him much. Only a tingling that something was off. Suddenly a thick fog hung in his mind like it did in the tops of the trees near the coastline.

How did I get here?

There was a pink plastic jug of water on the table next to him. He touched the white band around his wrist. *Kawai, John* was written on it in black ink. He looked at the stark white room with a white curtain pulled shut acting as some kind of divider.

A hospital?

He had no recollection of why he should be in a hospital

room. Searching himself, there were no bodily injuries that he could detect. Taking a deep breath, his chest was clear. He wasn't running a fever. Now that he was awake, he somehow knew he felt better than he had in a long time. He definitely wasn't ill.

He heard the footsteps before someone reached the closed door. As it opened, John tensed, braced himself for the unknown, trying not to fear what lay on the other side.

A woman entered—Caucasian, with short light brown hair, dressed in a nurse's outfit.

"Oh," she said. "You're awake."

John watched her, unsure if he should bolt or speak. She seemed pleasant, but nervous. His eyes looked to the hallway behind her, but he couldn't see anything there except more white walls.

She smiled at him, but he thought he detected a wariness behind it. Again he felt that something wasn't right. Like she was an actress in an elaborately staged play. He lay in a bed that was a set piece. Her clipboard, a well-placed prop.

"I'll let them know."

Them?

She backed out of the room, leaving the door cracked open. He felt woozy then, like if he could only wake up, he'd be out of the hospital. He'd be home in his own room or . . . wait, he should be in the tower. Wasn't he supposed to be on duty? They were watching for planes. How'd he get here?

Next thing John knew, his parents were rushing in. His mother, hugging him like she used to when he was young, close and tight, not the reserved way she'd started to when he'd turned fourteen. His parents looked tired, aged suddenly, as if he hadn't seen them in a long time, which was odd because he had just dove with his father earlier that day, hadn't he? He even helped him clean the boat before going to the tower. They spoke to him in Japanese, another oddity. In public, it was always English. His father wanting them to appear the same as everyone else, to make others comfortable.

Eigo dake, he would tell John and Gary, one of the many by-products of the years in the camp. *Only English*.

They pummeled him with questions. Was he hurt? What happened? He didn't know he said. Where had he been? His father was telling him not to say anything to the authorities. He would find a lawyer. Someone Japanese. Someone they could trust.

John wondered why he would need a lawyer.

Gary, who was never shy with him, stood a little to the side of his mother. Was she shielding him? John tried to read Gary's eyes. Tried to look for the message he could be sending so John would know how to interpret the situation, but the brim of Gary's baseball cap covered them.

His parents asked again, what happened? Where had he gone? Did he know where the others were?

The others?

John wondered who they were talking about. Then his father said a name. *Caroline*. The name filled his mind, pierced the fog that still clung, and his whole body went into shock. He started to shake. Someone called for help.

John felt himself falling and falling, like a bird with clipped wings, farther away from the multitude that was now in the room with him.

• • •

When he woke again later, they told John that he had been missing for almost two days.

He thought they were joking, but the presence of Sheriff Jones confirmed the timeline. It didn't make any sense to him. Sheriff Jones asked him to explain what happened a couple of times. John recalled how he'd gone to his Skywatch shift at the tower by the water. He had been very late. Caroline spotted something strange in the sky, some kind of light. They'd watched it until it looked like it fell or landed in the forest. After that they decided to go and try to find it. But he couldn't remember if they actually found anything. Why couldn't he remember?

"Okay, son," Sheriff Jones said, "I want you to think very hard. What exactly was the last thing you remember?"

John became frustrated because this was now the fourth time he had been through this and they were all so freaked out because he'd been missing for days with no memory of where he went or what happened. Even worse, John's confusion over why he couldn't remember was now giving way to fear.

It was like there was a hole now where the memory should be. Pieces of things poked through—like the adrenaline and fear he felt trekking through the woods with the others. Caroline's arm brushing against his, how he held her elbow steady, how scared she was, and how all he wanted to do was protect her. He remembered it was dark, except for the two flashlights. Their feet crunched on the forest path. Teddy had been leading them.

And then, nothing.

How did he get out of the woods?

"I'm sorry, sir," he said to the sheriff. "I . . . I'm not trying to be difficult, but I honestly can't remember. What have the others been saying? Maybe they can shed more light. Where's Teddy? He was the one leading us."

John wondered where in the hospital they were. Maybe they were in a room like him. He thought it strange though they would be kept apart.

John looked at his father for answers, but his father stood in the corner of the room, arms crossed. His face a trained neutral, but John read the fear in his eyes.

His father didn't fear anything. Not the ocean and how it behaved. Not when his mother got really sick two years ago. Not when they lived in the camp. But he was afraid now, and this made John feel like he was drowning. He eyes darted from face to face and they offered no help. He tried to breathe, but the air was too thin.

"John," Sheriff Jones began, and then hesitated. "Only you and Caroline have come out of the woods."

John stared at the Sheriff, not understanding.

"What do you mean only me and Caroline? Where's Teddy? And Bunny?" John raised his voice, as if to call them and they would appear from another room in the hospital.

The nurse came into the room again followed by his doctor.

"It's going to be okay, John. We didn't tell you at first because we didn't want you to worry."

But they were the ones who looked at him with worry. The nurse had a syringe. John again felt as if he were stuck in a terrible dream. He stared at the plant over by the windowsill. Its leaves were green but too glossy as though they were fake. He began to think again that it was all a farce. These people weren't real doctors. It wasn't a real hospital. He looked at the door. He could rush the sheriff. But what was beyond the door? The unnatural light above him swelled and pulsed, glowing as if he were looking at it from under water.

His father touched his arm then. He bent low and said, "*John. Watashi wa koko ni imasu.*" John, I am here. The soft voice calmed him. He knew his father's voice. That was real.

"Caroline?" John said. "Is she okay?"

"She was the first one found," the sheriff said. "Just like you, she walked out of the woods, doesn't remember anything. She's home now."

John looked at his father for confirmation. His father nodded his head. "It's true."

John didn't even remember walking out of the woods.

The sheriff continued speaking. "I know this is a lot to take in. We're doing all we can to find your friends. We need your help though. As soon as you start to remember anything—the smallest detail—I want you to call me. For now get some rest. We'll try again tomorrow. And hopefully . . . well, hopefully, we will know more."

John had a terrible feeling that tomorrow he wouldn't remember anything either, but he didn't tell the sheriff that.

He also didn't tell the sheriff about the strange little bump behind his left ear. It was small, and not something anyone would notice. But his finger kept finding it while talking to the sheriff. A tiny bump just underneath the skin. After being discharged, John rode in the front seat of their old Ford truck. He couldn't shake the odd feeling that had come over him ever since he had woken in the hospital. It was as if everything had changed, but as they drove through the streets he had known his whole life, nothing was different. The same store-fronts. The same people milling about. The same smell of the ocean and breeze stirring through the open windows of the front cab.

But as his dad drove on, people turned to stare.

Or maybe he just imagined it.

It was as if he were now a visitor, an alien in his hometown.

When they got home, John's mom put a small bowl of okayu in front of him, even though he wasn't feeling sick. It smelled good, but he wasn't hungry. He felt the eyes of all three of his family members on him. He didn't know what they were look-ing for, but they kept searching.

When he couldn't take it any longer he stood up. "I want to see Caroline."

John pulled up to the small yellow house and waited a few moments in the truck. He'd never been inside. Never had the guts to drive up and knock on the door. What made him think he had the right to do so now?

If Reverend Eddleston, Caroline's stepfather, was surprised to see John at the front door, he didn't show it.

In fact, he said, "Hello, John."

"Hello, Reverend Eddleston. Is Caroline here?"

"She's out back. John, how are you doing?"

"I . . ." John didn't know what to say. He looked down at the ground, wanted it to swallow him up suddenly.

"It's all right, son," the Reverend said. "You will both be all right. Most important thing is you're back safe and sound. We're all praying for you." He put his hand on John's shoulder and squeezed.

John thanked him and walked through the pale blue kitchen, and opened the sliding screen door to a patio framed by a beautiful garden full of white roses. Caroline sat in a chair underneath a tan umbrella. Her mother sat at the other end, painting. The portrait was the face of a little boy. John recognized Jack, Caroline's brother who drowned last year.

He hesitated.

John didn't fully understand why he needed to see Caroline. Maybe it was because she was the only other person who might know what he was feeling. She had been there. She had also come back without a memory of what happened. They were connected because of it, that much he was sure of.

But now that he was in her presence, he was nervous. They barely interacted outside of the Skywatch club. Coming here implied an intimacy they didn't have. He looked behind at the sliding door he had just passed through, like a threshold of their private spaces, thinking that he had made a mistake.

But Caroline looked at him then and smiled.

That was the invitation he needed. He crossed the brick floor and sat in the open seat next to her.

"The last thing I remember is you," she said.

They watched her mother for a few moments. Listening to the sound of the brush on canvas, back and forth, back and forth, like the fluttering of a small thing's heartbeat.

John placed his hand over hers on the table between them. It felt natural to do so. It felt like a coming home.

10

DR. BILL MILLER

....

DR. BILL MILLER STOOD ON THE EDGE OF THE WOODEN PIER WATCH-
ing the brown seals on the big gray rock off the shore. They
reminded him of that unusual spider he found in his kitchen a
couple of weeks ago. It had been a brown, nasty-looking thing
with a deformed, humped back. When he'd taken a broom
to sweep it up, the spider had exploded into hundreds of tiny
spiders that scattered across the floor. Turns out it had been
a momma carrying all her babies on her back. He had almost
thrown up.

That's what this rock looked like now with the seals clinging to it, except their big brown bodies slid in and out of the
water effortlessly. The seals were louder than he had remembered. And they stunk. Even from where he stood, he could
smell them. Like seaweed and fish and piss.

He took a drag on his cigarette. Dropped it on the ground
and crushed it with his toe.

The whole town smelled like fish.

He'd come right away, wanting to interview the subjects as
close to the sighting as possible. It was his belief this was the

best process. He wanted to document their experience as soon as he could. The more time crept on, the greater the room for error, falsehoods; memory had a way of distorting things, telling the truth, but from a slant.

Project Grudge, the Air Force's official program to investigate UFOs due to the odd rise in sightings across the country at the end of the war, had first come calling two years ago. Grudge didn't last long though and Bill wasn't surprised. Oftentimes evidence was ignored or skewed to fit a certain narrative—one that claimed practically all of the sightings were natural phenomena, hoaxes, or a result of post-war paranoia. The leadership had intentionally looked to debunk everything. Now, he worked for Project Blue Book, which had two objectives: to analyze UFO-related data and to determine if UFOs were a threat to national security. It was mainly about the latter, of course, but Bill was more interested in the former.

Out of all the cases he investigated, first with Project Grudge and now Blue Book, he'd come to find 80 percent of sightings were easily explained by all kinds of things—weather, balloons, stars, clouds, even human error. It was the other twenty percent that bothered him. The 20 percent that couldn't be accounted for, couldn't be solved.

The 20 percent almost made him a believer.

Almost.

But this. This case was strange right from the start. He had a premonition—not that he took much stock in such feelings, he was a scientist after all—that it would land in the other 20.

He took out a folded sheet of paper from his back pocket to review. Multiple UFO sightings spotted a couple of nights ago were of a greenish to bluish light in the shape of a triangle or V. Some even noted it had looked red at first before changing to green. Bill had a list of names he would be making his way through. All would need to be interviewed, responses documented and studied. He was methodical in his approach—his nature necessitated it, as did the Air Force.

Bill looked up and watched the seals some more. One lifted its head and yawned before letting out a loud primal call.

Bill chuckled. "Me too." He was tired.

The summer of '52 was proving to be challenging with UFO sightings escalating across the country. The higher-ups were nervous, which is why he was part of the team at Project Blue Book investigating. The goal was to try to understand what, if anything, was behind them. The CIA and the Air Force were worried a sneak attack could come from Russia disguised as something else, through the false sightings. Though Bill doubted the Russians would be that clever. He doubted Russian involvement at all. He thought it was both simpler and more complex than that, something in the public psyche, a kind of Jungian collective consciousness due to the fears of living in a post-nuclear society.

He'd gone to D.C. just the previous month because of two weeks of strange lights in the skies. Project Blue Book's official explanation was people were merely experiencing illusions due to temperature inversions. But headlines like "Jets Chase D.C. Sky Ghosts" from *The Washington Daily News* didn't help the situation. It was like the media was baiting the government.

They wanted aliens or the supernatural. Something that could explain their growing fear and anxiety of living in a world that could be here one moment, gone the next. They didn't want the banal truth.

Bill had interviewed one of the pilots who had followed the lights, the bogies, as he had called them. He was a reliable witness, not someone given to delusion. The man had obviously had an experience of some kind. He believed he saw something he could not explain away. It was the belief that was hard to argue with. It was also hard to argue with Navy specialists who believed the objects to be solid and not weather-related based on how the lights showed up on their radar. In the end, Bill thought the temperature inversion theory was likely, even with the credibility of the pilot and the radar specialists. It was a more objective view of the facts, in his opinion. It just wasn't what the public wanted to hear.

But did they really want to hear it was extraterrestrials? As if the world needed to add them to the growing list of possible disasters to face. People were terrified the world was going to end because the Russians had gone nuclear. Would hearing that little green men from Mars were plotting an invasion really make anyone feel better? It was one thing to answer the question whether human beings were alone in the universe. It was quite another to imagine the answer being hostile toward one's very existence.

Up until now, sightings of funny lights in the sky were the most popular that Bill investigated—primarily UFOs, sometimes odd-shaped humanoids. Bill often accredited this to something the witness had watched or read in some science fiction movie or book. He was quick to spot those who had been influenced by pulp fiction. Their minds literally projecting what they had read into their experience. They looked up, and instead of being in wonder, they saw the unknown as a threat—not the possibility that Bill saw. As an astronomer, he knew there was so much yet to discover in the field that it was hard for him to waste his time chasing imaginary aliens flying around the country. But it paid well, better than his current teaching assignment.

The cosmos were beautiful. Mathematically pure. Not some Wild West soap opera where aliens plotted to destroy Earth. Besides, if there were aliens, they would have to be so advanced to figure out how to travel by light. An impossibility, really. Would they come all this way only to play peek-a-boo with a few random members of the human race in the middle of the night? In corn fields? Or in the woods? Or in someone's backyard? Highly improbable. And Bill placed his belief in facts and figures. In numbers and probabilities. He was a man of science.

The main reason he came here to Monterey was because of the four Skywatchers. According to, he checked the name on his paper, Caroline O'Sullivan, one of the two who had been found first, after watching the UFO and trying to report it, they'd decided to investigate where they thought it landed.

All four teenagers went into the woods. Caroline O'Sullivan and John Kawai were the only ones to come out, more than a day later. They were each found separately at the observation tower, disoriented and hungry and with no memory of what had happened or where they had been after entering the woods.

They couldn't say where their two friends, Bunny Stapleton and Teddy Messina, were, either.

Chances were their disappearance had nothing to do with the light in the sky. But still.

He would start with the girl.

Bill arrived at the girl's home, a smaller, more modest one compared to those he'd seen driving in. When this was over, he decided he'd come back and play a few rounds at the beautiful golf course he'd passed along the coast. He exited the car and the red front door opened. A tall man stepped out. He crossed the lawn and held out his hand to Bill.

"Dr. Miller?" he said.

"Yes. Reverend Eddleston?" Bill said.

"Call me Charlie."

Charlie Eddleston stood there a moment next to Bill on a particularly well-groomed green lawn. With the hand that they'd just shook with, Charlie now grabbed the back of his neck and massaged it, as if he had a crick that needed working out. He was tall and broad-shouldered with short brown hair, looking more like a point guard than a minister.

Charlie looked down at Bill and kind of shrugged. "Well . . . You really think what they're saying is true?"

"What are they saying?" Bill asked.

"Flying saucers?"

Bill cringed at the words. They dismissed what Bill did as a joke. It also made people afraid to come forward with their stories. The term wasn't even an accurate description of the 1947 incident where the reference came from. The pilot who'd had an encounter with glowing discs said the objects he saw behaved "like a saucer if you skip it across the water."

A reporter is the one who called it a flying saucer, and the name had stuck. It infiltrated public consciousness, not to mention Hollywood and the alien and space movies that had come after. The aliens rained down terror. They probably had Orson Welles to thank for that. He was the one who'd started this war between the worlds.

"We call them Unidentified Flying Objects, UFO being the acronym."

"UFO," Charlie repeated.

As if to anticipate one spiraling across the sky, Charlie looked up. "And aliens?" he whispered, giving the word an almost holy affect.

"I don't think we can jump to any conclusions," Bill said. "Though I would find it hard-pressed to believe that aliens have anything to do with it. But I am here to collect the data, talk to people about what they witnessed. Your daughter was gone for over twenty-four hours. She obviously experienced something. I'm here to try and ascertain what, or even *if*, that had to do with the object she saw."

Charlie nodded. "We believe in God here, Mr. Miller." He kept his eyes on the clear blue sky.

A group of seagulls cried overhead as if echoing the sentiment.

"It's a miracle we got our Caroline back," he continued. "A twofold one. Janice, Caroline's mother, took last year pretty hard. Our son Jack drowned right out there at the beach. Ever since,

Janice has been . . . well, the best I can explain it is away. But the night those lights appeared and Caroline didn't come home, Janice got up and started painting again. She hasn't created anything new in a year. Somehow Janice has come back to us too." His eyes were misty. "I'm grateful I've got my girls again."

Bill would be wary to attach personal meaning to unrelated events, but he wasn't about to get into that with the minister. Instead he asked, "Did you see anything that night?"

"No. I was at the grocery store picking up some bread. I wish I had seen the lights. Maybe I could help a bit more if I had. Plenty of people are confused, scared. It's one thing to see lights in the sky. Another thing entirely when kids go missing."

Out of all the cases that Bill was sent to investigate, there had never been any missing persons. This one was certainly unique in that regard.

"And fear can be a strong motivator in how to interpret signs, coincidences. I'm just telling you that when you leave I'll be here. I'll be the one trying to help people make sense of what they saw."

"I'm not here to make meaning," Bill said. "I'm just here for the facts."

"Facts . . ." Charlie repeated.

Charlie studied Bill a moment before motioning that Bill follow him into the house. Bill noticed how neat and tidy the living room was with gray couches and a white throw rug. A vase of fresh wildflowers sat on the coffee table on top of a little white crocheted doily. He had one just like it on his own coffee table at home.

"Why don't you have a seat," Charlie said. "I'll go get

Caroline. Oh, and, Dr. Miller, we agreed to this interview because we want to do anything to help find the other two kids, but Caroline's been through a lot. Her best friend was killed the night she went missing. Her memories still haven't returned. Frankly, this is new territory. We don't really know what to expect. I simply don't want to give her any more stress than she already has."

"I'm just here to discuss the UFO," Bill said. "If she's uncomfortable in the slightest, I'll stop the interview."

Bill sat down on the couch, which was not as comfortable as it looked. He removed his black hat and placed it next to him. Big band music drifted into the room from somewhere—possibly another room. He was about to crane his head to try to locate it, when he heard steps coming from the hallway Charlie had disappeared down.

Caroline walked into the room. Bill noted she wore a blue skirt with a white belt and a blue button-down blouse. Her feet were bare, so he saw her toenails were painted pink. Her blond hair was in a ponytail. She looked like a typical teenage girl to him. She sat as if she was unsure the love seat across from him would hold her. In fact, she moved as if she were discovering the living room for the first time. When she set her eyes on Bill's, he was struck as if he were staring into the eyes of a much older person.

"Caroline, this is Dr. Miller," Charlie said.

"Hello," she said.

"Hello, Caroline."

"I'll be in the kitchen if you need me," Charlie said and left the two of them together in the room.

"Thank you for talking with me," Bill said. "Did your father—"

"Stepfather," she said.

"Stepfather, excuse me. Did he tell you why I'm here?"

"He said you're from the government and you're here about the light. Not about Teddy or Bunny. Or even Eleanor."

When she said Eleanor, her eyes pooled.

Bill knew who she meant. The girl on the bike. Killed instantly. A casualty of the UFO sighting, which was also a first for Bill.

"I heard about that," he said. "I'm so sorry."

"She was . . ." Caroline licked her lips. "She was shy sometimes, but not with me. With me, she told me everything. She was going home to make meringue. She didn't even like meringue."

Bill noticed a large scar on the palm of Caroline's left hand then. "That looks like it must've hurt." He wanted to get the focus off her friend's death or else he might not be able to get anything out of her.

She closed her hand. "Maybe."

"Can you tell me how you got it?"

"No."

"No, you don't want to tell me about it, or no, you can't tell me about it because you don't remember how you got it?"

"I . . . can't. I don't remember. Charlie," she called. "Can you get me some water?"

Charlie came in a few moments later with two glasses. He set them next to the flowers on the table.

"Thank you," she said.

"Do you mind if I record our conversation?" asked Bill.

"No."

He opened the gray box he'd brought with him from the car and placed it next to the water glass. He made sure the two spools of tape were aligned properly, adjusted the dials, and cranked the lever.

"Why don't we start with what you do remember. Can you tell me about the light?"

"I spotted it first. Off the coast. I knew they weren't regular plane lights right away."

"How did you know that?"

"Because I'd seen enough and had gone through the Air Force training. They were behaving differently. Moving strangely. Glowing, even. And it was more like one light . . . I think."

Caroline played with the side of the glass, wiping the condensation.

Bill proceeded with the same line of questioning he did with everyone when he investigated a sighting. "Can you tell me what other object, like an everyday object, the things you saw most looked like?"

Caroline stared at the glass. "It looked like . . . the bulb from a Christmas tree."

"So it was round?" Bill made a note. He thought it had been a V shape.

"I don't mean the shape, I mean the light. I'm sorry, I didn't really see a shape. I don't think . . ."

"That's okay. You're doing great."

"I am?" She leaned back. "It doesn't really feel like it."

Bill just looked at Caroline, giving her the space to continue.

He'd learned that sometimes subjects would reveal things they might otherwise not if he stayed patient and listened.

"I keep hoping and waiting for the memories to come back. I don't understand how Teddy and Bunny can just be gone." She paused. "Their parents both came to see me. Wanted me to tell them what happened." Her eyes welled with tears. "But I . . . I don't remember. How could I not remember?"

Bill didn't like crying. He pulled out the blue-and-white-checkered hanky from his left pocket, but Caroline didn't take it. He dropped it on the table between them and cleared his throat.

"Sometimes when a person has a traumatic experience, there is short-term memory loss."

She nodded, wiped her eyes with her hands. "That's what the doctor said. He told me, and John, to try to rest, not worry. It will all come back. But it's not coming back. It's like I have this space in my brain. Here." She touched the back of her head. "Where something is missing. I know that makes me sound crazy. But I'm not crazy. You can ask all my teachers." She broke into sobs, this time grabbing his hanky.

Bill stared at a piece of artwork on the wall, a watercolor of the coast, until she composed herself again.

"I'm an excellent student," she continued. "I'm never late. I sing in the glee club and in the church choir. I'm a member of the National Honor Society. . . . I even remember this time when I was three. I was with my father, my real father, not Charlie. We went to get ice cream—vanilla and chocolate scoops on a cone. On the way back, he let me sit on his lap while he drove the truck. It was blue and smelled like cologne and wood. My dad worked in construction. Even now when I close my eyes, I can still picture the scene, the memory of it." She closed her eyes.

She opened her eyes and stared at Bill, her fingers massaging a spot behind her ear. "It happened so long ago, but I can still see it. So why do I have no memory of something that happened just a couple of days ago?"

Bill knew he'd gone too far. He shouldn't have pushed the girl. She wasn't ready for the interview. He should have started with others.

"Caroline," he began. "Why don't we try this another time?"

"Wait," she said. "I do remember one thing."

"Okay," Bill got ready to take down her words.

"I was scared," she whispered.

The phone rang, causing Bill to jump. He immediately felt stupid. He let the girl get to him. What was wrong with him? Thirty-three years old, a professional, and letting a young girl unnerve him.

He heard Charlie answer the phone in the kitchen.

"Hello?"

"Caroline, I—" Bill began.

"Shh," she said and turned her head toward the kitchen, as if it would make her hear better.

Bill studied the girl. Though she was calm now, she exuded a nervous energy. He didn't know if she was telling the truth about not remembering. The way she acted made it seem like she was omitting something. Or that there were some psychological side effects to what she had experienced. Delusion? Paranoia? Could this be considered a first break? She seemed awfully young for that. He'd have to research the answer, but he didn't think schizophrenia manifested itself in one her age.

He went through a couple of likely scenarios in his mind: a) they'd been lost in the woods and due to dehydration and hunger they now suffered from memory loss. This seemed like a stretch because the woods weren't that large; b) they'd been kidnapped and only she and John had escaped or were set free. He hoped this wasn't the case because if it were, the odds were decreasing hour by hour that the other two kids would be found alive; and c) it was all a hoax, just some kind of sick game the teens were playing. A polygraph test might be needed.

"I see. Thank you," said Charlie.

He hung up the phone and walked back into the living room. He looked right at Caroline.

"They found another one."

11

BUNNY

BUNNY WALKED OUT OF THE PINES AND ONTO THE SMOOTH PAVE-
ment of the winding road.

Lost. The word scared her. She'd never been lost in her life.

Last thing she remembered was following the others and
then she wasn't and then she was alone in the woods and confused. She tried to get back to the tower, but she couldn't find
her way. Everything looked the same, making it hard for her to
get her bearings.

Back home she was used to concrete and brick and alleyways. Street signs and markers like the deli or the cigar shop.
The woods were something people visited on a weekend. Once
you left the city, the woods surrounded you, but the thing was
she hardly left the city.

Her feet ached and were dirty, covered with the dark soil
of the forest floor. Her new saddle shoes looking as if she'd had
them for a year already. How'd she get them so scuffed up? She
looked up and down the road, shielding her eyes because the
light was so much brighter. When did it get light? Wasn't it
nighttime? Her equilibrium shifted and she stumbled.

A funny feeling rose from the pit of her gut.

Did I stay out overnight? she wondered.

As her eyes adjusted, she noted that everything had a soft lavender color to it. Kind of like she was waking from a dream. She looked back at the woods and they seemed to expand and close in like an accordion. The motion made her dizzy. She squeezed her temples with her hand to steady herself.

Where was everyone?

She began walking down the street in what she thought was the right direction.

From what she could tell, it was early morning, just after sunrise. A couple of dogs barked from somewhere far away. They must have stayed out all night.

Bunny stopped. She looked around for the others, half expecting them to be following her down the road. But she was alone in the street.

"Teddy? John?" she whispered. "Caroline?"

An eerie silence answered her back. It was gray and chilly, like most mornings. The little sun hid now behind full clouds. It would rain today. Maybe not all day, but soon. She buttoned up her gray sweater.

She didn't remember drinking or doing anything that would mess with her memory like this. Not like that one night when she and Judy back home had met up with those guys from Queens. Bunny should have known they'd be trouble, right then and there. But she was looking for a little trouble that night. Her mother had left them. That's what the note said.

Her mother hadn't been happy in a while. She wrote that this was her chance and she had to take it. The chance was a guy she had met at a restaurant. She fell in love. It was that simple, she said. There was no apology, just a plea for Bunny's dad and Will and Bunny to understand.

Bunny didn't tell her dad or her brother about the second note. The one addressed only to Bunny with a salutation that said "Always follow your heart." The one that gave a number and an address. It was in Cleveland, Ohio. Cleveland. She left them for a guy in Cleveland. Bunny had imagined her being whisked off to Paris or London or even San Francisco. But Cleveland?

Bunny had torn up the letter, gone out with her friends, and partied all night. She had woken up on the couch in Judy's apartment with a bowl on the floor next to her. It already contained vomit. Bunny had vowed never to drink that much again. That whole night had been a blur. She remembered making out with some guy named Anthony. Singing on the subway. Running through the streets. Clearly, she didn't want to remember all of it. But she knew that if she really tried, she could remember. The scenes of the night, the feelings would all come flooding back, so she chose not to remember.

This was different. She had no choice in the forgetting. It was like it had been chosen for her.

Another odd thing was that she was sore too, as though she'd done calisthenics in gym class. She usually sat out during that part. She'd gotten a note from her "doctor" saying she couldn't do anything strenuous. It wasn't that she couldn't do it. It was that she didn't like being forced to do anything she didn't want to do. And gym class was something she just didn't want to participate in, plain and simple.

She stretched one arm and then the other across her chest as she walked, wracking her brain, trying to remember the night. But it was as if someone had taken a big marker and blacked out that part. She couldn't remember if she tried. Her mind was locked and it wouldn't cooperate.

And that really scared her.

What the hell happened?

As she walked she heard a lone car begin to approach. Normally, she'd keep her head down and ignore it. Her upbringing in the city taught her senses and body to be on guard when she was by herself. She knew she could easily end up as one of the missing girls she'd read about in the newspaper. Girls who slipped through dark alleyways and crevices in the city as if through a sieve. Even though this was practically paradise, she instinctively knew there were holes here. They were disguised by beautiful coastlines. But there were gaps just the same. The dark was the dark everywhere.

But why had the others left her? She knew she shouldn't have gone with them. Something in her gut said not to, that it wouldn't do any good. That would be the last time she ignored a red flag. When did she become the type of person to go on a wild goose chase after lights in the sky? Her stomach suddenly sank with a new understanding. Her greatest fear rose in her mind. The others were probably somewhere together, laughing, feeling like they had played a great trick on her. Especially Teddy. He acted like their leader. She wanted to know who put him in charge.

They'd gone into the forest together, and then they had abandoned her.

She did what she normally did when that happened.

She decided to cut bait. *Ha*, she thought. Before, she hadn't understood the meaning of that phrase. Now that she'd actually seen a fisherman cut bait, it had new meaning. In her mind's eye, she imagined Teddy, John, and Caroline hanging from a long thin wire. She took a pair of scissors, snipped, and watched them fall away from her.

The car approached more closely now, and when she turned around, Bunny was relieved to see it was a police car. She waved her arms. It slowed and pulled up alongside her. The officer rolled his window down and looked at her.

"Hello?" Bunny said.

"Are you Bunny Stapleton?"

"Yes," she said, startled. *This really is a small town.*

"Thank God." He stepped out of the car.

Great.

Her dad must've called the police when she didn't come home. That was just like him, having the whole police force out looking for his baby girl. She couldn't blame him though. She knew he sometimes checked on her in the middle of the night. She'd hear her bedroom door creak open. She'd always pretend to be asleep. He never mentioned it in the morning. She knew he was checking to see if she was still there. That he wondered if she would just disappear one day—like her mother.

It was partially why she felt guilty about wanting to return to New York. She had to think of herself, though. Her dad still had Will, even though he was old enough to be on his own. She needed to focus on getting back to her real home. Forget about this lame town with no friends and now real enemies.

"Yeah. Um, I'm sorry if my dad got you all worried, but I think I need a ride home."

"You okay? Here, come on, let me get you in the car." He helped her into the back. "There's a blanket you can put on."

She covered herself with it.

The officer ran around to his side and got in. He kept looking at her through the rearview mirror. His gaze made her feel suddenly exposed. She pulled the blanket tighter around her, even though it was scratchy and smelled like cheap cologne.

He picked up his walkie, pressed a button, and spoke into it.

"Hall to base." He waited until a voice crackled through.

"Base to Hall."

"You won't believe it. But I just picked up one of those missing kids. Bunny Stapleton."

Missing kids?

"Yeah, just out here walking along the road."

Bunny's gut churned again. She searched through her mind, trying to remember. She noticed a photo on his dashboard. It was her class picture. The one she hated because it made her look young and naive. She was neither. Teddy's photo was also there. He looked handsome, like usual, his grin revealing his confidence. She stared at his picture, his eyes drawing her in so much that she blushed and had to look away.

"She doesn't appear to be injured in any way. Just confused, like the other two. I'll bring her over to the hospital."

Bunny felt her heart race. *What was he talking about?*

He hung up the receiver and turned to face Bunny.

"Don't worry," he said. "You're safe now. Everything's going to be all right."

He put his lights and siren on. Bunny winced at the loudness of the sound.

When they rounded the bend, Bunny watched the ocean to the left of her stretching long and wide. It started raining. The side window streaked with droplets and soon she was looking through a gray watercolor painting.

She couldn't quiet the feeling in her gut that something was wrong. Or not wrong, exactly. Maybe the correct word was *off*.

The painting blurred and warbled the faster the car moved, making it harder for Bunny to see through to the other side. She sat back in the car and suddenly a wave of emotion hit, regret or loss, she couldn't tell which, but somehow she knew the others hadn't abandoned her. She looked at the picture of her and Teddy on the dash and fought back tears.

She needed to find them. If she did that, then everything would be all right.

She had no reason to, but she trusted that feeling. At the moment it was more real and true than anything else she'd once believed in.

12

FRANK

FRANK SHIFTED FROM LYING FLAT ON THE GROUND, HOISTING HIMself up onto his elbows, and peered through the binoculars.

"What're they doing?" Oscar whispered next to him.

"Walking around."

"In the tower?"

"Yes."

"What're they looking for?"

"Clues, probably."

"Like what?"

"I don't know. Be quiet."

The door to the tower opened and the man wearing the black hat, suit, and tie came down the stairs first. Frank kept his eyes on the government man; he knew who he was without being told. No one from around there dressed like him. He was way too formal. Besides, the government goons always looked the same. And this guy wore a hat. That was the final piece of uniform.

He watched the other men, mostly from the sheriff's office from what Frank could tell, follow him down the stairs. They didn't have any military personnel handling the case—Frank knew from his dad. Although he supposed the FBI could get involved the longer Teddy was missing.

"What are they doing?" Oscar asked.

"Standing in a circle, talking."

The government man lit a cigarette while the sheriff pointed to the trees.

"Now they're moving. Walking into the woods."

Frank waited until the four men disappeared from view before he got up. Oscar followed his lead. He stepped over the yellow tape, careful not to break it, and came to the tower, touched the brown wooden railing. He noticed the board to the stairs was broken in two and wondered when that had happened.

"We're going in after them?" Oscar asked.

"Yep."

"What do you think they're going to find?"

"I don't know, but they're going to lead us right to it."

Frank made sure to keep a good distance between himself and Oscar and the men up ahead. The padded forest floor acted as a sound buffer for their footsteps, and the trees were good cover. Thankfully the men didn't have any dogs with them, or else he and Oscar would be toast.

After what felt like maybe two miles, the trees began to thin and open into a small clearing with little shafts of soft light beaming in. The men walked out into it. Frank got as close to the edge as possible and lay on his stomach like he had when they were watching the men at the tower. More yellow tape sectioned off a spot toward the middle. Because it was so quiet, Frank could hear them talking.

"We searched much of the woods," the sheriff said, "and came up empty. I still don't understand it. But then we found this." The sheriff walked over to the yellow tape. "We might have missed it, except one of my guys, who was a pilot in the war, noticed something strange about the ground."

The government man bent down and examined the area within the tape. Even from Frank's vantage point, he could see the floor was blackened, as if there had been some type of fire.

"Campfire?" the government man asked.

"That's what we thought at first, but these marks aren't made by regular fire. Our guy says they've been burned by fuel. Jet fuel."

Jet fuel? What the heck did that mean?

"How jet burns got so far into the forest and at such a remote location is beyond me, but there you have it," the sheriff said.

The government man touched the burnt ground. He stood and walked around the markings. He brought his fingers to his nose, smelled them.

"I'm going to have to speak to your officer," the government man said.

"Of course."

The government man then stood and looked up at the clear blue sky. Frank followed his gaze. The clearing was a big enough area for something to land, but the object would have to come in straight down, hovering from above. As far as Frank knew, the U.S. military didn't have any planes that could land like that. Though he supposed a helicopter could, with a skilled pilot.

"Can we get someone to climb the trees?" the government man asked.

"The trees?" Sheriff Jones stood, hands on his hips, his stomach hanging over his belted pants. "What do you hope to find?"

"I'm not sure."

Frank would be looking for any damage. Broken branches. Singed leaves. Any kind of mark that could show an aircraft had landed.

"Look, Dr. Miller," the sheriff said. "I've still got a missing kid. A community that is in fear. I don't plan to let the public know of this."

Dr. Miller. Frank wondered what kind of a doctor the government would send. Some kind of scientist? A PhD maybe.

"I think that's wise," Dr. Miller said.

"But . . ." the sheriff continued. "Do you really think we have evidence of a *flying saucer* here?"

Frank noted he said the words *flying saucer* as if he were in a large cathedral, with emphasis and reverence, maybe even a bit of fear. He sounded like Mary who worked with his mom at the library. Earlier that day he'd gone to check out a book and Mary was worried that the aliens were going to come after her.

"Why would they want you?" Frank had asked.

"Frank," his mom had said. She made her *tsk-tsk* sound that she usually reserved for their dog when he behaved badly.

"Sorry," he said. "I didn't mean they wouldn't want to take you. I'm sure if I was an alien I would——"

"Frank," his mom said again and looked at the book he'd checked out. "*The Principles of Hypnosis*?" she asked him.

"Just curious," he said.

She'd given him a hug and kiss. "I'm just so grateful my boy came home early. That poor family. Their son is still missing."

"Teddy," Frank said.

It did worry him that Teddy still hadn't come back. He wondered when he would return. If the others had, wasn't it plausible that Teddy would have come back by now, too? There was also the fact that they supposedly couldn't remember anything that had happened. That was the craziest part. How could they all not remember what had happened to them? He was dying to speak to them, but he'd been shy, and when he went to talk to John, his parents had turned him away with fear in their eyes.

"Now don't go looking for trouble, *mijo*." Frank's mom gave him a hug and a kiss.

"Mom," Frank ducked and rolled his eyes at her intimate gesture. "I won't. Bye."

Frank thought his mom would probably think that he hadn't listened to her, but he didn't plan on getting caught. He planned on getting to the bottom of whatever was going on. Besides, it would be great to add more "true" details to his story. And these guys, the government man and the sheriff, definitely knew something.

"Flying saucers?" Oscar said.

"Shhh. They'll hear us."

"Highly unlikely," said Dr. Miller. "We won't know what we have here until we examine the evidence. Did you take samples?"

"Yes," said the sheriff.

"We will wait to draw conclusions then."

"All due respect, doctor, our town is small. If word gets out, every Tom, Dick, and Harry will come out of the woodwork with their own stories, especially the ones down in Carmel and Big Sur. There's some interesting people who live out there with strange ideas about the world. Artist colonies and spiritualists. We've already received calls from a group that is loosely tied to some kind of religion about aliens communicating to them through séances?"

"Yes. UFO cults. We are aware of the one in Joshua Tree," said Dr. Miller.

UFO cults? This was getting good. Frank couldn't believe it. Finally something huge was happening.

Dr. Miller and the sheriff bent down, examined the ground. Frank could no longer hear what they were talking about. They eventually straightened up and left the way they'd come.

Frank waited a good five minutes before moving. Then he and Oscar crept out into the clearing. Frank saw that the burn marks were scorched and not in a circle like a campfire, more like jagged lines. The area around it was flat as well, as if something big had made an indentation. Frank looked up. There was no way something could have shot straight down. Nothing from this world anyway.

A tingling crept up his spine.

This was real.

A spaceship had landed in the woods and he had missed it. He cursed under his breath again, wanting to kick himself for leaving early.

"So?" Oscar said. "You thinking what I'm thinking?"

Frank raised his eyebrows.

"First contact?" said Oscar.

Frank nodded, a huge grin spreading across his face. "Sure seems like it."

He and Oscar had spent plenty of time discussing the possibility of how a first contact would go down between humans and aliens after they had listened to *Dimension X*'s radio play about two spaceships meeting in outer space.

Frank stood. "Teddy, John, Bunny, and Caroline must have seen the UFO. They entered the woods because they saw it land or something. They came all the way here and saw a ship."

"A flying saucer."

"Whatever. It wasn't the Russians."

"Aliens," said Oscar.

Frank nodded. "They must have been taken aboard their ship. Later, they were released with their memories wiped of what happened."

"But how come they weren't all released at the same time? And where did they go?"

"There must be a mother ship with a cloaking device in orbit around our planet. Or maybe what they saw out here scared them so much they've blocked it out of their minds. The aliens were hostile and they had to separate and hide. Maybe the ship never left this area and they escaped in different times. I have no idea, Oscar. These are just preliminary hypotheses. We need to talk to them, find out if they are lying about their memories. Or lack of memories, I mean."

Frank couldn't believe he had missed out on the biggest event to happen in his lifetime. Why had he left early? Just because he was bored? He promised he'd never let that be a determining factor in his decision-making ever again.

"Come on," Frank said as he started to walk away.

"Wait a minute," Oscar said. He had been looking at the ground, now he bent to touch it. "Frank?"

"Yeah."

He lifted his finger to show the dried rust color now attached to it.

"Blood," he said.

13

CAROLINE

CAROLINE TOOK IT AS A GOOD SIGN THAT HER MOTHER WAS CREATing again, even if it was the same little face over and over. Caroline stared at the portraits. Amazed at how lifelike they were. She'd almost forgotten how talented her mother was. Caroline didn't share her mother's visual artistic skills, but she did play the violin. Years of lessons made her only proficient though. They hadn't given her a passion like the one her mother had for painting.

She stood behind her mother, watching each carefully laid stroke. Jack stared out at her from the painting like he knew a secret.

Tell me, Jack, Caroline thought. *Tell me the truth. Did you feel pain when you died?* And then she thought, *Is Eleanor with you?*

Her eyes welled up.

Eleanor.

The grief overwhelmed her. Caroline wished she'd told her friend how much she'd meant to her. She wished she'd insisted Eleanor stay. Or that she got a ride from Frank. It was cruel that Eleanor had been taken from her just like Jack. Two freak accidents in only a year, and she was the common denominator. She couldn't protect anyone. Had this been her fault too?

"Mom . . ." she began, but Caroline didn't know what to say. She touched her mom's shoulder. Her mom stiffened, but continued to paint.

Caroline felt a presence behind her and turned to see Charlie watching. He darted to the side, as if she'd caught him in some kind of act he wished to keep private. It had been like that lately, after the government man's visit. Charlie had become . . . distant. He looked at Caroline in a way that made her feel like she was a stranger now in her own home. It was the look he had when he was stuck and trying to figure out the path his sermon should take.

Charlie said she could stay home this Sunday morning, but he couldn't. He had a flock to help process. Many had seen the light in the sky and were worried about what it meant. His flock was about 125 regulars, which swelled to 205 on Easter Sunday, at a small Methodist church with a white steeple, exactly like one would imagine in a small town.

After he left, Caroline went inside the house, sat on the couch, and watched some television. She was glad not to be at church. She liked the people, it's just that she didn't want to deal with their looks or questions. Well-intentioned or not, she couldn't give them what they wanted. She couldn't give them answers.

The neighbors had come to the door after she was found. Caroline had watched them through the slits in her blinds.

They craned their necks, hoping to see her, as if seeing her would provide some clarity. They shared with Charlie their fears and concerns that kids had gone missing. They talked about kidnapping. About abduction.

Caroline knew they just wanted to hear all the dirty details they expected from a case where a girl went missing. How her face had flamed when the nurse, and later the police officer, had asked her those intimate questions. Had she been attacked? Raped? The word was so ugly.

Violated?

No. No one had touched her.

She ransacked her mind, overturning, digging, mining crevices, and she still came up empty. She couldn't remember. It was the most terrifying thing—the not knowing. She began to fill the holes with all kinds of possibilities—none of them good. Why else would her mind block her from the truth unless the truth was too painful to bear?

And Teddy. Where was Teddy? He should have come back too. But he hadn't. He'd walked into the woods that night, just like the rest of them, and disappeared. The dark had taken him. She tried not to think about it, but her mind kept circling back to the truth she didn't want to face—Teddy was dead. Just one more person she hadn't been able to protect.

Something had happened in the woods.

Caroline found her way out. She broke free.

But Teddy didn't.

She shuddered.

Why couldn't she remember?

She caught a strand of the dream last night. Cold and dark

and alone. No, not quite alone. Something with her. Something that made her cower in the corner.

The phone rang, making Caroline jump. She let it ring and ring. It stopped but started ringing again right away. After eight rings, she finally crossed the room and picked it up.

"Hello?" she said tentatively into the receiver, watching her mother from the kitchen window. She had started a new portrait. This time it was Jack on the beach, playing in the sand.

"Hello, Caroline?"

Caroline recognized the voice. A wave of nausea suddenly hit her.

"Bunny?"

"Yes." It sounded like she was about to cry. Bunny's voice was small and distant, like it had to travel far to reach Caroline.

She listened to Bunny's breathing. And for a moment she felt like she was in a dark quiet space, just the two of them. Their foreheads pressed together, the heat of their breath between them. The sound of a door being unhinged, and then Bunny's forehead was ripped from hers. Caroline was alone in the dark. Her singular breath rising in front of her.

"Can you meet me and John?" Bunny said.

"What?" Caroline stammered, confused by what she had just felt. "Where?"

"By the big tide pool."

"Is it safe?"

Bunny didn't answer. She had already hung up the phone. Caroline wondered why she had asked the question. Did anything feel safe these days? She left a note for her mother and took the bike.

• • •

It only took Caroline fifteen minutes to bike to the spot. She saw them, close to the water—Bunny and John, standing on the rocks, facing the ocean. She left her bike on the sand and walked to where they were.

Unsure of how to greet them, she stuck her hands in her pockets. To her surprise, Bunny grabbed her arm and embraced her.

She then stepped back. "Oh, that's strange. I'm not really sure why I did that." And then she asked Caroline, "Are you?"

"No."

Caroline didn't really like Bunny, not that she would have admitted it to her face—that would have been rude. She felt uncomfortable at how intimate Bunny had just been, hugging her like they were good friends. She and Bunny barely knew each other.

"Hi," John said. He held out his hand. When she took it, she felt the same feelings she had when he'd come to see her— tenderness, warmth, and, this time, loss. She dropped his hand quickly.

"How'd that happen?" John pointed to the scar on her palm.

"I don't know." Caroline rubbed the spot. It was sore as if it happened recently, but she couldn't remember. She moved a little farther away from him, confused by the way he made her feel—like she wanted to both go to him and run from him.

"I got this when my foot went through the board. Remember?" Bunny said, referring to a cut that ran up the side of her calf. "It healed pretty quickly. I don't even think it scabbed over."

"That was right before the four of us went into the woods," Caroline said.

The three of them didn't mention Teddy's name. They didn't have to. His absence filled their minds like the sound of the waves. Constant and in the background. In fact, the rushing and receding of the tide seemed to be repeating his name over and over.

Caroline heard it calling. She shivered, even though the sun was already out. Early. Shining on them. Like it too knew they would be there.

She watched the water.

Where did Teddy go?

She was beginning to think maybe they had dreamed him up. Maybe it had only been three of them in the forest. Maybe Teddy had never gone with them. Maybe he was somewhere, even now, waiting for them to get the joke.

Where did we all go?

Bunny removed a cigarette from a pack in her jeans, lit it, took a drag, and passed it to John who then passed it to Caroline. None of them stumbled with the intimacy. It was as if they had shared smokes for years. *Hadn't they?* Confusion darkened Caroline's mind. Being with them felt strange because the only time they were together was when they were with the Skywatch club. They would never hang out like this. Only she and Eleanor were friends. Her eyes watered again. She looked away at the small pool near her feet where two yellow starfish curved their arms over the side of a rock.

Eleanor.

Charlie was the one who told Caroline that Eleanor had died the night they disappeared. She'd watched him deliver such news before to others, even to her own mother. As a minister, he was often the bearer of loss and tragedy. He was expected to carry it, translate it with meaning.

Caroline appreciated the way he told her about Eleanor, without sentiment. Just the facts. He knew she would want it that way.

The facts were these. It was an accident. The driver, a man from Carmel, was distracted by the funny light in the sky. He didn't even see Eleanor. Just felt the truck hit something. Charlie was told that she died instantly.

Caroline thanked Charlie for being truthful, though they both knew that when you were told that someone died instantly, that was code for saying a person didn't feel much pain. That's what the doctor said when Jack died. Jack was so young that he just took all of that water in his lungs and went to sleep. No pain involved.

But no one knew that for certain.

Caroline imagined the shock Eleanor must have faced. One moment barreling home to please her mother and make meringue. The next being crushed by a truck. She hoped it had been fast. The driver said she already appeared dead when he checked her. But did he feel for a pulse? Did he back up in horror at her twisted body under the truck? (Charlie spared Caroline no details, knowing full well she'd find them out from someone else.) Did he watch the life leave her big brown eyes?

"I miss Eleanor," Caroline said, startled. She hadn't meant to say the words out loud.

"Me too." John's voice caught in his throat. Caroline took a sideways glance, but could only catch his profile. He was looking at the water.

"I shouldn't have let her go," Caroline said. "I should have made her stay the full shift."

"She passed me on the way home," John said. "I should have offered her a ride. I should have—"

"We should have never followed the light," Bunny said.

Caroline walked a little closer to the water's edge. "No, we should have stayed in the tower." They were all silent then. Caroline knew you could go crazy with should haves. Her whole year had been an exercise in should haves with the loss of Jack. Now with the loss of Eleanor, she was afraid she'd break. Become like her mother.

And then there was the other loss. The loss of time and memory. And Teddy. The loss that was working its way between her and John and Bunny. The loss that brought them together.

"What happened to us?" Caroline whispered, barely audible above the sound of the waves slapping the shore.

Bunny and John flanked her on either side. She tried not to pay attention to him, not to stand too close. Instead, she focused on Bunny's short hair flapping around in the wind. Caroline tucked one of her own stray hairs behind an ear. Her fingers found the small lump that was there on the left side. It wasn't noticeable to the eye, but she kept returning to it. Wondering how it got there.

"I figured since the two of you came back before me," Bunny

said, "maybe this memory loss has a time stamp or something. But you guys still don't remember anything?"

"No," Caroline said.

John shook his head. "Only . . . only that there was something. This big thing that we found. I think we found something in the woods."

"We did?" Caroline said. She didn't know if it was being with them or what, but she could feel her mind tingling as she probed around the dark spots, like small black holes.

"We did. We did find something," Bunny said. "But what about Teddy?"

"This is crazy," John said. "People don't just disappear." He picked up a small stone and threw it into the white, foamy water.

"People disappear all the time," Bunny said. "They just don't usually come home."

"I keep returning to that night, over and over," John said. "Thinking that if I just try hard enough, maybe I'll be able to remember a detail or a feeling or something that will bring everything else back. So that I remember what really happened. But it's like everything's been—"

"Erased," Caroline said.

Bunny and Teddy stared at her. The word just came to her without thinking. But once she said it, she realized that's exactly how it felt.

"Erased." Bunny repeated her, like she was trying on the word.

Caroline bent down and picked up one of the starfish. The top of it was rough. She pulled it out of the water and turned it over, running her fingers along the tiny suction cups on the bottom.

"I keep waiting for Teddy to come out next. I've even gone back to the tower, stood at the edge of the forest," John said. "You know they got it all taped off now? But I just stand there and stand there . . . he doesn't come out."

He's not coming out, Caroline thought. She shivered. The starfish bent the tip of one of its arms.

"You okay?" Bunny asked. She offered Caroline the cigarette. Caroline's hand shook as she took it.

"Yeah."

She didn't know why the thought had popped into her mind, whether it was a feeling or real. But she kept quiet. Trust had to be earned. She took a drag. After all, she barely knew these people.

Just because they went into the woods together didn't mean she owed them anything now that they were out. She passed the cigarette to John, careful not to touch his fingers. Being close to John made her nervous now. She found herself hyperaware of his presence, which was unsettling.

She liked John . . . as a friend. Besides, he was Japanese. It would never work between them. Not that she cared about their differences, but others would. There was a couple in town, a Caucasian man and a Chinese woman. She saw the looks some gave them. Caroline didn't know if she had the strength to face that kind of scrutiny. She wanted less attention, not more.

But there was something about John. Caroline first noticed him last year at a baseball game. He made playing shortstop look so easy, catching balls and throwing them to the bases with such accuracy. Then the first time he was up at bat, he hit a home run back past the scoreboard. The whole way around the bases she couldn't take her eyes off of him. He played as if he had been born to do so. There was something beautiful in watching purpose and intention come together like that.

Eleanor had noticed, of course. Eleanor noticed everything, which is why when John walked into the room for the first Skywatch meeting, she'd nudged Caroline so hard one of her books fell off the desk and onto the ground. John didn't miss a beat. He picked it up, glanced at the title, *Introduction to Calculus*, smiled, and handed it to her.

He did have a killer smile.

John gave her the same smile by the water just as she handed him the smoke. But there was something more in the smile now, too. A kind of understanding that she didn't know how to inter-pret. It made her uncomfortable.

Something had happened in the woods. Something between her and John. Caroline didn't know what, but it was still there now between them. She could feel it, the energy in the air.

"We need to go back," John said.

The boldness of his words startled the others.

"What?" asked Bunny.

"Teddy's out there, somewhere. We need to look for him."

"I'm not going back," Caroline said.

Caroline didn't want to admit it, but she was afraid. Before she might have been the one leading the charge, insisting that they find Teddy. But now . . . now she didn't want to step into the woods. They had become dangerous, the thing of stories.

Bad things happened in the woods. People got lost. People never returned. People changed.

She had changed somehow. She could feel it.

"If we stick together—"

"Like the last time?" Caroline said, cutting Bunny off. "We stuck together and then, well, who knows what happened. But I'm terrified of it."

"It's okay, Caroline," John said. "I won't let anything happen to you two."

"You can't promise that," Caroline said.

She dropped the starfish back into the water, watched it get taken by the swift tide. She hadn't meant to separate it from its friend, but she probably had. Just like her and Eleanor.

"This is so weird," Bunny said.

"What is?" John asked.

"This. You acting all John Wayne on us."

None of them laughed at Bunny's attempt at a joke. Instead, they passed the cigarette around again.

"Look," John said. "I don't understand what happed out there, but something did—"

"No. Something *is* . . ." Bunny said. "Can't you feel it?"

Caroline closed her eyes, and for a second she did. It was the sense of standing on a cliff. That feeling of staring down and suddenly wanting to jump. The pull so strong you had to fight to back away.

Caroline heard a car drive by slowly then, and she opened her eyes. It stopped and then backed up. Caroline didn't recognize the guy driving.

"Who's that?" Bunny asked.

The man raised a camera and started taking pictures.

"Oh, no." Caroline turned away. She didn't need her face in some newspaper.

"I don't know, but I'm gonna find out." John walked toward the car.

"See? John Wayne," Bunny said again. "You okay?" she asked Caroline.

Caroline shrugged. "Gee. My best friend just died. Another friend is missing. I can't remember a whole twenty-eight hours of my life, and everyone's treating me like a freak. But I guess I'm okay. You?"

"Same." Bunny gave a small smile.

"Wow. Never thought we'd have something in common."

Bunny laughed. She looked out at the ocean. "Actually, when I was lost and making my way out of the woods, my first thought was that you guys left me out there."

"What?"

Bunny shrugged.

Caroline remembered running through the woods. Confused about being alone, but knowing where she was going. She tried again to recall why she was there. Why she had been running even. But again, the memory wasn't there.

Behind them, Caroline could hear John yelling at the guy in the car. But she didn't turn to look. She watched the small waves with Bunny.

"You ever have a dream that you feel is so real, you don't realize you're dreaming?" Bunny asked. "You swear it's your real life? But then you wake up and understand the whole time it was a dream?"

Caroline nodded.

"That's what this feels like," Bunny said.

"Like you dreamed going after the light and going missing?" Caroline asked.

"No, like this is the dream part. I keep pinching myself, splashing water on my face in the bathroom, trying to wake myself up."Bunny reached her hand out in front of her. "It looks so real," she said.

A fear crept over Caroline because she knew what Bunny meant. It's why she kept staring at her mother's paintings. They were so lifelike. Just last night, Caroline had stood in her bedroom after waking from a strange dream. She had stared hard into the darkness, thinking something was there, but nothing was.

The car peeled off and sped away. Caroline heard John walking back to them. "Stupid reporter," he said, standing next to Bunny.

"Reporter?" Bunny asked. "What'd he want?"

"He wanted to know what the aliens said."

"Aliens?" Caroline asked. "Do you guys think we saw aliens?"

The idea was ludicrous. That was the stuff of those silly stories that Frank and Oscar were always reading from the magazines in the tower. They were fiction, not reality.

"We did see a UFO. It doesn't mean it's from Mars or something. But we all know it wasn't any plane," John said.

"Maybe we were taken," Bunny said. "What else explains us being lost for so long?"

"But where did we go?" Caroline asked. "And why?" Caroline shivered. She wrapped her arms around her body.

"You cold?" John asked. He began removing his sweater as if to offer it to her.

"I'm okay," Caroline said, even though she wasn't. The whole situation made her want to run away from the two of them. She couldn't keep her teeth from chattering.

"What would aliens want with us?" Caroline asked.

No one answered. Caroline was suddenly uneasy. She looked back at the road. She realized they were out in the open. Exposed. Anything could come swooping down on them.

"Maybe we shouldn't be here," Caroline said.

Why shouldn't they be outside? They hadn't done anything wrong. Had they? But the water was still whispering Teddy's name. And Teddy was still missing. Why were they here and Teddy wasn't?

"Do you think they'll find Teddy?" Bunny said, as if she had been listening to Caroline's thoughts.

"They have to," John said. "He's my friend."

Caroline wondered why he added that last part. She eyed him suspiciously.

"He was my friend, too," Caroline said. Not close, but they knew each other.

"Well." Bunny ground what was left of the cigarette into the sand. "He wasn't my friend. None of you were. But now . . . I guess that's changed, hasn't it?"

"Is that what we are? Friends?"

"I don't know what we are. But let's start with telling the truth. If anyone remembers something, we tell each other immediately," John said.

Caroline agreed along with Bunny, but she couldn't help

wondering what the others were keeping from her even now. Like how she didn't tell them about her dreams. The ones she started having the night she came home. The dreams that she couldn't quite remember either. All she knew was that they weren't good. How could they be if she woke from them screaming?

As they left the water's edge, Caroline glanced at the forest in the distance. It held secrets and it held Teddy. And it didn't look like it was going to give up either anytime soon.

14

JOHN

....

JOHN WATCHED CAROLINE PEDAL OFF. HE THOUGHT HE SHOULD follow her, especially after Eleanor's death only, what—a few days ago? It might as well have been a lifetime ago. But . . . Caroline wasn't his responsibility, no matter how he felt. He couldn't believe what happened to Eleanor. She'd been a friend to him, kind when other girls were stuck up or even mean. Since he heard of her death, he kept replaying the last time he saw her. She seemed happy, a little out of breath from biking, her face flushed. She'd stood up to get traction over the hill and then she was gone. He had no idea she'd be gone forever.

Eleanor had teased him about Caroline. How she knew he liked her, he didn't know, but John couldn't hide his feel-ings around Eleanor. Truth was, he didn't want to. Eleanor had become a confidant, a co-conspirator in whatever he hoped would happen between him and Caroline. Now that Eleanor was gone . . . John didn't think he'd have much of a chance. There was also this strange feeling that he'd already blown his opportunity. That he had let Caroline down somehow.

He tried to remember. Tried to retrace the steps in his mind of what happened that night. But every time he came up against the forest, it was like his mind shielded him. There was a thick veil—a membrane he couldn't break through. It reminded him of being underwater and looking up. The sky wobbly and grayish, but there on the other side. Only, John couldn't come up for air. He couldn't get to the other side of the water.

It scared him. Teddy still missing. The fact that he couldn't remember what had happened to them in the woods, or what he'd seen, or even more what he might have done. He felt out of control. His body even felt different. He opened and closed his hands in front of him. He had a strong grip because of playing baseball, but he'd noticed that his hands were faster now. No, that wasn't right—his reflexes were faster. They'd somehow acquired a muscle memory he couldn't place.

His finger found the spot behind his ear again. Then there was that. How'd he get that odd lump? He'd looked in the mirror and couldn't see a mark or anything, but something was there that hadn't been before. Or maybe it always had been, and he'd forgotten that, too.

His father told him not to try to remember. To just be present, go about his days, and then the memory would come. *Practice presence and breathing and being*, he said. His father advised that the mind and body and soul were all connected. Somehow there had been a fracturing and now John just needed time to heal.

But he didn't have time, did he? Every day that went by and they didn't find Teddy was another reminder of how dangerous John's amnesia was. What if he had the secret to Teddy's whereabouts? What if he had the information that could save

Teddy's life? John couldn't bear the weight of being responsible if anything bad happened to Teddy. He had the burden of being linked to Teddy his whole life. If Teddy didn't come back alive and well, John would snap like a twig, cracked in two.

When John arrived home after his meeting with Caroline and Bunny, he recognized Mr. Messina's car parked in front of his house. He knew they would come. Wouldn't his parents show up at the Messinas'? Wouldn't they demand the truth if the tables were turned? If he had been missing for days? John was surprised they hadn't come over sooner.

John entered the house and saw the four adults sitting at the kitchen table in a kind of tableau. His mother and father placed directly across from Mr. and Mrs. Messina. John had a flash of seeing them in the same position years ago. Hands gripping the small tea cups. The tea set that had been John's grandmother's, one of the few things of value his mother brought from Japan. For generations, the set had been witness to many conversations—from the joyous to the solemn. The way John's father's jawline moved. The way his mother was holding her head at a specific angle. John felt afraid watching them there.

The deal that sealed their fates together had been made around that table. The Messinas would take care of the home until their return. Keep their belongings, like the tea set, safe from looters. That the Kawais would return, there had never been any doubt.

The two fathers had shaken hands. There was comfort for John in that handshake. A handshake between two fishermen meant a binding loyalty. A cord not to be broken.

• • •

Now the four sat together again around the table. The Messinas were dressed formally—Teddy's dad in a black suit and tie, and his mother in a long black dress and a hat with a black veil that hung just past her eyes. Teddy's dad was a strong, wiry man like John's own father, with strong, calloused hands. His face had the look of a man who spent his time at sea—a dark olive complexion with already deep-set wrinkles around the eyes and forehead. John had a hard time looking him in the eyes—they were Teddy's, a pale blue.

Mrs. Messina smoked cigars and played bridge with a group of friends every Saturday. John knew this because he and Teddy had stumbled upon them many times. She laughed easily and long. Teddy's dad was also free with his laugh, as well as his anger. John was always struck by the way they revealed their emotions so publicly. He had to fight the thought that it was rude. John's parents, especially his dad, were very funny and light-hearted inside the home. In fact, his mother could be quite the joker. Gary had inherited her sense of humor. Outside the home, however, they were more *tatemae*—they did not expose their inside feelings. There really wasn't a good word for it in English; John thought of it as having two selves—one for public and one for private. The private was *honne*, or "true sound." Only family and maybe close friends saw one's *honne*.

John approached the adults sitting at the table as if he were encountering a wounded animal. The panicked anguish of Mr. and Mrs. Messina filled the room. His father motioned for John to sit in the empty chair at the table.

"John," he began. "Mr. Messina has some questions for you. I told him you would be more than happy to answer anything."

"Yes. I will try," John said. He kept his hands folded on top of the table like the others.

"We wanted to speak with you at the hospital, but the doctor said to give you some time," Mr. Messina said. "But we couldn't stay away any longer. Have you remembered anything about our Teddy?"

"I . . ." John swallowed. "I don't . . . it's like one minute, we were walking through the pines, searching for that strange light, and then . . ." John got a flash of Teddy up ahead of him, leading. Teddy stopped, held up his hand. He looked back at John, his eyes wide from the vision of something just up ahead. Teddy crouched down. John did too. He was crawling toward John, then a strange foggy nothing, like a dream. John's mind jumped to him running, stumbling through the woods alone. "Then, I was running through them. There's no in-between. Believe me, I want to know what happened to me, to Teddy, more than anything." John felt a sweat break out along his spine.

"But surely you remember something about Teddy," Mrs. Messina said. "It's not like Teddy to stay out all night. To miss work and practice. He's a good boy. He'd never want to make us worry this way." She started crying.

Mr. Messina put his hand on hers. He removed it to continue to ask about Teddy. He spoke with his hands the same way that Teddy did, accenting the ends of his words. John's hands remained still, like his parents'.

"Look, we won't be upset with anything you have to tell us. Anything."

"I'm sorry, Mr. Messina." John's heart raced. "I don't know where Teddy is."

John sat at the table with his parents until he heard the Messinas' car drive away from the house. His mother got up and started clearing the tea set. Gary, who had been in his room this whole time, came out and leaned against a wall, watching John. His father lit a cigarette and stared at the spot where Mr. Messina had been. An unfamiliar quiet settled over the house.

Unable to stand the scrutiny, John needed an escape, a distraction. But he knew if he left, they would be deeply hurt. His mother was already preparing dinner.

The piano, a long-ago gift for his mother from his father, stood in the far corner of the small living room. John walked over and sat down at the bench, ran his fingers over the keys. He began playing. It soothed him. Calmed his mind. His fears about Teddy still missing. The overwhelming thought that kept repeating over and over in his mind: *Teddy is dead. Teddy is dead.*

He meandered along the keys, letting his fingers find the melody that helped quiet his fear. The song was simple but beautiful. Something he knew inherently.

When the last note rang out he felt much better.

He stood, and turned to see his mother staring at him. She'd come up directly behind him while he was playing; he hadn't even noticed. His father and brother also watched him, their expressions the same as hers: confused and even worried.

"How . . . when did you learn to play like that?" his mother asked him.

John looked at her oddly. "What do you mean? I've always played. . . ." And then he realized that he didn't know how to play the piano. His mother played. She loved music, gave lessons to the neighborhood children, but she didn't force it on her own. John was never patient enough to practice the notes. But now he played. His hands hovered above the keys, knowing exactly where to go.

John backed away from the piano as if there was some magic possessing it. Something sinister now lurking in the keys or the wood.

But he knew it wasn't the piano.

Something had changed.

He had changed.

His family's silent questions filled the room, sucking all the air out of it.

"I've got to go."

John ran out of the house and jumped in the truck. He didn't know where he was going, he just wanted to put some distance between himself and whatever had just happened in his home. But he knew it wasn't the house that contained the problem.

The problem was something had happened to him in the woods.

The problem was Teddy was still missing.

In the rearview mirror, John spied a police car, so he slowed down. He took one of his hands off the wheel and wiped it on his jeans. He couldn't stop sweating. If he got pulled over, the cop would surely think something was wrong. They were following him, he was certain of it. But when John turned left at the next intersection, the police car continued going straight.

John took a deep breath, tried to steady his nerves. *No one is following you. No one knows anything.*

The thoughts invaded his mind as if governed by their own independent will, and surprised him.

What are you worried about them knowing?

He drove to the tower, parked his car a little farther up the road. It was abandoned. No one was using it for a Skywatch shift. He wondered when, or if, they'd start back up again. People were probably spooked. He didn't blame them.

He walked over and saw the yellow tape that told people it was a crime scene. John ignored the tape. He stepped over it and continued walking right up to the edge of the forest, stared into the pines as if they might give something up.

And he let himself indulge in a guilty thought that came to him whenever he realized Teddy really might not come back. The thought was that he would be free from Teddy's shadow. Relieved that he might not ever have to compare himself to Teddy, or feel like he could never measure up again. The thought wrapped itself around his heart like a snake. And now he felt shame for having it.

John fell to his knees at the edge of the wood.

"Teddy!" he yelled into the darkness. "I'm sorry!"

But only the wind answered.

15

BUNNY

BUNNY HATED *ALICE'S ADVENTURES IN WONDERLAND.* SHE preferred a certain realism over all the fantasy like *The Hobbit* and such. Her father loved them though and had read the popular ones to her as a child. She didn't want to disappoint him, so she listened and fell asleep rather quickly. This is probably why he chose them for her. Falling down holes into mysterious realms, talking rabbits and tea and creatures. None for her, thank you. She thought it very juvenile.

Bunny loved her mysteries though, *And Then There Were None* being her favorite. She read it at least once a year, that and *Pride and Prejudice.* She was also a sucker for a good romance, not that she had any romance in her life at the moment.

After meeting with John and Caroline, Bunny realized she was in a type of mystery herself. And she was determined to solve it. She ran back through the conversation in her mind. She walked and processed. Looking for clues. Holes in their story. But she came up empty. They appeared to be just as lost as she was.

Ever since she was found walking by herself along the side

of the road, Bunny had felt off. Why couldn't she remember what had happened to her and where she could have been for days? She felt powerless, and none of it made any sense. Why were the other two found before her? And where was Teddy?

Teddy. Before, the name wouldn't have meant anything to her. Now she felt, well, she wasn't sure what she felt, but something was there that hadn't been before. She chalked it up to general concern that she would have for anyone. Before she wouldn't have much cared about him or the others, but now they were linked. She couldn't break that chain in her mind if she wanted to.

They had experienced something together. Of that much, she was certain. Maybe Teddy was the key to their remembering. If they could just find him, maybe it would all come crashing through—the memories, the why, the reason for it all. But the more hours and days that passed without him returning, the more it seemed unlikely he'd be found.

Bunny refused to think that Teddy was dead. He was waiting for them . . . for her. That in itself was an odd thing to feel toward a boy she barely knew or even cared for. Just last week she'd considered him to be an arrogant jerk. But now something else was there. Emotion. The catch in her throat when she thought of him.

Something had happened in the woods. Something that made her feel close to Caroline, John, and Teddy in a way she had never been before. But what?

It was driving her crazy not to be able to piece it all together.

She felt that she had somehow become like Alice herself, that she had tumbled down a rabbit hole of her own. In fact, just thinking about it, she had to stop walking for a moment because she got a sense of nausea, as if she were actually free-falling. She looked around at the scene—the ocean and the rocky shore— certain that she could take her fingers and scratch through the veneer that surrounded her. She even reached out her hand, but all she touched was air. Invisible. Pure.

She inhaled a big breath of it now, blew it out in the direc- tion of the ocean. The sun was out, the morning haze having burned off, now warming her. The normal pleasant sea breeze was uncharacteristically missing today. She was suddenly very thirsty, hot, and tired. She should have asked John for a ride home. She had a ton of should haves.

The bell on the market door announced her presence when she opened it. Thankfully, it looked empty, except for the owner behind the counter. He nodded to her when she walked in. He was reading a newspaper. The headline something about North Korea and the Chinese. She glanced around the aisles and found what she wanted—a small bag of chips and a bottle of Coke. She didn't even notice Frank and Oscar were there until she practically bumped into them.

"Bunny, oh, wow. How are you?" Frank asked.

Bunny cursed herself for going out in public. She wasn't ready to face people yet, not that she knew tons, but Frank and Oscar were not on her list of people she needed to run into. The two boys stared at her. She took a deep breath. Sooner or later, she'd have to face others. She'd have to get used to the curious looks. Wouldn't she do the same if she had heard that some of her classmates had disappeared? She'd want to know what happened, too.

But the way Frank looked at her was with genuine concern. "Okay."

Frank and Oscar looked like they were expecting her to say more, but she didn't know what to tell them.

"You know how John and Caroline are?"

"Yeah, they're pretty shaken up, like me."

"I wish I would have stayed," said Frank.

"You wish you would have been lost in the woods for days and then come back with no memory of what you did or what happened to you? Or better yet, you wish you were like Teddy? What about Teddy?" Bunny tried to keep her voice down, but she couldn't. Just thinking about it all had her scared.

"Do you know where he is?" Frank asked.

"No. No, the point is I don't know anything. Do you understand how terrifying that is?"

"I'm sorry, Bunny," Frank said. "I didn't mean to upset you."

Oscar, who hadn't said a word, just nodded. He now whispered. "We know about *them*."

The way he said *them* and looked to the roof of the store gave Bunny a chill. She followed his eyes and they rested on a small crack in the ceiling she'd never noticed before. The crack appeared to waver and open, becoming sinister the longer she stared at it.

"Where'd they take you guys? To their ship? Couldn't have been far. You weren't gone long enough for light travel. Or maybe you were. Did you get a chance to look at their technology?"

"Oscar, are you kidding me right now?" Frank said, punching Oscar on the arm. "Real subtle."

Bunny looked from one to the other. "I gotta go," she said, immediately turning away.

She didn't feel like talking to them anymore, especially after Oscar's crazy speculation. Aliens and spaceships. Of course they would jump to that conclusion.

She left them in the aisle and quickly made her way to the counter.

She asked the store's owner, Mr. Chang, how much she owed him. He stared at her in an odd way. Maybe he didn't understand her.

"How much?" she repeated, digging into her purse for some change. "Wait, and I'll take a pack of gum, cinnamon."

Bunny felt a prickling on the back of her neck. She saw Frank and Oscar out of the corner of her eye watching her.

She turned around and gave them the look she'd perfected in the city when guys would give her attention she didn't want.

"What's the matter?" she asked.

"Nothing," Frank said. He looked down at the small bottle he held in his hand. Oscar leaned over and whispered something to him.

She was about to call them out again, but Mr. Chang spoke to her, so she gave him her attention.

"Sorry I was startled, Miss. Your accent is so good."

Bunny smirked. She knew she had a pretty strong New York accent, but people didn't usually comment about how good it was.

"Thanks. Born and raised in Manhattan. No one's ever complimented me on it, though."

"Is that where you learned Mandarin?" he asked her.

She looked at him funny, even laughed, and replied, "I don't speak Mandarin . . ."

But then the room tilted a little. Bunny reached out and grabbed the counter with both hands to steady herself. Suddenly, she realized she'd been communicating with Mr. Chang in Mandarin the whole time. One of Bunny's hands flew up to her mouth, as if she could feel the words. "Oh . . . I—" but she stopped. *What was she going to say?* She had a knack for learning new languages. This she knew she got from her dad, who was also gifted that way. But she couldn't speak Mandarin. She'd given it up because she'd failed at it.

Bunny picked her things up off the counter. "Thank you," she said. She walked quickly past the boys behind her, holding her head down. Outside, she leaned against the building and tried to calm her racing heart.

How could she suddenly speak a whole other language? What did it mean? She tried really hard to remember the woods. Or anything else. She couldn't learn Mandarin in a couple of days, could she? And what—she'd been captured by aliens that taught her Mandarin? Why? Were the Chinese behind the object they'd seen overhead? Not the Russians?

"Bunny, you okay?" Frank looked at her from the sidewalk.

She took a long sip of Coke before peeling herself off the wall.

"I'm fine." She was not fine. How did she suddenly speak Mandarin?

"Listen, sorry about Oscar, but you gotta admit it's not as crazy as it sounds. You did see a UFO. We all saw it, actually.

And today we followed a government guy to a spot in the woods where something landed."

Bunny's eyes narrowed at him. What was he talking about? She tried to rack her brain. Had they found something in the woods? They definitely had gone looking for something. She remembered they'd walked a long time. And then Teddy turned around, looked back at them because he was in front. His face glowing with excitement, not fear. He had seen something just ahead. He and John were going to investigate. But her mind couldn't see any further or hold on to the memory. It evaporated like a wisp.

"Maybe I can help is all I'm saying," Frank said.

"You can't look in here, can you?" Bunny pointed to her head.

"No, but I can try to help you remember."

She was about to ask him how he thought he could do that, when she suddenly had the feeling that she wasn't safe. Being out in the open where anything could happen. She needed to get home.

"No, you can't," Bunny told him.

She walked away and it felt like everyone she passed looked at her. And whispered. They knew who she was. She imagined them pointing, recoiling from her. As if she was now something to be feared. It was contagious, this fear. It went before her— up the street, announcing her presence to everyone nearby. It trailed behind her, too.

Her thoughts ran wild.

Maybe she had encountered some extraterrestrial presence like Frank and Oscar thought.

Maybe experiments had been performed.

Maybe they'd messed with her brain, made her smarter or something.

She tried to outrun the possibilities before they could consume her. But the terror held her in its grip, almost snatching her off the ground. She felt as if she were not in control of her own body and mind anymore.

She got to her house, raced to the bathroom where she shut and locked the door behind her. She turned and stared at herself in the mirror. She looked for something, anything that might give her a clue. It could be a tiny mark even. She pulled back her hair, examined behind her ears, her neck. She removed her clothes and studied every part of her body she could.

Nothing. Except—there. A small lump she hadn't noticed before, just behind her left ear. She craned her neck to see it in the bathroom mirror, but couldn't see any mark. Still, something was there now that she didn't remember being there before. She felt the spot; a little knot under the skin, like a small spot of fat.

What the heck?

She took a deep breath and stared at herself in the mirror. Her hair was the same—dark brown pixie cut. Her facial features—brown eyes, her father's straight nose and her mother's olive complexion, a couple of freckles scattered across her high cheekbones—were unchanged.

But in her mind she knew this wasn't true. Something had changed.

Somehow, she had come back different.

What had happened to her?

Her mind spun as she tumbled down a black hole. She stared into her own eyes and tried hard to remember. But she couldn't read anything beyond fear. The fear that said something bad had happened. That it was still happening, now. And that it was far from over.

16
FRANK

FRANK WROTE DOWN WHAT HE KNEW SO FAR. *UFO. DISAPPEARANCE.* *Memory loss. Teddy missing. Jet fuel. Blood. Mandarin.* It was a whole lot that didn't make sense, especially the last part. What did speaking another language have to do with anything? He thought Bunny could have been pulling his leg about not knowing the language, but the look in her eyes told him she was just as spooked about it as he was.

Frank had almost told his dad about the blood part, but he didn't want his dad to know he'd been snooping, following the government guy. His dad would probably ground him. So he kept that to himself, along with the scorched ground.

Something landed in the forest and took Bunny, Caroline, John, and Teddy.

Something still had Teddy.

Frank drew a picture of a humanoid with a large head and skinny body. It was the depiction of an alien in the eyewitness accounts he'd read. Supposedly these types of aliens had been seen so much, they even had their own name: the Grays, on account of their skin being described as pale gray in color.

Frank wondered if that was the extraterrestrial they were dealing with. Or maybe it was something in the insect category. Something like . . . He rummaged through a stack of magazines and found the cover with an alien species that looked like a large praying mantis with a human face. If that was the crea-ture that had abducted his friends, no wonder they'd blocked it out of their minds.

Frank made sure his bedroom door was locked, then he pulled out the large cardboard box he had hidden underneath his bed. He'd started collecting its contents five years ago when the story of the wreckage of a flying disk came out of Roswell, New Mexico, and landed on the local paper's front page. Frank didn't have that specific newspaper clipping, but he had plenty of others. Any time a UFO sighting or something unusual in the skies was reported, he located the article and filed it in his box, along with more scientific discoveries. New stars that had been found and named, or asteroids discovered, like 1788 Kiess at the Goethe Link Observatory in July.

But mainly it was filled with stuff his dad would deem nonsense. Frank held up a clipping from a newspaper in Los Angeles about a guy who lived at the base of Palomar—close to where the high-powered telescope was—and claimed to see hundreds of UFOs, even saying they were saucers and ships. He said he spoke to aliens. They visited him at night and told him that the world needed to get rid of all their atomic weapons and live in peace with one another. *What an origi-nal idea*, Frank thought sarcastically. He could count at least six stories he'd read recently with the same message from the aliens. But Frank read through it, looking for anything that sounded remotely like the situation he was now in. The article reminded him of *I Rode a Flying Saucer* by George W. Van Tassel. Another guy in southern California. Frank wondered if that was a coincidence.

He kept replaying in his mind the conversation he'd over-heard between the government man and the sheriff, claiming that maybe one of these types of cults could be involved. Could they have staged something? But why? What would they have to gain? It left him feeling uneasy about Teddy. That was the hardest to contend with. Teddy was still missing. And there was also the blood they'd found. Was it his?

The more days that passed without Teddy's return, the greater the likelihood that he was dead. Frank knew from his dad that once a person had been missing for more than twenty-four hours, it wasn't good. But more than three days? Frank's dad had avoided the answer when he had asked him about Teddy, if he thought he could still be alive. By not giving a direct answer, Frank already imagined a shallow grave some-where that the dogs would eventually find. Or—and this was what he and Oscar were beginning to indulge—maybe Teddy had been taken.

Frank tore through his stash. The data Frank collected was mainly about flying discs and saucers and lights in the sky. It didn't mention anything about abductions. The best work on the subject, in his opinion, was *The Flying Saucers Are Real* by Donald Keyhoe. It wasn't about Keyhoe's personal experi-ence being taken by aliens or anything subjective like that. It was more researched. Keyhoe compiled all kinds of arti-cles, documents, Air Force records showing the government's investigation into the phenomenon over the last few years. Keyhoe believed that the government must have some alien technology.

There was a knock at his door.

Frank froze. "Yeah?"

"It's Oscar."

Frank grabbed the magazines he needed from the box, put them in his bag along with his notebook, and shoved the box back underneath his bed. He and Oscar had fun sharing stories and talking about the possibility of aliens and other worlds, but he wanted to keep just how much he believed it all to himself.

He opened the door.

"Ready?" Oscar asked.

"Ready."

Frank stood next to Oscar in the small hallway. All the metal chairs were taken by others who had showed up at the sheriff's office around the same time as them. It was loud, and Frank could feel the energy in the air. Phones rang from the police desks in other rooms. Every few minutes someone walked quickly down the hall, passing him like a burst of air. People chatted about the UFO they'd seen, comparing observations.

"Exactly what I saw," echoed down the hall a number of times, as though the information was a beach ball being passed up and down the row of people.

A tall woman was explaining in an overly loud voice about how she'd seen this before, right after the war ended.

"I was out walking my dog, when I saw a metal object in the

sky that kind of whizzed by and it was spinning. And then it just kind of hovered and disappeared over the water."

"How big was it?" a man who Frank recognized but couldn't place asked next to her.

"Oh, I'm not sure. It wasn't a large ship, maybe just enough for one space man. They've been sending one-man ships for years. They're in the ocean. Underneath there's a whole colony of them."

Listening to her, Frank understood why his dad might think he was being silly with all of his talk about extraterrestrials. It was obvious this woman was a little off. Even he wouldn't go so far as to believe there was some alien civilization living in the ocean. Oscar patted Frank's shoulder and he made the crazy sign with his hands and crossed his eyes. Frank brought his hand to his mouth to keep from laughing.

The door opened and an old man stepped out. He put the hat he was holding in his hands on his head, and the government man said, "Next."

Frank and Oscar entered the room and removed their baseball caps. Dr. Miller sat behind a large brown desk, writing in a large yellow legal pad. Frank's eyes scanned the top of the desk, noting a half a cup of coffee in a Styrofoam cup, a pack of Lucky Strikes, an apple with a bite out of it, a tape recorder, and a framed picture of two boys and a woman. What Frank wouldn't give to get his hands on the recorder.

"Come in and sit down. I'll just be a minute."

Frank and Oscar sat in the two chairs on the other side of

the desk. The government man continued to write and Frank caught the words *Nocturnal lights?* at the top of the page. He almost gasped out loud. This guy couldn't be serious. It's what they first said the lights were in D.C. back in July. The term was basically used to make any kind of phenomena in the sky explainable, like aircraft, balloons, celestial bodies, meteors, northern lights, among other things.

But Frank was certain he hadn't seen the northern lights. The light he'd seen had moved with intention. Then he saw Dr. Miller write the word *unexplained*. That did leave it open, but still it said nothing about what the light might actually have been.

The government man stopped writing and looked up at them. Up close, Frank figured the guy was in his thirties. He wore thick black glasses, his brown hair short, almost military style. He smiled and straightened his black tie.

"Hello, boys." He flipped to a new page in his notes. "I'm Dr. Miller. Let's start with your names."

"Frank Rodriguez."

"Oscar Guzman."

Frank watched him write their names at the top of the page. He drew a picture of a mustache next to Oscar's name, making Frank smirk. All summer, Oscar had attempted to grow some facial hair. The result had been something that, according to his dad, looked like a small brown caterpillar had decided to rest on his upper lip. Oscar refused to shave it until he had to, which would be when they started back at school in the fall. He was damn proud of that fuzz.

"Okay, so why don't you boys start at the beginning?"

Frank looked at Oscar, who nodded.

"We saw the light," Frank said. "It was right after we had left our post at the tower."

"Tower?" Dr. Miller seemed to sit up even straighter. "You guys are part of the Skywatch group?"

"Yes. But we left early."

"Frank wanted to get home," Oscar mumbled.

"Not just me. You too. We were bored. There wasn't much activity that night, well, not until after. And then when we heard about the others going missing . . . We were both glad and upset that we left when we did."

"Why upset?"

"Missed out on the biggest thing to happen around here, that's why."

Frank saw Dr. Miller write *Skywatchers* on the page.

"Let's just start at the beginning. Where were you when you saw what you saw?"

"I had just parked the car at Oscar's," Frank said. "Got out and I noticed a funny light in the sky."

"It was kind of glowing," Oscar said. "A greenish glow. And it was moving fast."

"How fast?"

Frank looked at Oscar. He shrugged.

"I don't know, but faster than the planes we usually spot."

"Probably at least 100 mph," Oscar said.

Bill wrote *100 mph??* "How did it move?"

"Kind of in a line, or more like in one direction, and then it disappeared and appeared again."

"Do you mean the light was blinking on and off?"

"No, more like it was there and then it wasn't. Kind of like it jumped ahead."

Oscar took his finger and pointed in the air and then drew a semicircle and then another and another, like his finger was jumping in the air.

"There was a reddish dot in the center of it," Oscar said. "I raced inside the house to get my camera, but by the time I came back out, it was gone."

"Yeah, it passed over," said Frank.

"Passed. What does that mean?"

"I mean"—and here Oscar made a motion with his hand overhead—"it flew over us."

"Why do you use the word *flew*?"

"Cause that's what it seemed like it was doing," Oscar said.

"Just a light still?"

"More like a ship," Frank said.

"Yeah, like a spaceship. Or one of those flying saucers."

Frank thought he saw Dr. Miller's shoulders stiffen at the word *saucer*.

"If you had to compare the shape of what you saw to an ordinary, familiar object, what would you compare it to?"

"It was in a V shape, kind of like a flock of birds." Oscar connected his palms together to mimic the shape. "I could see the shadow of it on the ground."

V shape shadow? Dr. Miller scribbled the words quickly.

"A shadow? Are you sure about that?"

"Yes, sir," Oscar said.

"And what was the speed as it passed over head?" Bill asked.

"Slower. Like it was looking for something."

"Oh, and this is something I almost forgot," Frank said. "When I was in the house, the lights went out. They went out on the whole block."

"Yes. A transponder blew, shutting off the power in a section of town."

Frank knew this already from his dad, but he was testing the government man, seeing how much he knew.

"So after you saw it pass overhead, then what?" asked Dr. Miller.

"I left Oscar's house and went home to get to my telescope in the backyard. I was up most of the night looking, but didn't see any more lights in the sky."

"You have a telescope?"

"Yep."

Dr. Miller looked pleased. "I had one too at your age. Actually, even younger. You like studying the stars?"

"Yes, sir. I'm going to be an astronomer."

Dr. Miller smiled. "Good plan. I teach astronomy at a university."

"Ah, so you're a professor when you're not out chasing UFOs."

"I prefer the term ufologist. The study of UFOs."

"Who do you work for?" asked Frank.

"The Air Force."

"Project Grudge?"

"You've done your homework," said Dr. Miller, clearly impressed. "Grudge is no longer. It's Project Blue Book now."

"Were you down in Lubbock, Texas, last year?" Frank asked. He wanted to see what Dr. Miller would give up.

Lubbock was one of the unexplainable sightings he read about in the issue of *Life* with Marilyn Monroe on the cover. Almost two hundred people had seen a large formation of lights crossing the night sky. There was even a photo of it. The Air Force tried to debunk it all of course, saying the photo was a hoax. But two hundred people? That would be next to impossible to pull off.

Dr. Miller raised an eyebrow. "Seems like you're also a ufologist."

Frank shrugged. "Those were different than our light. At least, according to the reports. Supposedly there were twenty-five or so. In the shape of a V. Credible witnesses. We only saw the one light. You really think in Lubbock they were birds?" Frank remembered the name. "Plovers? Reflecting light off their undersides?"

"That seems the most plausible and possible explanation."

"Really?" asked Frank.

Dr. Miller shifted in his seat. "Maybe the Air Force has a jet bomber in the shape of a flying wing. Maybe that was passing over during a test flight."

"Without any sound?"

Dr. Miller grabbed a cigarette out of the pack on the table. He lit it with the yellow lighter and sat back in the chair.

"Are you going to make my life difficult here?"

"No, sir," Frank said. "We didn't just come here to give you another eyewitness account of the UFO. I'm sure you have plenty of those."

Dr. Miller smiled. "Why have you come?"

"We have a theory about what happened out there in the woods with the other Skywatchers."

Frank reached into the bag he placed at his feet and took out a magazine. The cover had a man in the foreground in a suit looking like a zombie with a city in the background. He pushed it across the table at Dr. Miller.

"'The Puppet Masters.'" Dr. Miller read the title out loud. "By Robert A. Heinlein."

"In the future, spaceships land with slug aliens from Titan, the sixth moon of Saturn, that attach themselves to humans' backs and take over their central nervous system. They invade the planet. It's way cool," Oscar said.

"I'm not sure what you want me to take away from this," Dr. Miller said, putting the magazine down on the desk.

Frank sat back and let Oscar take it from here. It was his idea anyway and he thought it a plausible one.

"What if the light was from a flying saucer and it landed in the woods?" Oscar said. "What if Teddy and the others stumbled upon it? What if they encountered aliens, who weren't friendly and . . ." Oscar pointed to the man on the cover. "What if they are now being controlled by aliens? That's why they can't remember anything. Their brains have been wiped clean."

"But wouldn't they know if there was an alien inside of them? Or better yet, wouldn't we know because they'd be acting strangely?"

"But they are," Oscar said. "Bunny now speaks Mandarin."

"What do you mean?" Dr. Miller asked.

"We were at Chang's Market, and we heard her having a conversation with Mr. Chang," Frank said.

"I'm sure lots of people speak to Mr. Chang."

"In Mandarin? She never knew how to speak Mandarin before."

Frank watched him jot down *Bunny. Mandarin?*

"How well do you know Bunny Stapleton?"

"Not that well. I mean, we're not friends. Just in the club together," Frank said. "But we know she speaks Spanish. Her mom's Puerto Rican or something. She caught Oscar and I talking about her the first time we met."

"Because you speak Spanish?"

"Conversationally, yeah. And we know she speaks Italian and French too, but not Mandarin. You should have seen her when she did it."

"Like she didn't even know she was speaking Mandarin," Oscar said.

"So you think that's what this is," Bill said. "The beginning of an extraterrestrial invasion?"

"Maybe."

"Could also be exploratory," Frank added. "Though it seems pretty hostile to take over someone's brain. The problem as I see it, sir, is that if it is aliens, we still don't know what kind of aliens we are dealing with."

"Kind?" said Dr. Miller.

"The good or the bad."

"And so what do you think happened to Teddy?"

"Taken," Frank said.

"Taken where?"

Both he and Oscar pointed up toward the ceiling.

Dr. Miller cleared his throat. "Gentleman, when I was your age, I read my share of stories from the pulp magazines. I loved how they led me to the stars and other worlds. But they were fiction. Not reality. 'The Puppet Masters' sounds like a great story. But I'm not sure that's what's going on here."

Frank picked up the magazine from the desk and put it back in his bag.

"Listen, I do think we need to be more vigilant," said Dr. Miller. "With the times being as they are, you never know who your enemy might be."

Frank tried to keep his face neutral. Dr. Miller was starting to sound a bit like that Senator McCarthy on television. If you believed him, you'd think one out of every five neighbors was a Commie. Frank didn't believe it. Neither did his dad, who muttered under his breath that McCarthy was nothing more than a bully.

"If you see anything unusual either in the skies or with the other Skywatchers, please let me know. Until then, let's not share this information with too many people. We wouldn't want to get the public more worked up than they already are." He wrote the number to the police station on the back of his business card and handed it to Frank.

"You've got it, Dr. Miller. You can count on us."

Dr. Miller stood up and shook the hands of both boys.

"Thank you," he said.

"No, thank you. We will report back as soon as we have something."

Frank opened the door and nodded at the tall woman. If Dr. Miller thought he'd heard a story from them, just wait until he got ahold of her.

17

CAROLINE

THEIR EYES BORE THROUGH HER RELENTLESSLY, LIKE LASER BEAMS from a space gun. She'd felt them the entire funeral. From the moment she stepped out of her stepfather's car and walked toward the building, to when she sat in the front pew. Everyone watched her. Like she was under suspicion. Like she was the reason Eleanor had been killed. It was unnerving.

Caroline stared at the closed casket, trying to ignore the heat.

Her stepfather spoke at the front of the church, but she wasn't paying attention to his message. She tried not to think about the body inside. A body that had been twisted and altered so much in the accident that an open casket wasn't possible. A body that had been her best friend since the third grade and the person she told everything.

Caroline thought for the thousandth time of Eleanor's last moments. How scared she must have been. Alone. In the dark. Did she scream out? Caroline wished she had insisted that Eleanor stay with them. That she hadn't let her go that night. But then, maybe Eleanor would be missing now instead of Teddy.

Even so, missing was better than dead.

Missing meant there was still a chance to be found.

Teddy . . . Caroline's eyes welled. Since returning, she hadn't let herself think much of him either. The last image she had was of him walking ahead of her. His back strong, solid, holding her up when she had tripped and stumbled. The expression on his face when he turned and looked at her—no fear at what they might come upon in the woods, only curiosity at the possibilities, and a set determination to defend their country.

Her stepfather sat down next to her in the front row. Now a woman was singing. Out of the corner of her eye, she spotted Eleanor's parents and sisters. Their grief crossed the aisle and pummeled Caroline like a wave. She struggled to stay above it.

Caroline's own mother didn't come. Charlie was worried that being at a funeral would be a trigger. But what was Eleanor's funeral if not a trigger for Caroline now? Her whole body ached as she had to endure one of Eleanor's favorite songs. Sung, if Caroline were honest, not incredibly well. If Eleanor were there, she would be cringing and whispering into Caroline's ear. In fact, she closed her eyes and tilted her head a bit, imagining. She felt Eleanor's breath and heard her laugh, and then she laughed too.

Charlie grabbed her hand. Startled, she looked at him and his eyes were stern. Had she laughed out loud? The smile died on her lips. She faced ahead again, but the fire making its way up the pews from the funeral attendees licked at her back, threatened to consume her. Caroline stood up and walked as fast as she could out of the church.

She ran around to the back of the building and sat down

in the dirt behind some bushes, ignoring her fancy black dress. And for the first time in what felt like forever, Caroline let herself feel the emotions, the absurdity of it all, everything. She didn't care that she was giggling. Eleanor would get it. Her poor Eleanor. And then Caroline was crying. She pounded the dirt with her fist.

Why did you have to leave me, Eleanor?

She wanted so much to talk to her best friend one more time. To have her share in the current terror she found herself in. The not knowing what had happened to her in the forest was beginning to make Caroline come undone. She felt helpless. Out of control and maybe even a little out of her mind. She was seeing and hearing things. She woke from dreams that seemed so real, but when she tried to recall them, she could only remember the feeling of having been somewhere. Somewhere far away. Awake, she was scared to leave the house.

She pretended like she was okay, but she knew Charlie watched her all the time—looking at her as if she were now someone else. She saw fear in his eyes when she looked into them. And her mind kept returning to the night she'd come out of the woods, flooding her with a sense of panic each time. She walked around on edge, as if she would suddenly turn a corner and run into something. The something that had been chasing her. Because in her fear and uneasiness, she now felt a shadow of something more. That she hadn't just been running toward something; she'd been running away.

If only she could remember what it was.

She heard the sound of footsteps. Had Charlie left the service? She tried to shrink farther against the back church wall.

She didn't need a lecture from him. She only needed a moment by herself, to try to keep her skin together so she wouldn't be washed away.

A pair of black shoes stopped and pointed in her direction. Her eyes followed them up to the black pants, black jacket, white shirt, and black tie into John's eyes.

"Can I join you?" he asked.

Caroline shrugged.

He crossed through the opening in the bushes and sat next to her on the ground. She wiped the tears from her face.

"It's so hard. I really miss her. I don't know what I'm going to do without her."

"I know."

His brown eyes were full of compassion. They were also sad in a way that surprised Caroline. Was he closer to Eleanor than she had realized?

Eleanor had liked John for Caroline. One of their last silly conversations had actually been debating his hair versus Teddy's on the way to their Skywatchers shift. Both boys had good thick hair. Eleanor argued John's black hair always fell perfectly, while Teddy's brown thick curls sometimes got the best of him. Oftentimes Teddy came to school with hair barely brushed, shirt needing ironing, while John was more put together. Even now, John's hair was perfectly slicked back, no strand out of place.

Caroline heard Eleanor's voice in her head.

See. Perfect hair. And come on, Caroline. Can't you see the way he looks at you?

She blushed and stared ahead at the shrubs.

"Eleanor would have been happy to see us like this," she said.

"What do you mean?"

"Sitting together. Talking. She liked you."

"She was always easy to talk to," John said.

"Yeah. Now I have no one."

"You can talk to me."

"That's different," Caroline said.

"Why?"

Because you're a guy, she wanted to say. And because she hardly knew him. Instead she said, "You're not Eleanor."

"No, I'm not Eleanor."

Caroline was tired. John sat so close, she could just drop her head on his shoulder.

"I feel like I haven't slept in days," she said.

"I feel like I can't wake up," said John. "Like right now, I'm not sure if I'm awake or in a really strange dream. Things are weird. The same, but different somehow. And the way my family is acting toward me—"

"What do you mean?"

"They watch me all the time. Observing. Like . . ."

"Like they're afraid of you?"

John turned to look at her. "Yes."

She nodded in understanding. "Thank you for being so kind to me," she said.

He took her hand, traced the lines on her palm, sending trails of shooting stars up her arm in a way she recognized. He had done that before. Surprised at how familiar it was, she touched his face, closed her eyes, and brought her forehead to his. Suddenly everything was fuzzy, spinning. She felt the dirt beneath her, but the wall of the church began to fade.

It was night. And the lights outside were coming in explosive flashes. The bushes were gone. They sat together, huddled by the door. John cupped her face with both of his hands and kissed her. The kiss felt like a question, and she answered it by pulling him closer. But the sound of an explosion made him pull away.

Then the door disappeared and she was back behind the church building, kissing John behind the bushes. The reality of the situation burst rapidly through her mind. They were at Eleanor's funeral. What was she doing? What would happen if someone found them? Caroline forced herself to push him away and stumbled to her feet.

"Caroline," John began, out of breath. "I'm sorry . . . I don't know—"

She cut him off. "No. No, it's me."

But she wasn't sure.

She dusted the dirt off her dress, thankful to have some-thing to do to avoid his eyes, suddenly shy with the way they had just been. Caroline had only been kissed by a boy one other time. It had been awkward and his breath had smelled like the hot dog he'd just eaten. He'd been clumsy. She'd been shy and nervous. It ended with him trying to feel her up and with her feeling empty.

John's kiss had been nothing like that. His kiss made her full and alive.

"I'm just messed up. I'm sorry," she said.

He took a step toward her, but she moved back and pushed through the gap in the bushes.

She had to fight the desire to let him comfort her. It was Eleanor's funeral. It wasn't right for her to be experiencing any kind of happiness. She should be crying and devastated, not kissing a boy she barely knew.

"Caroline," he said again, but she walked away from him toward the front of the building.

She sped up her pace, aware that John was right behind her, not wanting anyone to get the wrong idea, and all too conscious of the feelings he now evoked in her. A part of her wanted to escape everything and run somewhere with him, which scared her. What did that mean?

She fought the tears. This was what crazy must feel like. She was going crazy. Maybe her mom wasn't the only one. Maybe Caroline would end up just like her.

Caroline walked past the church and didn't stop until she was home. Her mother was outside, painting Jack. Always Jack. Caroline saw him running through the house. Heard him squealing with laughter as she chased him. She remembered picking him up and twirling him round and round and round.

Now he never moved.

In the painting, his eyes were accusatory.

Not you, too, she said to him.

She went straight into the bathroom and filled the tub. She lit three candles and turned on the radio station that played the greatest hits.

Soon, she was sinking into the warm water and covered

with bubbles. She lay back and closed her eyes, letting her whole body, and finally her head, sink under.

As she did, another image came to her. She was in the water, but it wasn't a tub. It was the ocean. She was holding a baby. She often pictured Jack like this; her memories frequently triggered by the slightest connection. His hands splashed in the water. The waves were calm as she waded with him. The water hitting her at waist level. The memory was cloudy around the edges, a bit blurry. But in her mind's eye, she turned him around to face her, held him at arm's length to get a good look. But it wasn't Jack who smiled up at her. A baby girl met her eyes and reached out her tiny hand. At the girl's touch, Caroline's eyes flashed open and she shot up out of the tub, gasping for air.

Who was that?

She squeezed her eyes shut and tried to conjure up the face again, but all she could picture was Jack.

Her heart raced as she dried off. She tried to calm her breathing by brushing out her hair and began putting it in rollers. But as she did so, her fingers kept finding the small bump behind her left earlobe. And she felt something there she was sure she hadn't felt before. The bump had a hard edge. She dropped her hand. Suddenly afraid.

How long had she had that bump?

She picked up a little handheld mirror and tried to get a better look, holding it up in front of herself as she looked in the bathroom mirror behind. She couldn't see anything. Still, she raised her hand again to the spot behind her ear. There it was. Small. Sharp.

She shuddered.

Caroline finished getting ready for bed, but she couldn't fall asleep. She was terrified to dream. The lump, her lack of memory, Teddy's disappearance, none of it made any sense. And then there was the baby girl.

Caroline tensed at the memory. She clenched and unclenched her hand to try to rid the feeling of the tiny hand in her own. But she felt it with her all night. Unable to stop it, along with the hot tears that fell.

18
JOHN

JOHN DIDN'T LIKE THE GOVERNMENT MAN. HE REMINDED HIM OF other government men. The ones in the suits and black ties. The ones with black, shiny shoes. The ones who'd visited every now and then at the camp. The ones he watched drive away from behind the barbed wire. Only this man, Dr. Miller, didn't have clean shoes. John noted mud on the bottom.

"John, I want you to know that I am here just to ascertain what you guys saw the night you went missing. I am not here to judge you or to make any assumptions. I do not work with the police department. I am a scientist. I am not 'working the case,' so to speak. So please, feel free to use this as a safe space to process what you saw and experienced."

A safe space. Was he joking? They were at the police station. John was told he had to come and do this interview, along with the others. And if they wanted them to feel safe, why did they have to talk separately? John glanced at the closed door, the closed blinds on the windows, the tapping of Dr. Miller's fingers, the notepad in front of him, the way he stared at John behind his black horn-rimmed glasses. In his mind, John imagined himself bolting through the door and never looking back, but he remained in his seat.

Dr. Miller stared at John, as if he had asked a question and was waiting for an answer.

"I'm sorry, can you repeat that?"

"I asked if you wouldn't mind if I recorded our conversation. Again, just for my notes."

"Sure. Yeah."

John had nothing to hide, but he kept thinking about Teddy. Where was he? Why didn't he come home? He felt like he should be doing something to find him, but he had no idea how or what to do. He tried to keep his feelings in check, but he thought of the way he'd played the piano yesterday, and how he was more acutely aware of his surroundings, constantly. He thought of the lump behind his ear.

There were other things too, but he didn't want to talk about them. Besides, they were more feelings than anything. Feelings about Caroline. And feelings weren't facts.

"So, let's start at the beginning. Can you take me back to the moment when you first saw the object in the sky?"

"Caroline spotted it. Or maybe I did, I don't remember exactly, but she was the one who called everyone over to see it. I was already next to her looking out. The light was coming from the northwest. At first, I thought it was a plane, but then it began to act really strange."

"What do you mean by act?"

"I mean, its lights weren't blinking and it wasn't moving in a straight line. It was kind of there and then it wasn't there. Like the light was turning on and off. So you had to follow its trajectory and then it would pop on again."

John stopped speaking and waited for Dr. Miller to finish writing on the yellow legal pad. It was difficult for John to make out what Dr. Miller wrote upside down, and it looked as if he was using a kind of shorthand, making it harder still.

"Keep going," said Dr. Miller.

"It was moving fast. Like a jet plane, maybe even faster," John said. "It was hard for us to track. Then it was like it started to come toward us. We braced ourselves for a crash or something."

"Because?"

"Because we thought it was going to hit the tower. I know that sounds weird, but the whole thing was weird. We ducked and nothing happened. Then it looked like the light went down in the forest."

"What shape was the object? If you could compare it to another shape you are familiar with?"

"I don't know about a shape. Maybe it pulled itself into two lines? No that's not right. It's hard to explain." *And my memory is all fuzzy*, John thought. The doctor at the hospital told him it would get better in a few days. He would start to recall what happened. But the more time that passed, the more this wasn't true. What was true was that there was a large space now in John's mind where there should be something solid, clear. He felt it all the time. His thoughts searching all around the edges of the space, trying to penetrate it, trying to unlock the secret.

What happened to us? And where is Teddy?

Dr. Miller waited for him to continue.

"It was greenish and it moved, but . . . it was kind of like a fish underwater when the light hits just so and everything glows. That shimmering body darting around. It kind of reminded me of that. Have you ever gone diving, Dr. Miller?"

"No. I've been fishing on a lake. But I can only imagine how stunning it must be. Especially in this area. So, this object you saw—was it kind of like a long fish or a short one?"

"Long and short."

"You said you felt it coming straight for you. Did the speed accelerate as it got closer?"

"I'm not sure. It was more of a feeling, I guess." The more John thought about it, the more evasive the details were, like a fish itself darting around. "It's hard to describe."

Dr. Miller nodded. "Were you afraid?"

"The girls were for sure."

"But not you and Teddy?"

Hearing Teddy's name made John's stomach lurch. He didn't want to talk about Teddy.

"Teddy was excited," John formed his words carefully. "He was the one who wanted to go after it. He talked about it being our duty as Skywatchers."

"And you didn't want to go?"

"It wasn't so much as not wanting to . . . I mean, we were in the club there at the tower. We didn't know what we saw. For all we knew it could have been the Reds, a bomb, anything. But Teddy was the leader. So we went in together."

"Teddy was the president of the club?"

"I didn't say that. I said he was the leader. The best leaders don't need a title, do they?"

"No, I suppose they don't."

Dr. Miller stared at John a few moments. John didn't drop

his gaze. He wasn't going to let the government man make him feel intimidated. He set his face in a calm, pleasant mask, the one his father had taught him to wear.

"Take me to the moment you entered the woods."

John had already been asked this over and over by the sheriff, his family, the Messinas, even Frank and Oscar. But he repeated everything again to Dr. Miller, the same as he had with the others.

"And how did you feel when you were in the woods?" Dr. Miller asked when John was finished.

Terrified. Excited. Anxious. Filled with love. Despair. Pain.

"Like something big was about to happen."

"What was the last thing you remember seeing?"

John tried to picture himself there. What he'd seen, and heard. There was a soft glow. A humming. Mechanical. *That's new.* He didn't remember recalling the sound when he'd tried to recover the memory before.

He thought harder.

Something in the woods. In the clearing. He and Teddy crouching low. He looked back and saw Caroline. Her eyes all wide in excitement. Or maybe it was fear.

"Teddy walking in front of me," John said, sticking with what he'd said before. Not sure if what he just remembered was accurate or not.

"That's it?"

"Yes. I've told you this over and over again. I don't know anything else after that. I don't know what happened. I don't know where Teddy is. I—" He looked away, ashamed at his outburst.

"Thank you, John, for talking with me. I can't imagine it's easy having to share what happened over and over again, especially with the memory loss."

"No, it's not."

"Can you tell Bunny Stapleton to come in?"

John pushed back the chair and stood up. He walked to the door, but stopped and turned around abruptly. "Is this normal?"

"Normal?"

"In your investigations, has this ever happened before? The memory loss, I mean?"

"Not that I'm aware of, no," said Dr. Miller.

"I didn't think so," said John.

He opened the door and nodded to Bunny, who was sitting in the hallway next to Caroline. Bunny stood up.

"What'd you tell him?"

John cocked his head to the side. It was an odd question. "Everything I could remember, of course." But this wasn't true. He didn't know why he kept the humming from the man and now from Bunny.

Bunny nodded. "Okay. Okay. I can do that." She straightened her skirt before entering the room.

John watched her close the door. He was free to go, but he took the seat he had started in, leaving an empty chair between him and Caroline. She had already been interviewed, too. They needed to stick together as much as possible. John felt protective over her and Bunny; maybe it was because Teddy wasn't here. And because things between him and Caroline were so confusing. The thing at Eleanor's funeral. John had seen a flash of something when they kissed. He wasn't sure what it was.

There was so much he was uncertain of, but he knew one thing for sure: he and Caroline had kissed before.

The thought sent a shiver up his spine.

How did you feel when you were in the woods?

Feelings aren't facts.

John glanced shyly at Caroline next to him. She was drawing in a notebook. It was a cypress tree, like the old one down by the water.

"It's gonna be all right," she said. "They'll find him. They'll get to the bottom of everything."

John didn't share her confidence. Something had happened to Teddy. He felt it in his gut. It was why he didn't return with them. John wondered if he was the reason for it. He thought maybe they should go looking for Teddy, but where? Every inch of that forest had been covered already by the police. No trail had been found.

"Do you think it's weird he wants to talk to us individually?" John asked, changing the subject.

Caroline thought for a moment. "Not really. Maybe he thinks we'll be more truthful or something. Isolating us is smart. It's what I would have done in his shoes."

John leaned back, extended his legs in front of him.

More truthful.

He looked at Caroline's drawing. Her version of the tree had a thick trunk, the branches were barren. A lonely tree, possibly even dead.

John saw the tree differently. He would have made the color lighter. Given it more branches. It stood alone, but it wasn't lonely. There was a difference.

Which was the truer image? The one in his mind's eye? Or Caroline's?

He thought about Bunny's question. *What'd you tell him?* It made him wonder if Caroline and Bunny were hiding something. Why would she ask him that if she told the truth? Did they remember things they weren't telling him?

If so, why?

Everyone had secrets, he supposed. Even him.

He watched Caroline draw the tree, watched as she altered the limbs, stretching them further and further from the truth.

19
BUNNY
....

DR. MILLER REMINDED BUNNY OF HER FATHER. HE WORE DARK glasses and a black suit and was the same general build. The difference was Dr. Miller smoked Lucky Strikes. Her father wouldn't be caught dead smoking those. She situated herself in the chair across from him.

"May I?" she asked, reaching across to grab the half-empty pack on the table. Not waiting for an answer, she removed one and put it between her lips. She tried to keep her hand still as she lit the end of it with the small lighter she kept in the pocket of her pants.

"Terrible habit," Dr. Miller said. "Especially for someone so young."

She inhaled deeply and blew a long stream of smoke out.

"I'm not that young."

She didn't need him to lecture her about bad habits, especially since he engaged in one himself. Not only did he smoke, but he bit his nails. That was a disgusting habit. If she unnerved him, he didn't show it. He launched right into asking her about the UFO. The experience in the tower and the woods. All the typical questions she had been bombarded with since the day she returned from wherever she had been.

No, she hadn't seen the light before.

Yes, it was a little scary, but exciting, too.

Yes, she thought they might have been under attack.

No, she couldn't remember what they saw in the woods.

Though, if she was being honest, this last answer was rehearsed and slightly off. She hadn't been able to remember anything at first. But now, a week since she'd been back, a few details had begun to poke through. She saw Caroline's back and Teddy's ahead of her. There was a glow in the clearing. *A clearing.* This memory was new. They had stopped on the threshold because of a sound like a buzz or a hum. She strained her eyes past Teddy to see what was making the sound.

"I'm sorry I can't be more helpful," Bunny said. She wanted to talk to the others, see if they were also getting new glimpses into what had actually happened. And if they too had kept any information a secret from the authorities.

When Dr. Miller shut off the recorder, she was relieved that it was over. Her armpits were sweaty; so were the backs of her knees.

"All of this is helpful," he said, mistaking her discomfort. "When we experience and see things that we don't understand, it's hard for us to process. Our brains are constantly trying to construct meaning, put everything into categories. This is just an unknown category."

Yes, she thought. He's talking about the somatosensory and frontal cortices. She suddenly pictured a map of the brain—a magnetic resonance image. And then it went away.

Dr. Miller watched her intently across the table, looking as if he were trying to understand something.

"Well," Bunny said, flustered, wondering where she'd seen that map of the brain. She had never studied that in school. She kept her cool, putting out her nub of a cigarette in the nearly full ashtray. "I hope that it becomes known. Soon. And I hope that Teddy is found."

Bunny hadn't meant to bring up Teddy so casually. In fact, she had wanted to avoid the topic of Teddy altogether. The longer he was missing, the sicker she felt about it. The more she couldn't sleep well because she saw his face when she closed her eyes. She woke with the same image of him—his eyes looking into hers, intensely. And a question on his lips: *Why'd you leave me?*

"Yes. The authorities are doing all they can, I'm sure," said Dr. Miller. "But you're new to this area, is that right?"

"We moved here last year." She knew why of course. Their home had become a nightmare for her dad. A constant reminder of her mother. It made him weak in Bunny's eyes.

"So were you friends with the others?"

"In the club? Sure," Bunny lied. She hadn't planned to lie; it was just a natural defense mechanism that kicked in when she encountered authority.

"Did you notice any tension between members?"

Bunny kept her expression blank, but inside she felt herself heating up. The back of her knees stinging from the sweat.

Bunny thought this was a strange question for him to ask, especially if he was only here for the UFO.

"No. Everyone got along fine. Am I done?"

"Just one more thing: Do you speak Mandarin?"

Bunny now felt the color drain from her face.

"No."

"Funny, I had a visit earlier today with . . ." He looked back in his notes on the legal pad. "Frank and Oscar? They came in with the strangest story. They are obviously science-fiction junkies. You should hear some of their theories. Aliens and such. Mind control. Of course with these cases, we sometimes get interesting folk who come out of the woodwork. The ones talking about aliens and how they are here with us now, sending secret messages. Regardless, they did tell me that they heard you speaking in Mandarin at Mr. Chang's grocery store."

Bunny would find them and kill them.

"No," she responded sweetly. "I do know how to speak Spanish and Italian, French, some German. You know, the European languages. They must have heard me trying some French with Mr. Chang."

"Oh, he speaks French?"

"He's learning," Bunny lied again. She had no idea if this was true. She'd never had a conversation besides how much she owed for her purchases.

"Strange. They seemed certain it was Mandarin."

She hesitated. Maybe she should tell him. He could help her, maybe he'd run across something like this before. But she was afraid of it all. Afraid of the dreams she started waking from. What if he took her away? Ran experiments? No, she needed to figure out what was going on by herself first, and with John and Caroline. As much as she didn't like it, she was in this with them. So she relied on her default—don't trust anyone. She drew herself up a little straighter in the chair.

"I haven't spoken a word of Mandarin in my life," she said. She held her hands folded in her lap mostly to keep from fidgeting. Fidgeting signaled guilt. She smiled as sweetly as she could.

"All right. They must have been mistaken. They were shaken up by something though." He paused as if thinking on something. "If you recall anything else, please let me know. That goes for when I'm no longer here, as well."

Bunny thanked him and exited the room.

Bunny stood in front of John and Caroline. She wanted to ask them. She didn't want to wait in case she forgot about the detail. Her mind was untrustworthy, something she wasn't used to.

"Do you remember the humming?" she asked.

Just then one of the officers passed by.

But Bunny saw it.

The slight nod from both Caroline and John.

They remembered it, too.

Bunny wondered what else they might be keeping from one another. Because she was certain of one thing—they weren't telling each other everything.

20

FRANK

FRANK SAT ON HIS BED READING THE BOOK HE'D CHECKED OUT AT the library. He heard the phone ring in the living room.

His mom called, "Frank, sweetheart, it's for you."

He left his room and grabbed the phone from her.

"Hello?"

"What do you mean telling the government cop that I now speak Mandarin?" Bunny whispered on the other end.

"Hi, Bunny. He's not really a cop. He works for the Air Force. More like a government agent, well, not really an agent. I guess you could say—"

"It doesn't matter." She cut him off.

He waited for her to say more, but she was quiet. Her breathing was the only thing he heard and she sounded like she was moving. Maybe she was pacing in her room. Frank wondered what her room looked like. What she had on the walls. What it would say about her.

"You really think there was a spaceship and aliens could be involved?" she finally asked.

Frank knew the practical answer was no, but he told her, "Yes."

"Meet us outside in ten."

"Us?" Frank asked, but she'd already hung up.

A huge smile spread across his face.

He was in.

Frank jumped in the bed of John's truck. They picked up Oscar too because Frank said he would never hear the end of it if they left him out of whatever it was that Frank was now becoming a part of.

"First things first, we're getting a bite to eat," said Bunny.

Frank was hungry, but he was also disappointed. He had hoped they would take him to some secret place in the forest. At least the clearing. But John stopped at Henry's, a popular soda and burger joint.

When they entered, all heads seemed to turn toward them. It was busy, like normal, especially because it was late afternoon. There was only one table in the back big enough and they walked through with all eyes and whispers following them. Frank wanted to yell *what're you looking at*, but his voice caught in his throat. Their looks made him ashamed and he didn't know what he had to feel ashamed of.

"Why is everyone staring?" Oscar said.

"We shouldn't have come," Caroline said.

"What? We can't get something to eat?" Bunny said. "We didn't do anything."

"No, but we're different now," John said.

They ordered burgers with fries and vanilla Cokes. Frank ate hunched over. He tried not to look around at the people. He hadn't expected to face the stares, the questions in the heavy silence. The feeling that every move he made was not just being watched, but also dissected and interpreted in a way he couldn't control. It made him uncomfortable, but it also made him feel a kinship with the others in a way he had never felt before. This was different than just being up in that tower together, looking for planes. This was something more, and even though he hadn't gone with them into the woods, he was a part of what was happening now.

"So," Bunny said. "Give us your theories. I told them you had some."

"The way I see it," Frank said, keeping his voice low.

Oscar cleared his throat.

"The way *we* see it," Frank continued, "there are a few possibilities." He took out a napkin and wrote down *1) Russians 2) government cover-up 3) hoax 4) nefarious persons 5) aliens 6) time travel 7) another world.*

He braced himself for Caroline's laugh, for her to dismiss it all as being crazy. But she didn't. Neither did John or Bunny. They stared at him intently.

"Seven?" Bunny asked.

"There could be more, but these seem the most plausible."

"I hadn't considered time travel. Or another world. Like we went someplace else?" Bunny said.

"Maybe that's where Teddy is?" Caroline said. "I mean, we made it out, but he didn't. He must be trapped somewhere, right?"

Teddy's continued absence reminded Frank that this wasn't a story he was making up or some mystery to solve for fun. The stakes were real. If Teddy didn't come back, then what? And where was he? Was he being tortured? Left for dead? Just bringing up his name made the others uncomfortable, Frank could see that. For a few moments they each went quiet. Frank tried to read their faces, to see if anyone would give up some information or even guilt, but all he could see was a mix of fear and sadness.

From what Frank could tell, they really didn't know what had happened to Teddy. For the first time he thought maybe it was a good idea that he had left the club early that night. Whatever it was that happened to Teddy, it couldn't be good. There was blood on the ground in the woods. They didn't know that part. Frank didn't want to think about the blood being Teddy's. He was beginning to think Teddy wasn't coming back.

"I . . ." John stopped himself. "Just go on."

"Let's start with what we can eliminate," Frank said, shaking his mind free of thoughts of Teddy. He drew a line across *Russians* and *hoax*. "Unless all of you are total psychopaths, I think we can safely say that this isn't a big elaborate hoax you're playing on the whole town?"

"Come on," John said.

"We can also cross out government cover-up. After all, they did send Dr. Miller, who's with Project Blue Book."

"Blue book? Like the notebooks used for testing in school?"

"Yep. It's the Air Force program that investigates UFOs. Have you seen any men in black suits around lately?"

"Yes," Caroline said. "There was a man parked across the street from my house today."

"Mine too," John said.

Frank looked at Bunny. "And mine."

"Damn."

"What do you think?" Frank looked at Oscar. "FBI?"

Oscar nodded. "For sure."

"They always send the FBI. Probably got a file started on each of us already."

"Don't you think you're being a bit paranoid?" John said.

"No. He's right," Bunny said. "My dad works over at the Presidio and even though its focus is language, they monitor all kinds of things—radio signals, transmissions. They have the equipment to listen in on conversations. Wiretaps. Bugs."

Frank looked around again at the people in the restaurant. Other than how often they tipped their eyes in the group's direction, everything seemed normal. As normal as it could be. No one looked like they were FBI. Unless the FBI had started employing teenagers, women, and families.

"Really?"

"You should check your homes for a wiretap," Bunny said.

"What does that even mean?" Caroline asked.

"Start with your phones," Bunny said. "Unscrew the receiver. It would be a small black attachment. Then span out across the house, looking at lamps and outlets."

Frank looked at her, impressed.

She shrugged and took a sip of her drink.

"I agree. I don't think it was a government cover-up," John said. "That doesn't make sense to me. What would they be doing in the woods? Frank, what's your dad saying? Doesn't he work at Fort Ord?"

Frank shook his head. "He's got nothing. No intel to divulge."

"Nefarious persons," Bunny read the napkin. "You mean, like we ran into some kind of trouble out there?"

"Yeah. Like maybe you were kidnapped or something," Frank said. "Somehow you each escaped, but they still have Teddy. It doesn't explain your memory loss, but it's plausible."

"That's not what happened," Caroline said.

They all turned to look at her.

"How do you know?" John said.

She thought of the flashes she'd seen—of the things she'd seen herself doing with no memory of having done them. "We . . . we were somewhere. I think we were somewhere." She touched the spot behind her ear.

"Somewhere," Frank echoed. "Okay, so aliens and their ship or time or—"

"A parallel dimension," Oscar said.

Frank nodded. That was an option he had thought of, but even he had to admit it was more fiction than science.

"Could be something like Einstein and Rosen's mirror universe," Frank said.

"What does that mean?" John said.

"You know Einstein?"

"Of course we know Einstein," said Caroline.

"He and another scientist, Rosen, speculated that there are these kind of holes in the fabric of space-time that link this universe to a mirror one. The holes are like a passageway, a tunnel, to another universe. Maybe you guys somehow crossed one."

"An Einstein-Rosen bridge," Bunny said.

Frank's face lit up. "You've read about it?"

"Of course, I study physics. But they dropped the theory,

didn't they? They dismissed it as a mathematical anomaly. Improbable."

"What if it's true, though? And what if when a red giant or—"

"Red giant?" John asked.

"A very old star that collapses and burns so much helium that it expands hundreds of times larger than our sun," Frank said. "Something of that magnitude comes apart—expanding and engulfing all within reach . . . somehow it punches a hole through the membrane of space and time."

"You think a red star exploded out in the woods?" John said. "That doesn't make sense."

"That's not what I'm saying," Frank said.

Bunny smirked. "I thought you were just a science-fiction guy."

"I thought you were a Nancy Drew girl."

"Agatha Christie," she said.

"Same thing," Frank replied.

"Not even close."

"Tell them about missing mass," Oscar said.

"So, when astronomers study galaxies, there's a certain observable mass," Frank continued. "But it's way smaller than the amount of mass that would have to be there for the current measurements of the gravitational pull. So the theory is that there's something else there in the dark. Some reality that is there, but we can't see it. If not, the numbers would be different."

They looked at Frank, waiting.

"What if that's what's happening now? This dark missing mass is what separates our world from others, or it's what prevents the worlds from colliding. Maybe you encountered the missing mass. You found an entry point, crossed through. Except on the other side, it's not missing."

"Let me get this straight," said Caroline. "You think we may have traveled through some intergalactic opening—"

"It's actually called a wormhole," Oscar interrupted.

"Wormhole," Caroline repeated. "To another galaxy?"

"Something like that," Frank said.

"Or maybe we stumbled into a mirror universe," Bunny said, looking out the window. "Like *Alice's Adventures in Wonderland*."

Frank followed her eyes. A woman walked by holding the hand of a little boy eating a chocolate ice cream cone.

"Well, that sounds ridiculous," John said. "And I can't believe I'm going to say this, but I'm starting to think aliens might not be that far off. We did see some type of craft—a plane or ship, whatever it was, in the sky. That's the reality we have to go on. All of us at this table saw it. And not only us, but there's a number of other people who saw it, too. Sure, they're scared that we went missing, that Teddy is still missing, which is something we're all dancing around right now, but they're also scared because the light was real. They saw something that can't be explained."

"He's right," Caroline said.

"And the humming," Bunny said.

"What humming?" Frank asked. He hadn't remembered any sound coming from the UFO.

"There was something in the woods. Wasn't there? We found it," Caroline said. "Didn't we?"

John nodded. "Yes, I think so. I keep trying to see it. It's just through a clearing, but I can't break through."

"Same," Bunny said. "You and Teddy went first, but we," she motioned to Caroline, "we were there too."

A clearing. Frank got goose bumps. Oscar stared at John as if he'd seen a ghost.

"They said clearing," Oscar said.

"What? Why is that a big deal?"

"The other day we followed Dr. Miller and the sheriff from the tower to a spot in the woods, a clearing, just like you said. They found fuel marks on the ground."

"Why didn't you say something?" Bunny said.

"I hadn't had a chance yet," Frank said.

"So something did land?" John said.

"I don't know," Frank said. "But they took samples to test it."

"Okay, okay," John said. "Are we really saying a spaceship landed in the woods? They took us onboard? Flew around and then let us loose one by one? Then where's Teddy?"

"We're missing something," Caroline said.

Oscar leaned in and said, "Suit in the back corner."

Frank yawned, stretched, and turned to look. Sure enough there was a man in a black suit and hat. Typical FBI.

Bunny and Caroline turned, too.

"Act natural," Oscar said.

"Natural?" Caroline asked. "How the hell is any of this natural? You think he's another government guy?"

"Probably," Frank said.

"I wonder how much of our conversation he's recorded," Bunny said.

"Did anyone notice when he walked in?" Frank asked.

They each shook their heads.

"Let's go," John said.

Outside, Frank felt like he could breathe better. He hadn't realized how suffocating the air had been inside the restaurant. The FBI guy didn't follow them, but Frank thought he was trying too hard to ignore them. Everyone else in the joint had followed their movements as they exited. The FBI agent still sat at the bar stool. His back to them.

"What do we do now?" Caroline asked.

"Maybe we don't do anything," John said. "We've all been trying so hard to remember, but maybe we just do something that doesn't require any thinking. We have fun."

"Fun? With all that's happened? Eleanor dying? Teddy still missing? Do you think he'd have fun if it was one of us? Do you think Eleanor would just forget about us so quickly?" Caroline said. Her voice broke and she started crying softly.

"No one's forgetting Eleanor. I miss her, too," John said, as he put his hand on her shoulder. "Fun was the wrong word, I meant—"

"A distraction," Bunny said. "I get it."

"There's a movie at the drive-in," John said. "A new Western."

"Yeah, I need to escape from my head for a few hours. I think we all probably do, right?" Bunny asked, looking at Caroline.

She gave a sad, slow nod.

Frank and Oscar jumped in the bed of the truck. As John pulled away from the curb, Oscar said, "You didn't tell them about the blood."

"No."

"Why?"

Frank waited for a few moments. The truck passed the ocean now, gray and churning as the surf seemed to be picking up.

"No use in freaking them out more than they already are. Besides, it could be anyone's."

"Teddy's?" said Oscar.

Frank gave him a look. "It could be anyone's," he repeated.

21
JOHN

THE FOG ROLLED BACK IN AS THE DARK DESCENDED AND JOHN drove to the drive-in over at Lovers Beach. He'd imagined going with Caroline before, but that had been under completely different circumstances. He'd wondered what it would be like to date her, even take her to one of those USO dances over at Fort Ord. Not that this was a date. It was anything but with Bunny sitting in the middle of them, and Frank and Oscar in the bed of the truck. Besides, she was still grieving Eleanor's death. That would take time—a lot of time. He would be her friend through it. He could do that, even though he wanted something more. He would wait for her.

John tried not glance at Caroline but his eyes kept roaming back to her. Her head rested on the passenger window. His mind returned to their kiss behind the church. *Did she regret it now?* he wondered. He hadn't planned to kiss her. The boldness of it shocked him. Especially since he'd felt a wave of unexpected emotion at Eleanor's funeral. He had actually teared up.

John had only cried a couple times in his life. The first time was when he had fallen and broken his leg. The second time was when he didn't make the varsity baseball team freshman year. He'd been ashamed of the latter. But the crying at Eleanor's funeral had nothing to do with shame. It was born of a sadness he didn't understand, and it moved him to follow Caroline, make sure she was okay.

John turned into the drive-in. HIGH NOON starring Gary Cooper was written in black letters on the marquee. He'd have to apologize to Gary later, since he'd promised to take him to see it. Gary Cooper was his namesake, after all. John's namesake—a friend of the family, one of the first Americans his dad had met when he immigrated—was boring in comparison.

"What's the deal?" Bunny asked.

A long line of cars were waiting ahead of them to get in.

"I forgot," John said "*Buck Night.*"

"But it's just a Western," Bunny said.

"Just a Western?"

When John was little, all he wanted to be was a cowboy. He'd run around shooting at people with his friends. His father had even bought him a cowboy hat that still hung in his room. He didn't want to be a cowboy anymore, but he did own a pair of boots, like the guys who came in from Salinas sometimes, the ones who farmed and worked the fields.

Once John had seen a samurai movie from Japan with his dad. It was the first time he'd seen Japanese depicted as heroes. The movies were kind of like Westerns, set in old Japanese villages. The samurai banded together to save women, children, whole towns. Cowboys, but with swords and armor instead of guns.

As they inched forward, John noticed some commotion in

his rearview mirror. He rolled down the window and looked behind. There was a small crowd gathering a few cars behind them.

"Something's going on," John said. He felt the truck wobble and saw that Frank and Oscar had jumped out of the truck's bed.

Frank paused outside John's window. "I'm going to check it out."

Bunny was already opening her door. Caroline followed behind. John turned off the truck and joined them.

In the center of the small crowd, John saw a young man lying on the asphalt next to a car. His eyes were closed and his legs twitched. A woman hovered over him.

Caroline pushed through the barrier of people and knelt next to him on the ground. John stood nearby on the edge of the crowd.

"What's his name?" Caroline asked as she put her fingers on his neck.

"Brian."

"Okay, Brian, I'm here and I'm going to check your vitals. Don't worry," she said to the woman at his side. "Brian is going to be okay."

Caroline forced his eyes open with her hands. John wanted to ask her what she thought she was doing, but her confidence and quick action held him back. It was like she knew exactly what to do.

More and more people were gathering around, pressing in on the man and Caroline.

"Can you tell the crowd to back up?" she asked John.

John did as she said and, surprisingly, the crowd listened. John, Frank, and Oscar helped secure more of a perimeter.

Everyone watched as Caroline checked the man's breathing, heart, and then she felt along his ribcage.

"Anyone have a knife? And a straw?" she asked.

"What are you doing?" said the woman.

"There's an obstruction," Caroline said. "Something is blocking his breathing. I have to help him to breathe."

"Have you done this before?"

Oscar handed Caroline the switchblade he carried in his back pocket. Bunny grabbed a straw out of a guy's drink next to her.

"Hey!"

"Are you sure you know what you're doing?" John whispered next to her. He knew that Caroline kind of freaked out around blood.

But Caroline didn't respond. Instead, she took the items and tilted the man's head back and cut into his neck right below his Adam's apple. A small amount of blood oozed out. Caroline put her fingers inside the hole she made. John thought he was going to be sick. Caroline didn't even hesitate. She put the straw inside and blew into it three times. She stopped and watched. The man's chest began to rise and fall.

"Okay. He's breathing. See?" Caroline comforted the woman. "He's going to be okay. Just talk to him."

The woman bent low and began speaking in Brian's ear.

An ambulance pulled up.

"Caroline, let's go," John said.

He didn't understand what had just happened, but he knew that people would have a lot of questions.

"An emergency trach?" one of the EMTs said when he got to the man. "Where's the doctor?"

The woman sitting with the man on the ground pointed to Caroline.

"The girl? Seriously?"

"No, it's true. She did it."

"Excellent work," the EMT said.

"Is that Caroline O'Sullivan, one of the girls who went missing?" someone whispered.

John felt the fear begin to spread through the crowd. He knew what could follow such fear.

"Let's go," he repeated and pulled Caroline away.

22

BUNNY

ONE BY ONE, THE SKYWATCH GROUP GOT BACK IN JOHN'S TRUCK.

Bunny spoke first. "Give me the knife," she said, taking the blade from Caroline's shaking hand. She wiped off the blood on a napkin she found in the glove department.

Then she didn't say anything more. None of them did. Bunny watched out the window as John drove fast through town, past homes, most of them dark, except for the white phosphorous light coming from the televisions in living rooms. He finally parked at a desolate spot, private and quiet, next to the woods.

Bunny peered into them and thought she saw movement. There was something there. Something in the woods. And then there wasn't. Was her mind playing tricks?

A bang on her window sounded then, making Bunny jump.

Oscar stood next to her side of the door. "What the hell was that back there?" he yelled in at Caroline through the rolled-down window.

"Shut up, Oscar," Bunny said.

John opened his door. Bunny opened hers and jumped out.

She held the door for Caroline, but she was already following John out on his side.

"What? No one else is thinking it?" Oscar said.

Bunny thought all kinds of things. How what Caroline did both fascinated and terrified her. How she was certain it meant something, but what? Mostly she thought about how she'd dreamt in Mandarin last night. Even now she could translate everything Oscar said into the language. How could she speak a language she had never studied? She was good, but she wasn't *that* good.

"Seriously, how did you know how to do that, Caroline?" Oscar asked. "I mean, it was amazing. Amazing. And gross. I've never seen anything like it. Can I have my knife back?" He pointed to Bunny's hand.

Bunny gave it to him. He turned it over in his hands, as if there was something magical about it.

Caroline stood next to John and kept her arms folded across her chest. Bunny wanted to reach out and put her arm around her. Comfort her. Bunny wanted to know how she'd known how to save that man, too, but she was distracted by the memory of her dream.

Last night Bunny had dreamed of a small room with a bed and desk and no windows. It was cold, dark, and she was afraid. She could hear muffled sounds coming from the other side of the door. Something was making its way toward her. She'd backed away from it as far she could because, even though she didn't know what was there on the other side, she knew that whatever it was, she was terrified of it. She looked down; her hands were dirty. She had marks on her arms as if she had been cut or scratched or maybe both. The thing turned the handle. Bunny woke up in a sweat.

Something told her that she should be afraid of the thing behind the door.

Frank pushed off the truck and stood facing them, positioning himself directly in front of Caroline. Bunny noted that John drew himself up to his full height and scooted closer to her.

"Someone want to tell me what's going on?" Frank asked.

"If Caroline isn't ready to talk about it, she doesn't have to talk about it," John said.

Somewhere along the way, John had become their protector, and even though he was talking about Caroline, Bunny felt included in his statement. Not that she needed his protection. She had always taken care of herself. Though here in the dark, with the woods so close, she was thankful not to be alone.

"This is going to get back to the police, maybe even the FBI," Frank said. "Don't you think they'll find it weird that Caroline can now suddenly perform complicated medical procedures?"

Or that I can speak new languages, Bunny thought.

If she and Caroline had new abilities—talents? She wasn't sure the word—she wondered what John was now able to do. Bunny got the feeling that he wasn't sharing the full extent of what he was thinking even now. He stood there with his arms across his chest, defensive posturing, her father would say, staring straight ahead into the woods. Like he was bracing himself for something. But what? Bunny watched as he rubbed a spot on the back of his neck.

"It's hard to explain," Caroline began, her voice a small hole in the darkness that surrounded them. "When I saw the man on the ground, I didn't even have to think. It was like I just knew what to do. Kind of like tying your shoelaces. Remember when you had to learn how to tie them and it was so hard at first, you had to concentrate each time? You had to practice that sing-song phrase about the bunny to get the loops just right? But now, you just tie your shoes. You don't even think about it. And if someone asked you to show them how to tie your shoes, you'd probably have to stop and think about it really hard to walk them through the simple steps."

The others just looked at her.

"It was like that. I knew what to do for him, like it was second nature. I knew how to examine him. I knew how to treat him. I know it sounds crazy, but I'm sure I've done that procedure many times. My hands have . . ." She held them out in front of her, covered with streaks of dried blood, and then clasped them together. "But that's crazy, right? I've always been squeamish around blood. How can this be happening?" She looked at both Bunny and John now, searching their eyes as if they could give her the answer she needed.

"How could I have known?" She started crying.

Bunny reached out and laid a hand on Caroline's arm. "Were you afraid?" Bunny asked.

"No. Well, yes, I was terrified after I realized what had happened, but in the moment I was actually helping him, no. I wasn't."

"Did you hear any voices?" Oscar asked.

"Voices? What do you mean?"

"I mean, in your head. A voice. Something that was speaking to you."

"No, that's absurd."

"No more absurd than you suddenly being a surgeon," Frank pointed out.

"I'm not a surgeon."

"No, you're not. Which is why Oscar asked about the voices." Frank and Oscar looked at each other like they were about to reveal the biggest secret. "We may have another theory."

"What?"

"The night you all went missing," Frank explained in a slow, steady voice, "what if you were taken?"

"You told us that already. Aliens. We get it."

"No. We don't think you were just taken," Oscar said. "What if you were implanted with another life-form? That would explain how you suddenly knew what to do. It's not you alone in there anymore." He pointed to her head. "It's you and something else."

Caroline let out a high-pitched laugh. It came out all warped and screechy, otherworldly sounding. For a split second, Bunny entertained the possibility. But that would mean there was an alien inside her, too, and that was ludicrous. She knew who she was. She was not an extraterrestrial. This was getting too intense.

"But wouldn't we know if there were aliens inside of us? Telling us what to do and stuff?" Bunny said.

"Not if they don't want you to know they're there. It's more like a symbiotic relationship. The alien is kind of like a para-site," Oscar said.

"You're basically a host body," added Frank. "And maybe

you weren't even taken, just implanted somewhere in the forest and then were hidden away or unconscious for hours before making it back."

"That could account for the memory loss," said Oscar. "Maybe your mind is blocking out the experience to protect you from the trauma of it all."

Bunny thought about this. No one said anything.

Then finally Caroline spoke. "You guys are crazy."

"Maybe," Frank said. "But if I hadn't just witnessed what you did with my own eyes, I would have thought you were all crazy. But first Bunny and now Caroline. You guys have changed."

They all looked at Bunny now.

"What do they mean?" Caroline asked her. "Did something like this happen to you too?"

"Not exactly . . ." She hadn't intended to keep it from John and Caroline. "But yes, something weird, like the shoe-tying incident."

To illustrate, she started speaking to them in Mandarin, telling them about what had happened at the store.

"It happened with Mr. Chang. I didn't even realize I was speaking to him in Mandarin. I was just talking."

"Why didn't you say anything?" John asked.

Bunny shrugged. "I don't know. It's not like . . . we were close before this, or even friends. Caroline, have we ever even spoken outside of the tower?"

"No. I didn't even like you."

"Me neither. I didn't like any of you. Just because we went into those woods together and came out doesn't mean we're all best friends now. In fact, I don't know who to trust."

"Look who's talking," John said.

"Really? Coming from the guy who never says what he's thinking."

Bunny wanted to stop herself, but the feelings she'd masked since having to move to the small town refused to be hidden any longer. Tears came now, which really angered her. She didn't like for anyone to see her cry. She hadn't cried since her mom left. This was a stupid thing to cry over.

She grabbed a cigarette from her purse. She'd been smoking way too much lately. But she needed something to help her nerves. God, she was sounding just like her mother. Her mother, who always had a cigarette dangling, and you felt like you wanted to run around after her with an ashtray. Now the house was full of empty ashtrays. Maybe Bunny had started filling them on purpose.

She inhaled deeply, pushing away the image of her mother.

As she did this, another image came to her. Or maybe it was more of a feeling. One that surprised her. She felt that they belonged together. She looked at John and Caroline to see if they felt it too, but they were staring off into the woods, each absorbed in their own thoughts.

"I played the piano," John said.

"Yeah, so? I play piano, too," said Bunny.

"I play the violin," said Caroline.

"No," John said. "I don't actually play the piano. I never learned. But the other day, I played a song from memory, like I'd been doing it all my life."

"What did you play?" Caroline asked.

"I don't know. But it was . . . just like you guys are saying.

I sat down and didn't even realize what I was doing. It was just something I knew how to do." He held out his hands. "My fingers knew the keys. Kind of like if someone were to give me a glove and a ball. And there are other things I can't explain." He glanced quickly at Caroline. "More like feelings. Like there's so much more on the edges. And when I try to reach for it, it's just gone."

Bunny noticed Frank and Oscar had backed up a little, giving themselves some distance, and they looked scared, like they were going to make a run for it.

"What's the matter?" John asked.

"That was . . ." Oscar let the words trail off.

"What?" Bunny asked.

"The three of you were just speaking another language together. It sounded like Mandarin."

"What—" Bunny started, but she knew he was right. As soon as she spoke, John and Caroline knew what she was saying. Her speaking to them in Mandarin was the most natural thing. And she hadn't even realized she was doing it. She'd just slipped into the language fluently, as though she'd been speaking it all her life.

"That's impossible," Caroline whispered.

"But they're right," John said.

Bunny faltered because now she saw fear in John's eyes, too.

"How can we know a whole language?" John asked.

"It's not out of the question to learn a new language quickly," Bunny said. "Some have learned a language in a couple of days."

"So we were in some language school in the forest?" Caroline said. "I don't understand. I don't understand any of this. I just want to wake up. I wish I'd never joined that stupid club!"

"I wish we would have stayed that night," Oscar said.

"No, you don't," said Caroline. "You want to feel like you're losing your mind? Like they're going to put you in an asylum? Because that's where we are headed. Or to some lab? And I'm so tired. I'm afraid to sleep. Afraid of what I might dream. Is it just me? Are you guys having weird dreams too?"

"More like nightmares," said Bunny. "Things creeping into my head that I know I didn't put there."

John looked at them both. "It's going to be all ri—"

"Stop that!" Caroline cut him off. She began pacing. "Bunny's right. We aren't really friends." She gestured between her and John. "There's nothing here. You and me, John, we don't even know each other."

John looked as if he were going to say something, but Caroline stopped him. "I'm tired. And I'm scared and I don't want to be here anymore. Please just take me home."

She got back inside the truck.

"It's late," Bunny said. "This is crazy. A total waste of time."

John stared at her a few moments.

"You're different," he said, and joined Caroline in the truck.

"I have an idea," Frank said.

"Frank," Bunny said. "Now's not the time. And I'm sorry, but you guys don't really understand what we're going through, so . . . I don't want to hear your ideas."

Frank held up his hands in surrender, and he and Oscar climbed into the bed of the truck. Bunny stayed facing the forest.

I'm not different, Bunny thought. But a voice deep inside whispered that wasn't true.

"You coming?" John asked.

She took one last drag and put out her cigarette in the dirt and got into the truck. She was careful to keep a little space between her and Caroline.

We're all different now.

23

CAROLINE

THE DREAMS STARTED THE NIGHT AFTER SHE CAME BACK. AT FIRST they were more like feelings. She'd wake in the strangeness of them and forget after just a few moments. But then they began to take shape. She woke and remembered and *knew* things—like she had woken from a past life, where she had known pain and love and joy and a sorrow so deep, she felt it in the marrow of her bones. She was afraid of this grief, which is why she tried not to sleep.

But the dream last night . . . Her face still burned from it. She'd never had a dream like that before. She'd lingered that morning in bed, eyes closed, trying to hold on to it as long as she could.

After breakfast, she got on her bike. She noticed a black car parked across the street. It was the same car that was there yesterday and the day before. She couldn't tell if anyone was sitting inside of it, and it could have been a neighbor's, but she didn't think so. There was something sinister about the way it sat there, like the vehicle itself was watching her.

She passed it, and it didn't follow. She went for a ride down by the ocean to clear her head. As she rode, her blond hair became frizzy in the damp air. She didn't have any plans for the day, just to pass the time and try not to think about Eleanor. When she was with others, it was easier to distract her mind, but on her own, she kept thinking of her friend. Of how lonely she felt without her. Of this incredible hole that was now in her heart, this ache in her chest, this loss that felt so familiar. The same wound she'd received when Jack died, open wider now and more raw.

She rode along the deteriorating row of canneries, noting how she used to love to come here with her father. He hadn't been a fisherman by trade, but he loved the hustle and bustle of the waterfront. He'd come and get himself coffee and her a donut and they'd sit and watch. She especially loved the whistles that signaled the boats coming in. Each company had its own signal. She was able to pick out all of them.

In a way she was glad her father wasn't here to see what had happened to the canneries, especially after the most recent fire. It would have broken his heart to see the skeleton of what remained.

Up ahead, Caroline spotted Mrs. Messina standing near an open doorway. She froze, hands gripping the handlebars of her bike. The woman wore a black shapeless dress that came to her calves. Her long hair was tied back in a black kerchief. If Caroline didn't know better, she'd almost mistake her for a nun. Caroline thought she could turn around before Mrs. Messina spied her, but she was wrong. The woman motioned for Caroline.

"Hello, Mrs. Messina," Caroline said as she approached.

"Hello, Caroline."

Teddy's mother held a cigar and stared at Caroline. It was only a couple of seconds, but Caroline felt hours pass. Her eyes darted around, looking for a way out of the situation. But no one else was around. They were essentially alone.

"You have become very pretty," Mrs. Messina said. She shifted her weight to her left hip, the cigar a small stump gesturing to Caroline's hair. "Blondes have more fun, isn't that the saying?"

Caroline had heard that before. There were advantages to being pretty. Her face always got her in the door. She'd rather be pretty than not. But she had just as many problems and insecurities as the next person. A nice-looking face didn't solve what she struggled with on the inside. It was still a mask. It just happened to be a mask people liked to look at.

But Mrs. Messina wasn't giving her a compliment.

"You and my Teddy would make a cute couple," Mrs. Messina said. "I think he always liked you."

Caroline felt the heat rise to her face. "Oh, Teddy and I were"—she corrected herself—"*are* friends. Always have been."

"Friends . . . yes." The woman took another puff and then flicked the ashes onto the deck floor. Mrs. Messina moved close to Caroline. "Have you remembered anything?"

Caroline smelled coffee and ash on the woman's breath. It reminded her of her grandfather. He used to smoke cigars all the time.

"No," Caroline whispered.

She saw Teddy walking just ahead of her. He crouched down

low, motioning for them to do the same. There was something in the clearing. Something humming . . . and glowing.

Teddy's mother grabbed Caroline's arm.

"You think I don't know about you and your ways. But I know. What did you do? Pit those two boys against each other? You act like a tease, don't you. Maybe you make it so they fight over you?"

"Mrs. Messina, I—"

"You know what I think? I think something happened out there and it didn't come from the skies."

"No, that's not true." Caroline tried to back away, but the woman held her tightly.

"They say maybe Teddy ran away, but he would never do that to us. So the only explanation is something bad happened in that group of yours."

"Mrs. Messina, we never—"

"Don't tell me any more lies. This crazy talk about lights in the sky and flying saucers and things from outer space. It's all to distract from what really happened. One of you killed my boy."

Caroline stared at her in shock. "I, no, that's—"

Mrs. Messina pulled her in closer and said, "You can't hide forever."

Caroline yanked her arm free from the woman.

"God sees everything," Mrs. Messina cried after her.

Caroline didn't even try to get back on her bike. She ran, pushing it. The tears came fast, blinding her. She moved quickly, keeping her head down, hoping that no one would recognize her. But the smaller she tried to make herself, the more people watched. Their eyes peeking out of windows, of buildings, doorways. Following her up the street like a slow-moving fog of bulging eyes. The eyes opened and shut and turned into mouths that voiced the same thing.

Murderer.

But that wasn't true. There was no way she could have murdered Teddy. Still, the eyes were relentless.

Murderer.

She got back on her bike and picked up the pace. The word like a crescendo in her mind.

Murderer. Murderer.

"Caroline?"

From behind, someone called her name. She pedaled faster. Away from the docks, back toward town. Her heart pounded. Someone was chasing her. She could feel it. She turned down a street and hid behind a building.

Murderer.

Teddy was alive. He had to be. She would know if he wasn't. Wouldn't she? She thought as hard as she could, and then quickly, an explosion happened in her mind. A bright light. It was as if she saw him clearly then. In her mind's eye, Teddy raised his hand to her in greeting. He walked toward her, a slight limp in his step. Even with a thick brown beard, she'd recognize his wide smile anywhere. The sky was blue and tall trees stood in the background. He was happy to see her.

"Caroline?"

Caroline collected herself like a spring, ready to attack or flee from whoever was rounding the bend.

But it was just John, out of breath from coming after her.

"Oh, John." She leapt off her bike and ran into his arms.

He let her fall right in. She buried her face into his neck, inhaling his salty, sweaty scent. The smell stirred images and feelings from the dream she'd woken from that morning. Her face flushed again, thinking of it.

"Caroline," he said. This time his arms wrapped around her, and she felt safe. For the first time, she felt safe.

She turned her face up toward him and he bent down to kiss her—just in the way, she was suddenly sure, he'd done a hundred times before.

24

BUNNY
....

THERE WEREN'T TOO MANY MOMENTS IN BUNNY'S LIFE THAT SHE looked back and wondered what the hell she was thinking. But this was one of those moments.

She blamed her poor decision-making on what had happened last night. She'd come home from the drive-in feeling lost. And confused. They were still no closer to figuring out what had happened to them, and Teddy was still missing.

So when Oscar had called and asked for her help, she'd said yes.

Now she sat in an uncomfortable wooden folding chair in a garage, beneath a hanging light and aluminum foil that was molded to her head like a swim cap. Frank sat across from her in a softer, older padded chair, which looked much more comfortable. Oscar fiddled with something in the corner behind a car that looked like it was missing half of its body. Oscar asked the extra-terrestrial, who he insisted lived inside of her body, a question.

"What do you want with us?" He spoke loudly, as if he was worried that the thing inside Bunny couldn't hear him otherwise.

Bunny scratched an itch underneath the foil at the base of her head.

"Try not to move, okay, Bunny? We need to isolate the being's thoughts from yours," Frank said. "Ask another question, Oscar."

The garage smelled of grease, oil, and sweat. Bunny crinkled her nose, careful to keep her head still so the aluminum hat wouldn't tilt to the side.

Oscar peeked his face out from behind the hood of the vehicle. "What is your name?"

Bunny stared at him blankly, thinking again about how she had come to be here.

When she got home last night, she'd walked in on her dad sitting at the kitchen table, reading a letter.

"Dad?"

"Bunny." He tried to hide the paper, but she recognized the pale pink stationery that her mother wrote on. "What time is it?"

"Not too late."

Bunny wondered if the paper carried her mother's smell: Chanel No. 5.

He looked at his watch. "Kind of late."

"I'm okay, Dad." She walked to the sink and got herself some water. She drank a full glass without even taking a breath, the night's activities and revelations still reeling in her mind. "What did the letter say?"

"Oh, nothing. Just something from a friend."

"Dad."

He handed it to Bunny. It was dated last week. She was looking for absolution, forgiveness. The priest told her to write, so she was making amends. It didn't smell like anything.

"That's real generous of her."

Her dad caught the sarcasm. "I'm all right, Bunny. You have enough to worry about. Really, you don't need to concern yourself with me. I'm fine."

She wanted to tell him that he wasn't at fault, that her mother had chosen this path. She wanted to say that he needed to forget her and ask out the woman who worked in his office at the language institute. The one who smiled widely at him whenever he was around. The one who'd sent him home with baked cookies on more than one occasion. And even though they were a little hard and overdone, it was the thought behind them that Bunny felt was sweet.

Bunny knew her words could give no comfort to the wound her dad continued to patch over. After her mother first left, he'd reopen it nightly. Every so often, he did so again. Bunny figured he preferred the pain to the numbness.

Her dad needed to perform this ritual of reading the letter until it was done doing its work. The work of forgetting and mending took time. It surprised her, this truth. But she knew it somehow, deep in the core of her being.

"Dad?"

He looked up. Eyes out of focus as if he were off somewhere in a dream.

"I love you."

He smiled at her. In the past, she might have been hurt that he didn't say the words back, but she understood that he had difficulty in expressing his feelings. That didn't mean he loved her less.

But she woke the next morning feeling off. She wasn't sure if it had to do with how they'd left things the night before or if maybe she'd had a strange dream she couldn't recall. But she felt like there was a blanket of darkness covering her. Fortunately, the light streaming in through her window helped her get her bearings. She was in her bedroom. The one she had known for almost a year. She was safe. That's what was important.

The only plans she had for the day were to finish a book. She picked *And Then There Were None* by Agatha Christie. She didn't know where her latest Miss Marple book had gone, and this one had been on her list to reread for a while.

"Hey," her brother's voice called from outside her room. "You up?"

"Yeah."

Will opened her door and walked in, already dressed nice in a white button-down shirt and striped tie.

"Where are you going?" Bunny asked.

"Job interview."

"Really?"

"Really . . ." He looked around the room. "So, everything good?"

She nodded. Their conversations were always an exercise in brevity over depth.

"See you later."

"See ya."

He left her room, closing the door behind him. She couldn't

say that her brother had become more present since she'd disappeared and all, but he did check in on her more than he used to. It didn't make up for all the crap that he'd done back in New York, the gambling, making her parents sick with worry, or turn him into a loving older brother all of a sudden, but it did make her feel like he cared.

Afterward, she'd gotten dressed, ate some breakfast with her dad, and then settled into the couch with her book. But she found herself reading the same sentences over and over again. Normally she flew through Christie's prose, but this morning, she was distracted. When she'd finally had enough of trying and failing to focus, she closed the book. She'd come back to it another time.

Alone in the house, she went from room to room. Looking for what, she wasn't certain. But she did feel like she was missing something. Her fingers found the bump behind her ear and massaged it. A wave of intense loneliness hit her. She felt more lonely than when they'd first moved. Lonelier than on the first day of school when she walked in those doors, the students milling around her, glancing sideways, wondering who she was, but walking past. Only Teddy had talked to her directly. He had introduced himself in first period and asked what New York was like. After that he wanted to know what she thought about the atomic bomb.

Bunny smiled at the memory. Teddy was always talking about the Russians and bombs and war and basketball. Tears came to her eyes, but they weren't just for Teddy. They were for her own sense of loss. She didn't know which loss she was mourning, because there had been a lot lately, but the emptiness filled up the whole house. Bunny suddenly found it hard to breathe, and that's when the phone rang.

Frank. Wondering if she had time to come over so he and Oscar could run a few tests by her. She said yes, thinking anything was better than being in the house by herself.

Now she wasn't so sure.

Now she was stuck in a garage with two boys she had written off months ago. She almost laughed out loud thinking how ludicrous it all was.

"I'm not getting through, Frank. We may have to try something more drastic." Oscar came out from behind the hood of a car with jumper cables. "I just had to clean out some of the rust, but the battery should be good to go."

Bunny stared wide-eyed at him. "Oh, no. You are not coming anywhere near me with those."

"Bunny, this is serious," Oscar said. "It's no longer about just you. Think about the community. Hell, think about the whole United States of America. You could be saving the world."

"So what? You're going to jump-start my brain?!" Even as she said the words, though, she knew it was impossible to do so. At least she thought it was.

She stood up and yanked the aluminum foil off. Bunny crumpled it up in her hands. Frank started laughing.

"You think this is funny?"

"I'm sorry, Bunny. I let Oscar try his way." He motioned to the car battery and cables. "Now, can we try another?"

"What does that mean?"

"I thought we could try hypnosis."

"Hypnosis? You know how to do that?"

Frank shrugged. "I've been doing a little studying. It's worth a shot."

"I don't know."

"Look, your memory still hasn't come back, right? Nothing else is working. What have you got to lose?"

Bunny pointed her finger at him. "If you do anything else weird or—"

"Trust me."

Bunny thought about it. The worst case scenario was that she'd waste a few more minutes. The best was that she'd actually remember something.

She sat back down so that Frank could begin.

Frank took out a book and started reading it out loud to her. Telling her to close her eyes and to start breathing. He counted to ten. He took her through a couple of breathing exercises. Bunny thought that she might fall asleep she was becoming so relaxed.

And then she was somewhere else. She was no longer in a garage, but a small, tiny room. She could barely stand in it. And it was dark; she couldn't see. There were no windows. The sides were cement, cold and rough to the touch. She had a scratchy blanket that she tried to pull in closely around her torso and bare feet. Her whole body ached with hunger and cold. She imagined her breath rising above her in a small cloud.

She lay on the cold cement ground with no pillow. As far as she could tell, she was the only person in the room. She didn't know how long she had been there or where the others were.

The bowl they placed water in was empty. She wondered how long she could go without water. Wasn't it only a couple of days?

A noise came from behind the door. She moved as far away from it as she could, pushed her back up against the wall, and ignored the pain that now came from being pressed up against it. The person on the other side spoke to her, but she couldn't understand him. She was terrified. He opened the door and she screamed. In the shadows, his face appeared gray and mouthless.

Her eyes stung from the light. She squinted, tried to see where she was. She was grabbed on both sides, and something or someone helped her walk down the hallway because she couldn't stand on her own. Looking down, she saw her ankle was swollen and there was a gash on her calf. They were bringing her to the other room. She tried to resist, to yell, to get away. But she was too weak.

"Bunny," she heard her name being called.

The images began to fade. She left the hallway and the room and the darkness.

She was back in Oscar's garage.

"It's okay," Frank said. "We're not going to hurt you. It's okay." He held out a bottle of Coke. "Here, drink."

She could barely hold it she was shaking so much.

"Something was after us," she said.

"You remember?" Frank asked. He and Oscar exchanged looks.

"Yes," she whispered. "I remember."

25

JOHN

JOHN WALKED ALONGSIDE CAROLINE, PUSHING HER BIKE UP THE hill. He was quiet, not sure what to say after the way she had kissed him. The way he had kissed her back. And yet it didn't surprise him. His body responded as if by muscle memory. They had kissed this way before. He was certain. Not after Eleanor's funeral—before that, way back somewhere, someplace.

He thought he should say something, but he didn't know what to say. This was all new territory for him. He'd never had a girlfriend, not that Caroline was his girlfriend, but she was something. Wasn't she? She was more than what she'd been to him a week ago for sure.

"I'm sorry," Caroline finally said.

"For what?"

"For . . . you know . . . back there. I don't know what's the matter with me."

John matched her pace a few steps, wondering what the right response would be.

Finally he said, "Don't be sorry. At least, not for kissing me."

She kept walking. "Is this weird?"

"Kind of."

"I mean, is it more weird that it's not weird? Us? What does that mean? I feel like . . ."

"Like we know each other much more than we actually do?"

She stopped. "You feel it, too?"

"When I woke up in the hospital room, the first person I thought of was you. Now, don't get me wrong, I may have thought about you from time to time before . . ."

Caroline laughed.

"But this was different."

"Different," she repeated. "That's one word for it."

But also amazing, he wanted to say. Caroline O'Sullivan. Just saying her name had always had an effect on him, but now the name contained meaning. Part of him wanted to pull her aside and make out with her for hours. The other part, the one that played it safe, told him she was still out of his league, even in the way she kissed him. But here she was now, walking with him as if it was the most normal thing in the world for them to be doing so.

They passed two women who gave John a cold stare. He knew what they were thinking. It's why he didn't hold her hand or stand too close. Some people would have trouble with a relationship like theirs. His parents wouldn't even want it. They expected a nice Japanese girl for him. Many times over dinner, his mother brought up how kind and pretty Keiko, the Yamamotos' daughter, was. John agreed with her. Keiko was pretty and smart and funny. She was practically perfect, but she wasn't Caroline.

He picked up the pace to get away from the women.

"Wait up," Caroline said, running a little to match him.

"Come on," he joked. "Don't tell me this is too fast for you?"

"Oh, yeah?"

He goaded her, knowing she would rise to the occasion. Caroline and competition always went hand in hand. In every class he'd had with her, she always wanted to be the best. Some thought it was annoying, but John liked her confidence and drive. It was so opposite from him. He was competitive on the baseball field, but he was more methodical about it. He never wanted to draw attention to himself. This quality he knew he got from his father. Work hard. Keep your head down. Be excellent at what you do. Become someone who others want to see.

Caroline started running ahead of him. Since she didn't have a bike to push, she made it to the intersection at the top of the street before he did. She turned around, hands on her hips, looking at him in triumph.

A wave of recognition bowled over him, almost knocking him down. She'd been wearing different clothes—a heavy brown jacket. Her hair had also been shorter, darker, cut in a kind of bob. A long angry scar marked her left cheek.

And then the image was gone.

Just a flash.

John stumbled with the bike and fell to the ground.

"Whoa, are you okay?" Caroline said, running to his side.

He picked up the bike and dusted himself off. "Fine." Embarrassed more than anything, even though it felt like the wind had been knocked out of him.

"It's just a couple more blocks," she said.

He steadied himself, hating that she'd seen him in a moment of weakness.

They kept walking, and John's attention was pulled to a parked car across the street. He saw a Caucasian man yelling at a person through the rear window into the backseat. The yelling turned to beating on the hood of the car and waving his arms around wildly. John slowed down, trying to see who was in the backseat, but then thought better of it.

"Come on," he said to Caroline. He didn't need the trouble or attention drawn to them. They had enough of the two on their own.

But as they drew up alongside the car, John saw the man force open the door and yank out a young woman with curly brown hair. The man pushed her up against the side of the car and continued to yell.

"What'd I tell you? You trying to embarrass me? You think you're so much better?"

The woman said something inaudible back and that's when he slapped her.

Everything in John's head said to keep walking, to ignore it, to not get involved. But John didn't listen.

"Stay here," he told Caroline and handed her the bike.

"John?" Caroline asked, taking her bike from him.

He saw worry in her eyes, but he couldn't let that stop him. For a second he thought of the Western they would have seen the night before. He pretended Caroline was his fiancée, pleading with him to go, not to face the bad outlaws.

"Heroes stay," he said, more to himself than to her.

"What?"

"I've gotta help her."

John crossed the street, his resolve growing with each step, walked up behind the man, and said, "Excuse me? Is everything all right?"

He addressed his comments to the woman, who he could now see was probably not that much older than he was. He could also see that she was scared. The man turned abruptly toward him.

"This is none of your business." He had black hair and stubble, and smelled like cigarettes and beer. His eyes warned John of what would happen if he didn't keep walking.

A bruise was already forming underneath the woman's eye. Yellow coloring underneath her chin spoke of an older one.

"I wasn't speaking to you," John said, keeping his eyes on the woman.

"I'm fine." She folded her arms across her chest, stared down at the ground.

John knew this was his moment to leave. He had behaved honorably by trying to help her. She wasn't asking for his help, he could say that later to anyone who would tell him that she had been beaten or worse. Besides, it was a domestic dispute. He knew Caroline was watching him. But he couldn't walk away.

John took a deep breath. "I'm sorry, but it doesn't look like you're fine, miss."

This time, the man turned around and got up in John's face. He puffed his chest out, towering over John. Up close, he now realized he had seen this man working down by the docks many times.

"Look, kid. There's nothing to see here."

"Doesn't seem that way to me, sir." John moved to position himself at a better angle slightly away from the man and close enough to the woman that he could grab her if he needed to.

"Hey, I know you. You're Kawai's kid. One of those kids who went missing?"

Out of the corner of his eye, John saw the woman begin to ease herself down the side of the car, her back sticking to it like a snail's.

"Yeah, that's me."

He needed to keep the guy distracted so she could get away. He could even help her go to the police station if she wanted. He positioned himself so the woman was blocked from the guy's view. She continued to slink away.

"How do you know my dad?" John asked.

"Work."

The guy noticed the woman was trying to get away then, and he grabbed her arm, sliding her back toward him.

"Where do you think you're going?"

"Nowhere," the woman said.

John knew this wasn't going to end well.

"Sir, please let the woman alone."

"Don't you tell me what to do," said the man.

"I'm only going to ask you one more time."

"Oh yeah? And what do you think—"

John didn't let him finish his sentence. He grabbed him, turned him around, and threw him up against the car, pressing the man's face to the glass window of the driver's side. He wrenched the man's arm around and held it behind his back. The maneuver was instinctual.

"How does that feel?" John whispered close to the man's ear.

"What the hell?" the man spit out.

"You can go now," John said to the woman.

Instead of leaving, she yelled at him, "Let him go, you're hurting him."

"I'm simply restraining him."

"Well, stop it. I don't need your help."

John looked at her and realized that if she didn't want to be helped, there was nothing he could really do. He let the guy go and backed away.

The man pointed his finger at John. "You'll be sorry you did that." He pulled down his red T-shirt that had gotten all bunched up. The woman came to him with soothing words. "Baby, come on. I'm sorry. Let's just go."

John looked at Caroline across the street and was surprised to see there were a couple other people who had stopped to observe the commotion. He'd drawn too much attention to himself. But he couldn't help it. With his judo training, he knew how to handle himself physically, and he would subdue the guy if he had to. That was the art of judo. Control, not force. But seeing how the guy had manhandled that woman had unlocked something within John. Now he stood a little confused at what to do.

He was thinking about it when Caroline's hands reached out to him and she yelled, "Look out!"

He felt a quick searing heat in the spot just below his shoulder blade. Something sharp. He saw the blood spread across his shirt first, then the knife in the man's hand. Before the guy could get another cut in, John turned and faced him.

"Baby, don't. Don't. Come on," his girlfriend screamed at him, but the guy pushed her away from him.

"Just gotta teach this boy a lesson." He was crouched low, knife still pointing at John.

"Please, don't," John said.

But the guy swiped at him again. This time, John was ready. He faced the guy, crouched, hands out front so he was able to dodge the blow. He waited for the man to do it again. When he did, John lunged and grabbed the man's arm that held the knife. He brought it down on his leg, knocking the knife to the ground. The man acted predictably then. John antici-pated his next move, so he blocked the punch with his arm. John punched him in the gut and gave him an upper cut that sent him backward. To finish the guy off, John brought him in closer and hit him with two more jabs to the face and the abdomen.

"Stand down," John said.

Even though the guy was bleeding in the mouth now and clearly favoring his right side, he came at John one more time. John bent down and threw him over his shoulder and onto the ground. John held him down with his knee in his back, but he didn't really need to apply much pressure. The guy moaned.

"Get off me," he muttered.

"If I ever see you beating a woman again, I'll come find you." John shook with rage as he said the words.

The woman came at him, swinging her purse and striking John in the face. "Leave him alone! You're killing him!"

John stood up as she dropped to the ground to help her boy-friend. The guy's face was bloody, and his nose looked as if it were broken. Fear traveled up John's spine. Even with years of judo, he hadn't learned to fight like that.

Conscious now of others who had stopped and were gawking at the scene, John crossed the street to Caroline and said, "Come on, let's get out of here."

He walked next to her, ignoring the pain that now radiated from his shoulder blade. He felt the stickiness of the blood on his shirt. He reached up and tried to tame his hair. He'd already been a mess after working all morning; now he was sure he looked worse. It seemed to him that cars slowed as they passed.

When he reached Caroline's front yard, John put the kickstand down on the bike.

"Well, I guess I'll see you later."

"What're you talking about? I need to get a look at that wound."

"I can't go in your house like this." John motioned to the blood stain. "What'll your dad say?" He wondered what he'd tell his own parents. He'd have to throw away the shirt. Hide it at the bottom of the trash can.

"His car's not here. And my mom, well, who knows if she'll even notice. You need help. Come on."

"I'm fine," John said, but he wasn't. With the adrenaline tapering off, the pain was becoming intense.

She cocked her head to the side. "Aren't you tired of playing the hero?"

John looked at her. He was right the first time; somehow, they knew each other very well.

26
FRANK
....

FRANK WAITED WITH BUNNY IN THE BUSHES WHILE OSCAR USED HIS knife to open the window.

"Tell me again why this is a good idea?" Bunny asked.

"You want answers, don't you?" Frank said.

"I don't want to go to jail."

"Then be quiet so we don't get caught."

After seeing what happened to Bunny when she was under hypnosis, first of all, Frank was shocked it actually worked. And second of all, her behavior freaked him out. She had started crying and clearly remembered something that scared her. But she couldn't articulate it. Just that something scary had happened to them in the woods. Since they didn't have much to go on, he figured it couldn't hurt to see what Dr. Miller knew. He supposed they could have gone to him, told him about Bunny's experience, but Frank didn't think he would suddenly give them his confidence. To him, they were a bunch of kids. The government would swoop in and classify everything. Frank felt like they were on the verge of a great discovery and he wasn't about to be bumped out. He wanted to know.

And if it was aliens, well, he wanted to be there when they returned. Because if they came once, the likelihood of them coming again was plausible. And that meant they had probably taken Teddy. He only hoped he was still alive.

Any knowledge he had was leverage. He didn't want to give that up.

Oscar gave them the head nod. The coast was clear.

"Come on." Frank and Bunny crept to the window. Thankfully Dr. Miller's motel room was on the bottom floor. Oscar and Frank helped Bunny up first, then Frank followed. Oscar stayed outside as lookout.

There was a twin bed, a desk, and a small bathroom. Everything was neat and tidy. The three of them began looking around. Bunny went to the desk and opened the top drawer.

"Bingo," she said. She pulled out a yellow note pad. "He was writing on one of these during my interview."

"Ours, too," said Frank.

She began to read out loud:

"With the time and the behavior of the lights, it can be concluded that it was a possible sighting of the planet Venus. According to the weather report, the skies would have been clear enough. Unknowable still is the source of the fluid and the burns. But the report of the analysis of the gas is inconclusive at best."

Bunny kept reading but to herself.

"What's it saying?" Frank asked.

"Just a sec. Something about how the fuel found in the woods was kerosene based with a 50/50 gasoline to kerosene blend. This was something different from the avtag used in typical aircraft. This fuel was synthetic, like nothing ever seen. Containing seawater, hydrogen, and carbon dioxide."

"Seawater?" Frank said. "Strange. Let me see if he has the photographs."

Frank rummaged through the drawer and found the photos of the scorched ground. "Here," he showed Bunny. "This is what it looked like."

Bunny took the photo from him.

"Look familiar?"

"No."

Frank opened other drawers while Bunny continued to read Dr. Miller's notes. There was nothing significant inside. On top of the desk there was the recorder Frank remembered from when he'd visited Dr. Miller at the police station. Frank rewound it and pressed play. There was the sound of a chair being pushed across a floor. Some shuffling. Someone coughed.

"Can I have your full name?" the Project Blue Book guy said.

It must have been one of the many interviews Miller conducted.

"Spenser Wayne Williams." The man's voice was soft with a slight rasp.

"Spenser, I'm not here to ask you about what you saw in the sky that night. I'm not a police officer. I'm only here to investigate the lights. Many people saw something. You wouldn't be alone in that."

The chair moved.

"I was outside, enjoying a smoke. Actually, it might help my memory if I had one now."

Frank heard the sound of a lighter and someone taking a drag.

"Thanks," he said.

"You're welcome."

"I was having smoke when I saw this crazy-looking light. It kind of flashed like an airplane, but then it went away and then flashed again. Almost like a big firefly up in the sky."

"Was it any particular color?"

"Green, I think. Maybe blue, too. But what was strange was that it suddenly hovered and then shot down."

"An object hovered or the light hovered?"

"I'm not sure. It was too dark to really see. I guess just the light."

"How fast do you think it went?"

"I don't know. Fast. Like maybe a missile. That's what I thought it was. A bomb sent over by the Red Commies. I've got me a bomb shelter out underneath the garage, and I had half a mind to get inside of it."

"Did you?"

"No, I was too curious. I grabbed my gun and went to go see what it was."

"What kind of a gun?"

"The one I go hunting with, a rifle. My dad gave it to me when I turned twenty-one."

"You've had it a long time. Says here you're fifty-six."

"Yep."

"And was it loaded?"

"Of course it was."

"And you went after the light?"

"Yes. I walked into the woods, and it was . . . odd."

"Odd how?"

"Well, just . . . everything was quiet. Even the animals. Like they was watching, or waiting for something. I followed the quiet. There was something there that wasn't there before. Something in the woods that didn't belong. Or . . . sorry. I'm not explaining it right. But I could sense it, and it led me to . . . a light just through the trees."

"Can you describe the light?"

"Kind of like a flashlight whose batteries are dying. Not too bright, more like it was fading. But by that point, I was following the voices."

"Voices?"

"Yeah, I heard people talking."

"What were the voices saying?"

"I couldn't make them out at first. Then I think they were talking about helping someone. I don't know. It's all confusing . . . like static. And then . . . and then the light just goes, along with the voices."

"Goes?"

"Yeah. Just disappears." He snaps his fingers. "Like the flashlight went out."

"Did you see who was talking?"

"No, it was fuzzy."

"What was fuzzy?"

"The woods . . . or maybe it was more like the air or something. I don't know."

"Was it foggy?"

"No. I couldn't really see anything. Look, you don't have to believe me. These guys in here don't." There was the sound of the chair moving, and muffling, like the guy was putting out his cigarette in the ashtray. "But I haven't seen anything before like what I seen there. And I tell you, it wasn't natural. That light wasn't natural."

"You said before you found a blanket. Where did you find it?"

"When the light went out and it was quiet again, I crept forward for a better look and there was a blanket on the ground."

"Why'd you take it?"

"Why not? No one else was there to claim it."

The tape stopped.

"What a weirdo," Frank said.

"That was our blanket," Bunny said. "Caroline brought it with her from the tower."

"The red one?"

Bunny nodded.

"So we know you definitely went to that clearing. Oscar and I can lead you to it."

Bunny flipped ahead and kept reading the notebook while Frank looked around the room.

Bunny sat down on the bed. Her face drained of color.

"What's the matter?" Frank asked.

She looked up at him slowly. Pointed to the notebook. "They found a body," she said. "And blood. In the woods. Just out past the clearing." Her voice shaking and small. She pointed to the notebook.

This time Frank took it from her and read. He could feel each of them holding their breath.

"This says it was a female. Bone analysis revealed that the body had been dead for years."

"Oh," Bunny lifted her hand to her mouth. She turned away from him.

A knock on the window made both of them jump. Oscar signaled that someone was coming. They quickly put everything back exactly as they found it and left through the window.

When they were few paces away, Frank turned to look at Bunny and noted the tears in her eyes. "It wasn't Teddy," he said.

She nodded. "It wasn't Teddy," she repeated. "But it could have been."

"But it wasn't."

"But we still have no idea where he is! If he's even still alive. We've wasted so much time," Bunny said.

She stopped walking.

"We need to find Teddy. We need to go back."

Frank looked at Oscar.

"All right," he said. "Count us in."

27
JOHN

JOHN FOLLOWED CAROLINE UP THE WALKWAY AND INTO HER HOUSE. She led him into the bathroom and immediately began rummaging through the cabinet. She removed a bottle of hydrogen peroxide, cotton balls, and a bandage.

"Lift," she said.

"What?"

"Your arms."

As he did so she carefully helped him remove his shirt. His whole back was soaked in blood. He was surprised. He had no idea the cut was that bad.

Her hand lightly touched his back. His whole body shuddered.

"Sorry. Am I hurting you?"

"No," he said, embarrassed by his reaction. It wasn't the pain that made him shudder.

She grunted. "You're going to need stitches. We should probably go to the hospital."

"Can't you do it?"

"Yes, but I only have some ibuprofen here. It'll hurt."

"It already hurts. I don't want to go to the hospital. They'll call the police and then my dad."

His father would be furious with him when he found out about the fight and John causing such a scene. What the hell had he been thinking? In his gut, John knew as soon as he crossed the street that it was going to turn into a fight. And just as he knew that, he also knew he would win.

"Okay. You probably need about ten, maybe twelve. You're lucky that guy didn't get you any deeper. Just stay here for now. I'll be right back."

Caroline left the bathroom. John turned around and tried to see the wound in the mirror, but he could only see dried and fresh blood down the side of his back. He stared at his face, hardly recognized the person looking back at him. He was thinner somehow, his cheekbones more pronounced, as if someone had sculpted deep grooves. His eyes were still a deep brown, but they seemed more vibrant. Dark circles lined them.

What the hell happened out there?

John had never been in a fight in his life. He didn't count the time that Stu Nakamoto rushed him on the field after he hit him with one of his pitches. When confronted by his father, John had lied and said it had been an accident. But even at age ten, John had excellent aim. Stu knew this, of course, which is why he rushed him. There'd been other scuffles on the baseball field, but John had never ever been in a fight like the one he just had. A fight with a knife. A fight where he could have been killed.

But . . . his body had known just what to do. How to block and defend, how to throw a punch and defeat his opponent—as though it wasn't his first fight. Which was impossible.

Caroline returned and closed the door behind her. She carried a small sewing needle and pink thread.

"Sorry," she mumbled. "It was the only color I could find."

He smiled. "Pink's my favorite color."

He looked up and caught her eyes in the mirror. Feeling suddenly exposed, he crossed his arms across his naked chest.

"Okay, let me clean this up first."

She used a dark towel to wipe away the blood. Then she applied peroxide to the wound. Her face focused and concentrated, looking kind of like it did when she was taking a math test. Every time she touched him, his body twitched. He couldn't help it. Her hands sent a charge through him.

"You shouldn't have to do this," John said, trying to get his mind off the fact that he was half naked in Caroline's bathroom.

"Yes, I should. You can't stitch yourself, can you?"

"Well . . . thank you."

"You're welcome. Okay, this is the part that's going to hurt."

His skin burned as the needle pierced through. He clenched his fists, barely taking the pain. He just hoped he didn't cry or do anything stupid.

"So, what was that out there?" Caroline asked.

John answered through gritted teeth. "I couldn't just let that guy beat on his girlfriend."

"I know but . . . you fought like you've been professionally trained."

"Says the girl stitching me up right now like a surgeon."

"Touché."

"What's crazy is that I knew the moves he was going to

make before he made them. I also knew how to counter them."
He tried to talk through the pain. "So yeah, maybe I have been
trained . . ." John trailed off. *But how? And when?* He wondered.
It didn't make any sense.

"I know what you mean. I feel like I've been trained too.
How else could I know how to do . . . this? And blood. I used to
be squeamish around it. Now," she held up a couple of bloody
cotton balls, "this is nothing."

She finished the last stitch and tied the thread. "John," she
continued, but then she paused and stared off a bit.

"I've been having these dreams that I'm working in some
kind of hospital, tending to the sick and injured. There are so
many bodies." She grabbed a bandage to cover the stitches and
began taping. "But it all seems so real. Like I've done these procedures hundreds of times."

He reached out and touched the top of her cheek—the place
he'd seen that scar when his mind flashed to her earlier. That
had seemed so real, too. *How did she get it?* he wondered. Her
face was smooth now; no sign of what he'd seen. Was that just
a dream as well? He decided not to tell her about it. He didn't
want to alarm her.

He dropped his hand and she finished taping the bandage.

"If you get a fever or if the wound starts getting red and
hot, let me know. It could be an infection, though I doused it
really well with the peroxide. Hopefully you don't get tetanus.
We have no idea where that knife has been."

"Okay, doc," John saluted.

"Actually . . ." She placed her hand on his forehead. "You're
feeling a little warm. Clammy too." Suddenly she dropped her

hand and backed away from him. "Everything about this is so familiar. Like déjà vu."

"Oh, yeah. I've sat here in your bathroom, letting you stitch me up after a knife fight?"

"Exactly."

John stood up. His back was sore. He didn't want to admit to her how much it had hurt when she'd stitched him up. It was like a small knife going through the same spot over and over again. He held his T-shirt in his hands; there was no way he'd be able to put it on.

"Umm . . ." he said.

"Oh right. A clean shirt. You can wear one of my dad's."

John wanted to protest, but there was no way he'd walk around outside with his shirt off. Down by the water, maybe, but that was with the guys, or when he was going to the pool or the beach to swim. Not out in public. Besides, his family would be humiliated if they found out he'd been so indecent, especially his mother.

He followed Caroline to her parents' room where she rummaged through the top drawer of a dresser. On top of it was a photograph of Caroline's mother holding a baby Jack at the beach. Jack was so little. Her hair was up in a green and blue scarf. She and Caroline had the same color eyes, hair. A similar smile.

Caroline handed him a white undershirt.

"Here."

"Thanks." His gaze returned to the photo. "Your mom looks so young there."

"I know. Hard to believe it's already been a year."

She picked up the frame, traced her hand over Jack's face.

"Sometimes, after his bath, I'd chase him around the house yelling, 'Nakey baby!' He'd giggle and squeal. It was so funny to see his little butt tearing around the corner."

John smiled. He lifted the shirt, but he could feel the skin on his back stretch and pull.

"You have a little brother, right?" she asked him.

"Yeah. Gary."

"You're lucky."

She placed the photo back down on her father's dresser and saw him struggling.

"Oh, what was I thinking. Give me that, let's do a button-down instead."

Caroline located a navy shirt that John probably wouldn't ever wear, but it didn't matter. He just needed it to last him until he made it home.

He moved to grab it from her, but she said, "I'll help you get it on." He let her direct his arms into the sleeves. Then she stood in front of him and buttoned it up. She was so beautiful.

When she got to the top button, he held her hands.

"Thank you."

"You're welcome," she said softly. "Can I?" She reached up and touched the spot behind his ear. He flinched.

"Does that hurt?"

"No, but what're you doing?"

"I've just seen you rubbing there. And I wanted to check something."

Caroline took his hand again and directed him to the same area behind her ear. There was a bump, just like his. They stared at each other. John couldn't help but feel like they were on the edge of discovering something.

"What do you think—" he started to ask, but the doorbell chime startled the both of them.

John followed Caroline to the front door. She opened it. Bunny, Frank, and Oscar were standing outside.

"We've got to talk," Bunny said, and she pushed her way in.

28

CAROLINE

....

"BUT IT WAS A GIRL'S BODY. NOT A BOY'S. NOT TEDDY'S," CAROLINE said, after hearing Bunny's story of what they found in Dr. Miller's motel room.

Frank and Oscar sat on either side of Bunny on the couch across from Caroline and John in her living room.

"Exactly," Bunny said. "Which means that Teddy could still be alive. He's in trouble. And we owe it to him to try to help. You know we do."

"I don't *know* anything," Caroline said.

She didn't like the way Bunny was making her feel. As if she didn't have a choice.

"Maybe if we go back to the clearing, our memories will be triggered," Bunny said. "Have you thought of that? Aren't you tired of not knowing?"

Caroline got up from the couch. She didn't want Bunny or the others to see the tears that had started. Going back to the forest sounded like the most logical plan. She did want to find Teddy and if he needed their help, she would gladly give it to him. But she was terrified of the woods. No, not the woods, of whatever they had found there. It was still out there, she was almost sure of it. And it was waiting for them.

"Is that blood on your shirt?" Oscar asked her.

Caroline bent down to look at the stain. She hadn't had time to change since helping John. She hadn't even thought about it. She'd just reacted.

"Yeah. Probably John's from when I stitched him up."

"What happened?" Frank asked.

"Nothing," John said.

"He was in a knife fight," said Caroline.

"Really?" Oscar said.

"It wasn't a big deal," John said.

Caroline didn't know why John was trying to hide what had happened from the rest of them, but she wasn't going to.

"This guy was going to hit his girlfriend and John told him to knock it off. The guy didn't like it. He pulled a knife on John, so John had to, um . . ." How would she explain what she saw John do? "John restrained him."

"You never fight," Frank said.

John shrugged.

"You stitched him up?" Oscar said. "Like gave him real stitches?"

"Yes."

"Let me see," Oscar said.

Oscar and Frank stood up. John sighed, but he got up from the couch and showed them the stitches. As they admired her work, Caroline noticed Bunny's hand massaging the top of her neck.

"Bunny," she said. "Do you have a small lump just behind your ear that you didn't have before?"

"How did you know?"

"I have one. So does John. Can I see it?"

Bunny turned and Caroline touched the spot and felt the bump.

"Same as mine. See?"

She took Bunny's hand and placed it on the bump behind her ear.

"John?" Caroline asked and John was on his feet, allowing her to do the same with him.

"What does this mean?" he asked.

Even though she was scared, Caroline ran to the kitchen and grabbed a paring knife.

"Come on." She went to the bathroom down the hall. The five of them crammed inside and Caroline shut the door behind her.

"What're you going to do?" Frank asked.

Caroline poured some peroxide on the knife.

"We're going to get to the bottom of this." She grabbed a hand mirror from the cabinet and pulled the hair back behind her ear. "Can you hold this?"

Bunny did as she was asked and held the mirror in front of Caroline.

"Are you sure?" John asked.

"Trust me," she said.

Using the bathroom cabinet mirror behind, she now had a full view of the back of her head. Caroline found the lump with her fingers and made a cut. It stung, but she breathed deeply, tried to relax. Blood oozed down the side of her neck.

"I'm gonna be sick," Oscar said.

"You think something is in there?" asked Frank.

Only Bunny and John were quiet, as if they were afraid speaking would distract Caroline.

Caroline squeezed the place of incision and something poked out of her skin. She squeezed again and a small piece of metal bulged out.

"What the hell?" Oscar said.

"I knew it," Caroline said looking at the object in her hand. "I . . ." Suddenly a sharp pain erupted behind her eyes and she couldn't see. She bent over.

"What's the matter?" Bunny asked.

"Caroline!"

She felt John's arms around her.

"Her brain's going to explode!" Oscar said.

"Shut up, Oscar!" said John.

Caroline tried to straighten, but she was too dizzy.

"I'm okay. I'm okay."

Was the ground suddenly moving? She felt a rolling in her gut. A familiar sensation in her mind made her feel like she was back in the woods, running. The same thread was pulling, but instead of unraveling, it was now knitting, forming something in her mind.

"What is that?" Frank said.

Caroline straightened up and held the object in the palm of her hand. It was small, about the size of a pinto bean and oval in shape. Dark gray, metallic in color. Wrapped in blood like a membrane. Caroline wondered if it was actually metal or some other mineral. It was—

"Oh!" Caroline exclaimed.

The force of it all made her head snap back. She fell into John, who was already trying to help steady her.

It came to her then. Like a huge wave. All at once. Crashing into her.

"Caroline."

She heard someone calling her name, but she was drowning. Her mind couldn't make sense. There was no category. No compartment for the narrative. She was slipping into a bottomless deep where they were there waiting for her. The terrible monsters that existed in the darkness.

"Caroline?"

She recognized the voice. Bunny. Caroline reached out her hand. Bunny grabbed it and pulled her to shore.

She sat up, panting, trying to get her bearings. Looked around at the faces staring at her, worry on their foreheads. *Frank. Oscar. John. And Bunny.*

Caroline grabbed her by the shoulders.

"We . . . we made it home," Caroline cried.

The images assaulted her. Some had leaked through to her dreams, but she realized in that instant that they were not dreams. No. They were memories.

She saw a figure rise in front of her, terrifying, huge—its wingspan the length of a car.

"We can't . . ." she whispered. She looked all around, afraid they were here already. She listened for the roof. No footsteps. She pushed past John, Bunny, Frank, and Oscar, ran out of the bathroom to her room. Nothing was at the window. Nothing was trying to get inside.

"Caroline, you're okay," John said. "You're safe."

She stared at the boy in front of her. Safe? She looked around at her room. At how everything was exactly as she'd left it. There were no monsters here. And she began to cry.

Her mind was still fragmented and there were gaps, but she understood.

She remembered. Her body shook as terror and then relief took hold. She remembered.

She almost wished she could put the device back in. Knowledge came at a terrible price; with it came the loss of everything else.

John stared at her with both fear and concern on his face. Caroline sucked in her breath at how he looked. He was young, brave, handsome. The boy she fell in love with. The boy he was before he lost everything.

She remembered. Again tears welled in her eyes.

The grief rose slowly from within like a gray wisp, curling and unfolding, threatening. No, she wouldn't let herself think it even now. She caught it just in time. Stuffing it back into the recess of her memories. There was no place for that here. Here where there was only life and no death. Where they were just kids.

"Do me," John said.

She wiped her eyes.

"This will hurt."

Caroline's hand shook as she cleaned the knife in the bathroom sink and held it up to John's neck.

"I trust you," he said, echoing what she'd asked of him earlier.

Trust. Such a fragile thing that could be broken in a moment.

She knew all about the tearing. It was the mending that took the work and delicate stitching together.

John turned his back to her and tilted his head down slightly.

"Take a deep breath," Caroline said. Then she made the incision. John didn't even flinch. She pulled out the same-looking device that was in her neck and then held a bandage over the wound. He lifted his head and looked at her. She kept her eyes on his, waiting for the moment—the moment shame replaced innocence. The moment the boy he'd been became the man she knew.

And then she saw it. The flash of pain.

29

JOHN

JOHN HELD HIS HEAD, TRYING TO STOP THE RINGING AND THE PAIN that had started when Caroline removed the thing from his neck. The memories he had tried so hard to recall bowled over him. They swelled and filled the bathroom until he had to get out. He bolted from the room.

"John," Caroline called.

But he didn't stop. He had to get away from her, from Bunny, but especially from Caroline. He couldn't see her crying. Not again. He couldn't face his pain and carry hers.

He reached the front door, hesitated. A new feeling overwhelmed him. The fear climbed his spine, radiated to his outer limbs. His hands were suddenly cold and stiff on the knob. What if they were out there now? Waiting for him somehow? On the other side of the door? His heart raced.

"Where are you going?" Bunny yelled.

John thought about turning around, but he didn't. Behind him was Caroline. Behind him was a past filled with pain and suffering and something like rage. He held back the desire to yell, to fight, to break something.

Instead, he opened the door.

The sunlight met his body, thawing some of the terror. He stopped at the edge of the street. Looked down both sides. No one was there, waiting for him. He was alone.

John sat down on the curb and cried.

30

BUNNY

....

"LET HIM GO," CAROLINE SAID.

Frank and Oscar peered out of the curtains at the window.

"He's just sitting there," Frank said. "What is going on?"

Caroline ignored his question, instead asking Bunny, "Ready?"

"Wait, what do you remember?" Bunny asked, doubting for a moment if she wanted to discover the truth.

"It's better if you see for yourself," Caroline said.

Bunny followed her to the bathroom.

She held her breath as the knife pierced her skin. But even as she braced herself, she wasn't prepared for the intense shock of pain. Caroline and John had made it look easy. She forced down the bile that rose in her gut. Closed her eyes. Caroline's fingers found the object, making Bunny's stomach churn. And as Bunny felt it leave her neck, the splinter that had lodged itself in her mind was plucked out.

Bunny bent over from the new pain that began to radiate from her head. It spread across in a wave that seemed to move down her whole body.

And then she knew. The knowledge made her legs shake. She held onto the sink to keep from falling.

"Oh." She looked in the mirror and barely recognized herself. Her face was fuller somehow. She turned and faced Caroline, who had also changed. But she would know Caroline anywhere. She'd been her friend through everything. And then she thought about the boys and . . .

"Teddy," she said.

Where's Teddy?

Caroline's eyes were full of sadness but also pity. Bunny wanted to shake her. Tell her not to look at her that way. What gave her the right?

Bunny's memories were fuzzy as they returned. She could see the whole webbing but not the individual strands. Teddy was running with them and then he wasn't.

Caroline handed Bunny a washcloth. She wiped the blood from her neck and behind her ear. She sat still while Caroline bandaged her. Caroline rinsed the three implants in the kitchen sink and set them on a plate.

After a few moments, when the ache in her head began to fade, she, Caroline, Frank, and Oscar sat around the table. John was still outside. She couldn't blame him. Out of all of them, he had suffered so much. Both he and Caroline would be experiencing their loss all over again.

But she had lost someone too.

The last thing Bunny remembered was Teddy—yelling, waving them on. He turned to run, to create a diversion. But he looked back at her. Just for a second, but his eyes said it all. And then he was gone. And she was tumbling.

Bunny's eyes welled.

She had lost Teddy.

Bunny took one of the implants and placed it on top of the others. Liquid-like strands poured out of each one as the three melded together and formed a singular oval shape.

Oscar and Frank jumped back from the table.

"Shit!" shouted Oscar.

"What's it doing? Is it alive?" Frank asked.

"You really think this is safe out in the open?" Caroline said. "What if they're listening?"

Caroline stood and went to the door but didn't open it, as if she were worried they would be found. But Bunny didn't think it worked that way here. If it did, wouldn't they have already been discovered?

"They can't hear us here." That much she knew.

Bunny didn't have the technology available to her to get a thorough reading. She'd have to try to build her own, but she had no idea if she could actually do that, or how long it would take. She knew this device could tell her the status of the four of them. They were designed that way. To keep them on the same monitor. The same neuro inhibitors. Mind control. To influence their conscious memories. They must have been triggered to block their memories again when they returned. Bunny hadn't anticipated that. She had removed the devices when they figured out how they were being used to control them, then Bunny had uploaded her own tracking program, and Caroline had reimplanted them so they could keep tabs on each other if they got split up. Refashioned like homing devices, they were uniquely crafted to their individual biorhythms and designed to give off a red light when movement or heart rate was detected.

Bunny touched a spot on the tracking device that the implants formed. Three red lights powered on. Teddy was number four.

She fought back the tears.

Bunny got up from the table and walked to the front door. But instead of listening for what might come as Caroline had done, she opened it. She stepped outside. John still sat on the curb. Bunny breathed the fresh air. Noted the empty blue sky. No dark thing hanging above. No fires burning in the distance. Nothing streaking through the air except for the occasional plane. She threw her head back and breathed in deeply.

She held out her hand in front of her. Her nails were pretty and painted. Her palms were soft. They hadn't known much work. This was unexpected. It was like she had never left. She supposed it had something to do with how time passed here as opposed to where she'd been. She didn't understand it, but now all she had was time. She was seventeen again. Her whole life ahead of her. It was as if none of it had happened.

She felt the grief rising again. She did her best to push it back down.

"So blue," Caroline said as she came out and stood next to her.

John stood up from where he sat and walked over to them.

"I'm sorry," he said when he reached them.

Bunny hugged him. "For what?"

"I don't know. Not handling this well." He moved to hug Caroline, but when she stiffened, he stopped.

"Your face," he said and reached out his hand.

Bunny knew he was looking for Caroline's scar, the one that covered her whole cheek.

"It's gone," Caroline said. "Like it didn't happen."

John dropped his hand.

"It's like we never left," he said. "How is that possible?"

"I don't know," Bunny said.

"But it did happen, right?" John took a sideways glance at Caroline, who had both arms protectively around her chest.

"Yes. We . . . we had a life together," she whispered.

"And Teddy?" John asked.

Bunny nodded, then exhaled. "His light isn't registering," she said. She hated saying the words. They all knew what that meant. She wanted to scream, to run around the house and break everything. She wanted to go back, to never leave.

Caroline turned to look at her. "Are you certain?"

"Yes."

Caroline grabbed her hand and squeezed it.

"It was always a risk. We all knew it," Bunny said.

Inside she steeled her heart. She would have time to mourn later. The breaking would come. When she was alone and able to process all that she had given up to get back. But then she realized something.

"Wait a minute," she said.

The others turned to look at her.

"If we found a way to remove our devices, what if Teddy removed his, too? What if he's out there somewhere? What if he's waiting for us to come find him?"

Bunny saw something like hope flicker across John's face.

"So what do we do?" Caroline said.

Bunny had imagined a future with Teddy. She couldn't let that go just yet.

John spoke first and said exactly what Bunny was thinking. "We go back for Teddy."

"But the light," Caroline said.

"Screw the light. I think Bunny's onto something. Maybe there's some other explanation. As long as there's a chance for him to still be alive, we owe it to him. *I* owe it to him."

Bunny smiled at John, grateful for his loyalty. Caroline didn't say anything, but her silence was full of disapproval.

"Sun'll be down soon," John said.

"Then we should go tonight," said Bunny.

"How about Frank and Oscar?" John said. "What do we tell them?" He looked back toward Caroline's house, where Frank and Oscar peered out at them through the window.

"The truth," Bunny said. "Even if they'll never believe us."

31
FRANK

....

WHEN FRANK WATCHED CAROLINE SQUEEZE THE OBJECT OUT OF HER neck, part of him had wanted to throw up. It was one thing to read stories about other life-forms, another to actually see a tiny foreign object come out of a person. It was disgusting. But the other part of him wanted to scream, *I knew it!* He and Oscar had been close to the truth all along. Maybe an alien hadn't taken over their brains, but they had been implanted with alien technology. That was clear. Still, he had so many questions. Who had done this to them? Had they been willing participants? Had it happened on Earth, or aboard a spaceship? What did the aliens look like?

Frank wracked his brain, trying to remember any story he'd read where something similar had happened. He couldn't. No one wrote about visitors from space implanting someone with something.

He wondered if Bunny wasn't who she said she was. What if the implants weren't alien technology, but Russian spyware? Bunny, a sleeper agent in New York, recruited at a young age because of her intelligence and aptitude for languages. But that didn't make much sense. Why would her family move to Monterey and infiltrate the life of typical American teenagers? As if *they* were a threat? Unless . . . she was a plant here because Russia was planning an invasion beginning on the West Coast. Even if that wasn't true, it might make for a great twist to the story he was writing.

But it didn't explain Caroline or John. Frank had known the two of them most of his life. He couldn't believe that they, too, might be Russian spies.

All Frank knew was that as soon as those things came out of Bunny, Caroline, and John, they were different. Sure, they looked the same, but their eyes said they had seen things, done things. There was a hardness to them that wasn't there before. There was also a fear.

While the others were outside, Frank and Oscar stared at the device on the table. It hadn't moved since Bunny made the three smaller pieces come together somehow.

Oscar touched it.

"Don't do that," Frank said.

"What? It's fine. Try it."

Seeing that Oscar didn't get electrocuted or anything, Frank touched it too. The device was smooth and cool to the touch. No sign of it ever having been separate pieces. No movement. It just lay there, dead, an ordinary piece of metal.

"Maybe it's some kind of alien," Oscar said.

"Like it's sentient?" Frank said.

"Do you think it's been controlling them all along?" Oscar said.

"I don't think so. Bunny seems to know what it is. Sounds like it definitely has something to do with their memory loss."

"Should we go to Dr. Miller?" Oscar asked.

"Are you serious? Why?"

"Because . . . we are in way over our heads here. This is real alien stuff. The government should know about it. What if this is the start of an invasion?" Oscar lowered his voice. "How do we know we can trust them? They went somewhere, had this stuff in their heads."

Oscar did have a point.

He grabbed Frank's arm. "What if they killed Teddy?"

The door opened causing Frank to jump up from his seat at the table. Oscar was out of his mind. There was no way they killed Teddy.

John, Caroline, and Bunny walked into the living room. Frank and Oscar met them there and for a moment they all just looked at one another. Frank waited for them to say something.

"You probably have a lot of questions," Bunny said.

"Yes, we do," Oscar said. "Like what the hell happened to you guys in the woods. Who put those things in you? And where's Teddy? I'm serious. You need to tell us now, or I'm going to Miller."

"Look, we know you're scared," Bunny began and stopped. She looked to John.

"It's complicated, and even we don't completely understand everything. But the night we saw the UFO and went into the woods, we found something."

As John talked, something caught Frank's peripheral vision coming from the table in the kitchen. A blinking light.

"Hey," he said.

"What was it?" Oscar said.

"Well, let's just say it—"

"Hey," Frank said again, a little louder, cutting off John.

"What?" Bunny asked.

"You probably want to see this."

Frank walked to the table. The others followed him.

Bunny picked up the oval metallic object. She did something to it that made it shimmer and open. At least that's what Frank thought it was doing. It was hard to tell because it was moving again, like putty instead of solid metal.

Frank couldn't tell if it was the soft reddish light coming from the object that was making Bunny's face appear brighter, or if it was something else.

But then she spoke and he knew.

"He's alive!" she said. "Teddy's alive!"

32

JOHN

"I MEAN, IT COULD BE TEDDY, SURE." CAROLINE LOWERED HER
voice to a whisper and continued. "But it also could be . . ." She
gestured her head toward the front door, to where *they* might
be waiting, as if she was afraid she could be heard, even now.
"There's no way to tell."

"If there's a light then Teddy is alive," Bunny said.

"Let's say you're right. He could be alive and in captivity,"
Caroline said. "What if it's a trap?"

John nodded. He thought of those last moments before they
returned. Something breaking in the woods, which had signaled they weren't alone.

Teddy had pulled John aside. "John, get them through.
Take care of Bunny."

John was about to protest, but he saw the resolve in Teddy's
eyes.

"I will."

And then Teddy ran off in the opposite direction. John had
to resist everything within him not to go with his friend.

"If they got him, he's as good as dead," Caroline said. "You know I'm right, Bunny."

"But he's not dead," she said.

"You don't know that," Caroline said.

"What if it were you?" snapped Bunny. "Wouldn't you hope that we would come for you no matter what?"

"It's not that simple," Caroline said. "We're free. Finally free. It's like we've been given a chance to start over. With all that we know, with everything we suffered, we can make a real difference here. Why would we ever go back?"

Because it wasn't all suffering, John thought.

"And what if Teddy needs our help? What if he's . . ." Bunny choked back a sob. "Look, you know that I love you both like family, even more than family, but I'm going to do this with or without your help. I can't live my life here knowing that I didn't try everything I could."

"If we go with you, can you guarantee we'll be able to get back?" Caroline asked.

Bunny started to say something, but then she stopped herself. "No."

Before he might have felt a certain obligation for Teddy. One that was driven by jealousy and fear, but after all they'd been through . . . Their friendship didn't have room for obligation. Not anymore.

Caroline's back was to him. He had lost her long ago. He understood her not wanting to go back. She was broken, but she was also a fighter. He couldn't decide for her. In the end, she'd have to live with her own conscience.

"I don't know why we're even discussing this," John said. "We have to leave tonight."

"Can't we just be here, pretend like none of it happened? I can just be Caroline O'Sullivan. Seventeen years old. Starting my senior year of high school. Can you imagine?" She laughed, and then after a moment, her laughter turned to crying.

Ignoring any awkwardness he might feel, John walked over and put his arm around her. To his surprise, instead of shrugging him off, she leaned in, rested her head on his shoulder.

"How did everything get so messed up?" she asked.

John didn't have an answer for her. He motioned for Bunny and she stood on the other side of him where he put his free arm around her. They wouldn't all need to go, just him, and Bunny if she really wanted to. Caroline was too shaken up to go. He knew she would if Bunny asked her to, but he would tell her not to. He wanted Caroline safe. He couldn't keep her safe if she went with them. Especially not when she was so vulnerable.

"Something has been pulling me back to these woods," John said. "Maybe it's been Teddy all along."

Caroline stiffened and straightened next to John. She ducked out from under him. He couldn't worry about disappointing her. He hoped that he would make it back. Hoped that they could still have a future. But he couldn't base his decision on that now. Bunny was right. If Teddy was still alive, then he was in desperate need of help.

"Um, so is anyone going to fill us in?" Frank asked. "'Cause we should know what we're going to face when we go back in the woods with you."

"Don't look at me," Caroline said and left the kitchen. John heard her walk down the hallway and enter her bedroom.

"Bunny, you want to tell them?" said John. "Oh, and Frank?"

"Yeah?"

"We're gonna need one of your dad's guns."

IN THE
WOODS

33
TEDDY
....

TEDDY'S HAND SHOOK, SENDING THE FLASHLIGHT'S BEAM AND THE shadows it cast jerking along the forested path in front of them. The other hand held onto the Saint Peter medal around his neck. He prayed that the saint would give him courage and protection. He didn't want the others to know that fear flowed through his whole body, making his feet a little numb. He told himself it was just the dark playing tricks like it often does. But his mind imagined a train of malicious creatures lurking, waiting for the right moment to strike. Russians crouched low behind the bushes, aiming rifles in their direction.

A twig cracked.

He stopped suddenly, making John crash into him.

"What?" John whispered sharply.

"I thought I heard something." Teddy strained to find the sound again, but it wasn't there.

"I don't hear anything," John said.

"Me neither," Caroline said. But to Teddy, it seemed like her eyes transformed into giant, round bugs—the whites glowing in midair.

"Maybe we should go back," said Bunny.

Teddy suddenly felt protective and big brotherly, even though Bunny annoyed him. He walked over and put his arm around her. "We won't let anything happen to you, right, John?"

"Promise," said John. But he didn't look at Teddy when he answered. His eyes darted off to the right and seemed to focus on something in the trees. Teddy's gaze followed. There was nothing there. Only the outline of pines and bush. Only the promise of something being there, which just made Teddy more paranoid.

It was the promise of the unknown. Surely, there had to be something lurking there in the darkness. If not, what were they doing? Chasing ghosts? No, they had seen something real and tangible fall from the sky. Teddy wouldn't stop searching until they found it. No matter what.

"That's great and all," said Bunny, "but what if something happens to *you* guys?"

"Nothing's going to happen to us, Bunny," Caroline said, the timbre of her voice shaking just a little, betraying her own fear. "Besides, where's your sense of adventure?"

"I like adventure," Bunny said. "In the city. Where there are lights and people and civilization."

"If you're really that scared, you can walk back to the tower," John said. "We're not that far."

"I didn't say I was scared. I'm just . . . just bored with all of this." She gestured toward the whole woods with her hands.

"Bored? Yeah, right." Caroline rolled her eyes. "Which way do we go, Teddy?"

They all were looking to Teddy to guide them, even John.

Normally Teddy would have wanted that responsibility. But tonight? Tonight there were too many possibilities where he didn't come out on top. Too many unknowns. But he didn't falter. He pointed in the direction they had been heading, uncertain if it was the right one, but aware that someone needed to make the decision.

The others followed him. This time, in a new order, with Bunny directly behind him, then Caroline, and John in the rear. John had a large stick that he swept across the ground to the sides and in back of him.

If anyone was out here, Teddy thought, they were either gone now, or lying in wait. He couldn't tell which direction he was headed anymore. He'd lived in Monterey all his life, but he didn't know this part of the woods.

"What if it is the Reds?" Caroline whispered.

"Then we're doing our jobs," said Teddy.

"Our job was to watch for planes," she said.

"Our *job* is to protect this country," he said.

"We'll be lucky if we can protect ourselves," said Bunny.

If it was the Russians, they were terribly underprepared. They would be captured, possibly tortured for stumbling upon the first stage of an invasion. But there was also the chance that they wouldn't be caught. If so, they could spy, maybe even bring back crucial information. They would be heroes, saving their country from the brink of war.

"Light ahead," John whispered.

Teddy saw it, too. In the distance, a soft glowing light broke through the dense trees.

"Everyone down," Teddy said.

Teddy crouched close to the forest floor. He and John turned off their flashlights.

"Listen," he said. "John and I can go and check it out if you girls want to stay here."

"We can go, too," Caroline said.

"You're not just going to leave us here," Bunny said.

"Okay, then we have to be very quiet. No one make a sound. The first sign of any trouble, run back to the tower and call for help. Okay?"

Teddy couldn't help but think about the article he'd been reading less than an hour ago. The one about the different reports of UFOs and flying saucers.

"Say it's not the Russians. You think it could be something from up there? From outer space?" Caroline pointed toward the night sky. It was as though she could see inside Teddy's thoughts.

"I don't know," he said.

"Does anyone speak Russian?" Bunny asked.

"Yeah, Bunny. We speak Russian," said Caroline. "This whole time we've been sleeper agents posing as regular high school students."

"It was a legitimate ask. I know a few words."

"I don't think it's Russians," John said.

"We're wasting time," Teddy said. "Let's go."

Teddy got up and this time tried to walk as lightly as he could. He zigzagged through the trees, never taking his eyes off the light. As he got closer, he noticed a low humming sound that he hadn't heard before.

They curved around a bend to where the cluster of trees opened on a small clearing. And what they saw there made them pause. They hid behind the narrow trunks of the trees, but they could clearly see that below was some kind of crashed aircraft. Teddy watched for movement, but he couldn't see anything.

"Oh my gosh," Bunny whispered. "Is it Russian?"

"I don't think so," John said. "What *is* that?"

Teddy didn't know. It was made of a smooth black metallic alloy and shaped like a V. No propellers. No outer evidence of what would make it able to fly.

"That's definitely not something we've been trained to iden-tify," Caroline said. "Unless it's a secret American government plane, which I guess it could be. It's not like they'd tell us every-thing that's out there. But I don't recognize that symbol."

On the side of the plane there was a bird of some kind. Teddy could make out wings.

"I wish it would stop buzzing. It's driving me crazy," said Bunny.

Now that they were closer, it sounded like a swarm of locusts on a summer evening.

"Maybe that's the engine."

"Looks like it crashed."

"But how? Wouldn't it leave a trail of wreckage? Look at the trees," John pointed up. "They haven't been touched."

"It must've come straight down through the small opening."

"That's impossible. What kind of aircraft can do that?"

Teddy's gut churned.

"None on this earth."

Movement from inside the craft caught his eye. Teddy stared at the spot where it looked like a cockpit of some kind might be. There was someone—or some*thing*—inside.

"Is that—" John asked right behind him.

"An alien?" Caroline finished his thought.

"I don't know." He tried to make out the shape of the figure behind the glass. But it was covered in a type of black film.

"We really shouldn't be here," Bunny said. "What if it blasts us or something?"

They hesitated, watching the thing in the craft.

"If it wanted to kill us, it probably would have done so by now."

"Or maybe it's waiting until we get closer," Bunny said.

"Maybe," Teddy said. "Or maybe it's hurt."

"Good," said John. "Then it can't kill us."

"Is it green?" Caroline said. "Aren't Martians supposed to be green?"

"I can't tell what color it is," Bunny said. "But I don't want to find out."

"Well, I do," said Teddy.

"What if this is a trap?" John said. "There could be more than one of them in that thing."

Teddy looked all around him. The others did the same. There was no one else on the edge of the clearing. It was just them and the downed aircraft.

"Guys, seriously," Bunny said. "This is crazy. We need to get the army in here or something."

"No time for that. John and I will take a closer look," Teddy said. "You girls stay here until we make sure it's clear."

"Why do we have to stay here?" Caroline said.

John touched her arm. "Caroline, just listen for once. Please. For me," he pleaded with her.

Maybe it was the way he spoke to her, but Caroline nodded.

"Ready?" he asked John.

John gave a curt nod and they headed for the downed craft.

"Cover me," Teddy said to John.

"Cover you with what?" John asked, but he held up his stick as Teddy began creeping forward, glancing from side to side as he walked toward the craft. The smell of burning fuel became stronger, along with something else he didn't recognize. Closer now, he could see there was a pane of curved glass covering the cockpit. It was cracked.

Just then a loud hiss erupted from the craft as the cockpit began to open.

34
BUNNY

BUNNY LAY ON HER STOMACH AND WATCHED THE TWO BOYS maneuver slowly toward the large black aircraft. Could it really be something extraterrestrial? A possible spaceship? She couldn't believe she was entertaining that idea. Just a couple hours ago she would have thought that type of thinking was juvenile. It was something that Frank and Oscar would have come up with. They'd be wetting their pants if they were here right now.

Why didn't she just stay in the tower? Inside she'd be safe. Bunny could never admit it to them, but she didn't like feeling left out, even by a dumb group like theirs. There was also the fact that she'd read enough books to know that girls alone at night, wherever they are, don't make out well.

She wondered what Miss Marple would do. Of course Bunny wasn't an old lady like her, but she was observant, a reader of human behavior, and didn't trust people, just like Miss Marple. But what would Miss Marple say about finding a downed, possibly alien, spacecraft? She would take in the scene. Make mental notes. Ask questions. Remain calm.

Bunny crawled forward in the calmest way possible, ignoring how the debris of the forest floor pierced her skin.

"What're you doing?" Caroline asked. "They told us to wait here."

"I know, but they're taking too long and I wanna get a better look," said Bunny.

"Me too, then," Caroline said, and crawled alongside her.

"What do you think they'll find?" Caroline whispered, close to her.

"Probably a pilot," Bunny said, thinking that to be the most logical answer.

"Do you think the boys are okay?"

Bunny wanted to go after them. As much as she didn't like traversing through the dark in the forest, she didn't like being left alone, in the dark, in said forest either. Besides, she had the odd feeling that they were being watched. Every so often, she glanced over her shoulder into the anemic, still trees, where shadows stared back at her. At one point Bunny thought she saw yellow eyes, but then she blinked and they were gone.

"I can't stand this," Caroline said. "Let's go. Maybe they need us."

Feeding off of Caroline's courage, Bunny stood up with her. Even though she felt in her gut that they never should have stepped into the forest to begin with, never should have gone after the light, she wouldn't be left out now. Miss Marple would go. She'd be drawn into the mystery. So Bunny vowed to be astute and keep her eyes open, no matter the danger she faced. If only she had something to quell her shaking hands.

She understood now why Miss Marple always carried yarn and needles with her.

Up close, the craft looked even sleeker than she'd first thought. Teddy and John stood over what looked like a busted cockpit. Pieces of dark glass littered the ground. But what drew her attention was inside. The pilot had a human shape and wore what looked like a gray flight suit and helmet.

"You should go back," John said when he saw Bunny and Caroline.

"You guys are taking forever," Caroline said. "What's happening?"

"We're trying to talk to him. He's unresponsive."

"Hello?" Teddy said to the pilot.

Bunny stared at the helmet, trying to make out the face it hid, but she couldn't see inside due to some gray-colored protective outer layer.

"My name is Teddy. You crashed in the woods. In California. We are here to help you."

The strapped-in pilot now raised his hands to lift off the helmet. Bunny held her breath, bracing herself for all kinds of creatures—the ones they showed in the movies or what she glimpsed from Frank and Oscar's comics. Something green with large eyes. Maybe even a face without eyes. A giant squid from a movie poster popped into her mind. She didn't know what it would look like. But she was determined not to cry out. Not to show fear.

The pilot pulled off his helmet and John raised his stick. Bunny felt the other three tense around her and they all seemed to hold their breath. The first thing she saw was long, black hair. The next was a face of an Asian woman. Bunny was shocked. She hadn't been expecting a human, let alone a female.

The pilot began speaking, but it wasn't English. The language was foreign to Bunny, but she recognized it. The woman's eyes darted from face to face and stopped on John, widening. Teddy motioned for John to lower his stick.

"Mandarin," Bunny said. The three looked at her, surprised. "My dad's a language specialist over at the institute. He doesn't speak Mandarin, but I recognize the language. I'm pretty sure it's Mandarin."

"Mandarin?" Caroline asked. "Since when do the Chinese have aircraft like this?"

"As far as we know, they don't," Teddy said. "But obviously they've got some top secret technology."

"At least she's not alien," John said.

"What is she doing all the way out here?" Caroline said. "Are the Chinese planning something? Is this some reconnaissance mission? And check out that dash."

Bunny edged closer.

"It looks like some kind of computer," she said. "But this technology isn't . . . well, it isn't possible."

"How do you know?" Teddy asked.

"I've read about computers," Bunny said. "But they're huge. Not small like this. They can't fit inside a plane."

"And she's a woman," Caroline said, sounding a little in awe.

Bunny knew what she was thinking. How did a woman get a chance to fly a plane like this one? Sure, there were women pilots, but not many. Bunny had read about the WASPs, the Women Airforce Service Pilots during the war. They had helped the war effort, but as soon as it was over, the program was dismantled. The men had returned; they had no more need for women pilots.

"This doesn't make any sense," Teddy said.

The woman looked at each of them in turn, speaking slowly.

"Do you speak English?" John asked her in Japanese and then English.

"A little," she croaked in English.

She tried to see past them. Her eyes darted around, as if she were afraid of what was outside the craft.

"Hello," Teddy said. He moved closer to the woman. "It looks like you're hurt. We can help you." He bent toward her.

"Oh, no. She's bleeding."

Caroline turned away and covered her mouth with her hand.

"What's the matter?" John asked.

"I get queasy with blood."

Bunny strained to see. The whole left side of the woman's uniform was stained a dark red. "She looks pretty bad. Maybe we should run and get help."

Though as she said it, she doubted she could find her way back out of the maze of the forest. Even if she had a compass, it would be hard. She would brave it, however, if someone went with her.

"By the time we find someone she could be dead," Caroline said. She straightened. "Look at how much she's bleeding."

The woman winced in pain, closed her eyes, and leaned back.

Again Bunny had the strange notion that they weren't alone in the forest. She turned and faced the pencil-thin trees as the others discussed how they could get the pilot some help. Suddenly a face appeared between two of them. Bunny froze. The face disappeared. Had she just imagined it?

"Let's you and I lift her out of the cockpit at least," Teddy said to John. "We can use the blanket as a stretcher to carry her back." He held out his hand for the blanket. Caroline passed it to him.

"Guys," Bunny said. "I think I saw something."

"What? Where?" John asked.

"Over there. It looked like a face, maybe." She pointed to the trees. They all turned. John raised his stick again.

"I don't see anything," Teddy said.

But they all heard a snap. The breaking of a branch. John flashed the light, scanning the woods. It was difficult to make out anything; the light only stretched so far.

"There's nothing there," Caroline said. "Right?"

"Right," Bunny echoed, confused by what she had—or hadn't—seen.

"Maybe other people saw the light in the sky and they had the same idea as us—to get a closer look," John said.

"Or maybe she wasn't alone," Teddy said.

Bunny felt a chill run up her spine. "Let's hurry."

"This is going to take all of us," Teddy said. "Come on."

The four of them climbed up onto the roof of the aircraft. Teddy positioned himself behind the woman, John took one side, Caroline and Bunny the other.

The woman moaned when Teddy reached underneath her arms.

"It's going to be okay," Caroline said. "We're going to get you out of here."

"Just don't move too much," said John. "Let's lift her on the count of three. One . . . two . . . three—"

The woman cried out as they began to lift her, making them stop and lower her back down.

"I don't know if we should move her. She's in so much pain," John said.

"We can't just leave her here," Caroline said. "We've got to try."

"Yeah, and we have to let the military know," Teddy said. "As soon as we get back to the tower, I'll call it in. They're going to want to see the plane and talk to this pilot. The Chinese could be working with the Russians. Maybe this is some kind of bomber. Think of that. Why is it so black and streamlined? Perfect design to go undetected. I bet if we opened up its belly we might even find an atomic bomb."

Bunny looked at the ground and the fuel that had probably leaked when it crashed. Maybe it was even seeping into the forest floor now. She couldn't tell because it was so dark, but if that were true, just one match and it would all explode. She may have wanted out of this little seaside community, but she certainly didn't wish for it to be decimated into oblivion.

"Let's be careful, then," John said. "And quick." He looked at the ground, too. Was he thinking the same as Bunny about the leaking fuel?

The faster they got back to the tower, the better. They could solve the mystery in a house, around a table in the light. Or even at Fort Ord, the military base. She would feel more secure with military presence.

She, Caroline, Teddy, and John repositioned themselves around the woman.

"Okay, on my mark. One," Teddy said.

Bunny felt a vibration under her feet. Did the engine just come on? She looked at Caroline, who didn't seem to notice. The three of them kept their focus on the woman. But the woman looked directly at Bunny. She'd felt it too.

"Two."

There it was again. A slight rolling.

"Did you guys feel that?" Bunny asked.

"No. Feel what?" Caroline asked.

"Three."

As they hoisted the woman up, the air around Bunny began to wobble and shimmer. Distracted, she almost dropped the woman's leg.

"Bunny, be careful!" John said.

She reached out her hand to try to touch the wave. That's what it looked like—small, greenish-blue ripples in the air.

"What're you doing?" Teddy asked.

There was something beyond the ripple. She almost felt like she could part it like a curtain. As she stuck her hand through, she saw the forest change. Saw it fade into another place entirely, more barren and with mountains in the distance. But then she withdrew her hand and the forest was the forest again. And Bunny saw those yellow eyes.

She didn't have to ask the others if they saw them too. They all stared at the same spot in the trees, even the woman.

That face, thought Bunny. Someone, or something, was there. Watching them. Its eyes floating in the dark.

And then they disappeared—along with everything else around them.

35

GONE

THE MAN RUBBED HIS EYES THINKING HE WAS HAVING HALLUCINA-tions again. The visions usually came at night when he was alone in his room. Never outside. And never as big as this.

He'd followed the light and came upon the voices. The girl had seen him. He was sure of it.

One moment the spacecraft was there.

One moment the kids were there.

The next they were all just gone.

It was impossible, he knew, so it must not be real.

He rubbed his eyes hard, until they burned a little when he opened them again.

If momma were still alive, even she wouldn't believe this. She, who told him stories of the creatures that lived in the woods. The ones who took small children and ate them for dinner. She was also the one who told him to talk to the voices.

It wasn't his fault that she didn't like what they said.

He crept slowly out from behind the thin trees and stood where the black plane and the kids had just been but now were not. He walked all around the area. The only evidence there were some burnt marks on the ground, a blanket, and a flashlight.

The man picked up the blanket, placed it around his shoulders like a cape.

He held the flashlight in his right hand.

He looked up in the sky for the light he had followed, but that was gone, too.

Only the stars bore down upon him in the clearing.

He left the way he had come.

36

CAROLINE

CAROLINE LOST HER BALANCE AND FELL TO THE GROUND. A RINGING began at the top of her spine and swelled in her head. She had to squint and shade her eyes because of the bright light. That didn't make any sense. It was nighttime, but she found herself looking up at a big blue sky.

As Caroline's eyes adjusted, she saw the forest around them had thinned. No. It had been burned. The trees that remained poked out of the ground like used matchsticks. They were marked by black char. The heat was beginning to make her sweat.

"Teddy?" she called.

"Here."

"What is this? What's happening?" Bunny called out.

Caroline stood and her legs wobbled as if she hadn't used them in a while. Everything was a little muffled, so Caroline yawned as big as she could, trying to pop her ears. Once she could hear again, she noticed the ringing had stopped. She scanned her surroundings and saw scorch marks on the ground. She turned in the direction of the ocean, but she couldn't see it from here.

The woman in the aircraft groaned.

"Let's just get her to the tower, then we can figure out whatever the heck is going on," Teddy said.

Caroline scrambled back onto the aircraft with the others. Little beads of sweat marked their brows, just like hers. They lifted the woman as carefully as they could, but they were all a little weak. They placed her on the ground. She sat with her back against the downed craft.

John knelt down next to her. "You're still bleeding."

The woman nodded. "It's okay. I can walk. I just need to catch my breath and then we have to—" She stopped speaking and craned her head as if to listen.

Caroline watched as her expression turned from pain to fear.

"Run!" she yelled.

Caroline spun around, looking in every direction. Run where? And then Caroline heard it—a whooshing sound coming from the sky. A large shadow spread across the ground toward them. John grabbed her hand, pulling so hard it almost yanked her shoulder out of the socket. She stumbled after him and the others.

She worked her hand free from John so she could run faster. The shadow grew above until it blocked out much of the sun. There was nowhere to hide from whatever was making it. A huge presence bore down on them. She didn't dare look up. The whole air was filled with the sound of giant wings beating, like an enormous brown owl had descended and was chasing them.

Suddenly whatever was in the sky dove straight down at Teddy and picked him up in the air. His screams were joined with Bunny's as another one came for her. To the right of her, John turned his head, like he was going to tell her something, but he was snatched, too, taken up overhead. Then Caroline felt the force of her own body being jerked and almost snapped in two, before everything went dark.

She woke in a small room. A tiny crack of light came in from underneath a door. It was cold, so Caroline pulled her legs in close, but her midsection hurt when she moved. She felt around her left side and thought a rib or two was probably broken. Once her eyes adjusted to the very dim light, she could see the room was all concrete walls and flooring. No windows. Nothing else was in there with her. She fought against the claustrophobia that began to gnaw its way up from her gut.

Her mouth was dry. When was the last time she'd had any water? She felt as though she hadn't had a sip in days. How long could a person go before they died of dehydration? She knew she'd had some apple juice before heading to her shift at the tower. But who knew how long ago that was? She'd lost all track of time.

Her mind battled through the haze and disorientation. Where were the others? Why was she in a room all by herself? How did she get out of the forest? A train of questions sped through her mind.

"John?" she whispered. She hoped he was close by.

No answer.

She wracked her brain, trying to figure out what was going on. But there was no category she could put the limited information she had into. They had been lifting the pilot out of her craft when suddenly the air felt thick and wobbled. And then they were in another place. A forest, but not the same forest. The same sky, but a different blue—more turquoise than the blue she'd known her whole life. Everything was off. Even the smell of the air—gone was the salty ocean scent; this wind carried ash and dust. But everything was also familiar, like the same canvas, only painted with different materials, changing the essence of the landscape.

Then *they* came.

Caroline shuddered and backed up to the wall behind her. The creature that had grabbed her wasn't a bird, but it wasn't human either. At first she thought she'd been caught in its talons, but when she was finally put down, she realized she'd been gripped by some kind of mechanical appendage that protracted from its midsection. The creature had two legs and arms, stood upright like a man. It wore red body armor and a mask with large bug-like eyes. If it weren't for the huge wings and append-age, she would have thought it human.

After dropping Caroline and her friends in a pile in front of a building, the four creatures flew away. The dust from the ground stirred at their takeoff. Caroline stared at their huge wings—a mixture of blue, green, and yellow that shimmered and reflected the sunlight, almost like a peacock's plumage. They were beautiful in the terrifying way that untamed beauty can often be. She watched them in the sky until someone came behind her and put a bag over her head, threw her in a vehicle, and drove with her to another location, where she was dumped into the concrete room.

She had no idea where she was. All she knew was that she had somehow been transported to another place. She didn't even know if it was Earth. From the look of the flying creatures, how could it be? But people didn't just walk into the forest and stumble into another world, either. Especially in Monterey. Did they?

"Bunny?" she tried again. "Teddy?"

Only silence answered her. Along with a dripping. Water. Maybe there was a leak somewhere. Her hands felt along the wall, cool and damp to her touch.

The door opened then and the light crawled slowly across the floor until it found her body, curled in on itself against the far wall. A man stood in the doorway. She hid from him, pressing against the concrete as if it would offer her protection. She prayed to go back home. But the air didn't wobble. The room didn't morph into anything familiar.

In the end, it didn't matter what she did.

He came for her anyway.

The heat radiated from the gash on her cheek in equal measure across her face. She felt the blood ooze out, tasted it in her mouth. He hadn't even spoken. Just held her face in his hand, took a knife, and made the cut.

She stood now, hands tied behind her back, in another cement room. The position made her ribcage throb. She was certain now she'd broken her ribs. Every time she breathed, it hurt.

The man with the knife sat in a small chair in front of her.

"Who are you?" he asked. He wore a red mask, similar to the winged creatures.

"Caroline," she tried to say, but it was difficult to speak through the pain.

"Where are you from?"

"California."

"What is California?"

"Um, it's a part of the United States."

"If you do not cooperate, I promise you, another cut will come."

Caroline tried not to cry, but she couldn't help the tears from falling, both from the pain and the terror she felt.

"I'm telling the truth," Caroline gritted her teeth, tried to take short, shallow breaths. His voice was muffled behind the mask, and it also had an accent she couldn't place. "I'm American."

He bent close to her face.

"I am told that you prefer we wear these masks. That it makes you feel more comfortable, but maybe we would get somewhere faster if we speak face to face."

With both hands, he removed the mask.

Caroline let out a scream.

37

JOHN

....

JOHN PASSED IN AND OUT OF CONSCIOUSNESS. THE LAST INTER-
rogation session, what John was now calling them, had left him
reeling and with a broken leg. The doctor had at least put it in a
stint so it would heal correctly. He had no idea how many days
had passed since that winged creature had picked him up in the
forest. Because he was kept in constant darkness and solitary
confinement, his body couldn't find a correct equilibrium. He
never knew if it was day or night. Every now and then, they'd
drag him into another room, handcuff him to a hard wooden
chair and the creature in the mask would pepper him with the
same questions. *Who was he? Who were the others? Why had
they been in the area? Where was the Resistance?* He never gave
the interviewer the answers he was looking for. So John was
hit, lashed. Two of his fingers cut to the bone and then bandaged
up to heal, only to be cut again at a later inquiry. They gave him
enough food and water to keep him alive. But just barely.

The interviewer wore a red mask most times. John shuddered thinking about the first time he revealed his face. It
had been the color of ash, shaped like a human's, but not at all

humanlike. The features were all wrong—the eyes were overly large and resembled those of an insect, and they were in the middle of the creature's face. The irises yellow instead of dark. Its mouth was outlined in black, the teeth small and sharp. The creature had no eyebrows or eyelashes, nor any hair on its head. Its ears were double the size of a human's and lay flatter against the side of its head. But it was the nose that John found the most distressing. It was a small triangular shape with two small holes, just above the mouth. It reminded John of a skeleton.

The alien, for John assumed that was what it was, wore gloves, also red. John noticed that he had three fingers. He had two legs and two arms, and John would have easily mistaken him for a human from a distance.

John lay on his back, stared at the ceiling. He passed his time reciting baseball stats, having imaginary conversations with his family and Caroline, and dreaming of a way out. He refused to give into the despair that he would never see anyone again, that he would die in this terrible nightmare. He didn't know where he was, but he'd begun to think of this place as Yomi, the land of the dead—the place he'd heard stories about from his mother as a kid.

He heard steps in the hallway then. They were coming for him again. So soon. This was out of their routine. He steeled his mind and tried to draw on the strength he had left. He stood when the door opened. Faced his tormentors.

This may be Yomi, he thought, *but I will not die here*.

The guard came and put a bag over his head. He led John down a short hallway. John counted the number of steps, only twenty-four. His broken leg made the journey difficult.

They entered an elevator. John felt it rise; he counted the seconds until the doors opened again—thirty. He made sure to count the steps he took from the elevator, but he lost track of the turns they'd made. The guard stopped him at fifty-seven. He removed the bag and John saw he was in a large room with a window that had been covered with a black curtain. In a few moments, one by one, Teddy, Caroline, and Bunny were led into the room the same way. Then the door was shut—locked—and they were left alone.

John stared at them. They each looked so different than the last time they'd been together. Skinny, circles under their eyes. Bunny's head was shaved and there were nicks on it, as though whoever had done it had botched the job. Teddy's hands were bandaged, like John's. He had a yellowing bruise underneath his left eye. And Caroline. Her beautiful face was now marked with a long scar. He had to look away or else she might see the tears that filled his eyes.

Teddy was the first to move. Once he did, they all followed suit, grabbing one another, crying. John held Caroline forcefully but carefully, all pretense now gone.

"I never thought I'd see you guys again," Teddy said, his voice full of emotion.

"Where do you think we are?" asked Bunny.

No one had any answers.

"I don't know what they want me to say," Caroline's voice was a small whisper. She crumpled into a seated position on the floor. John wondered if she was too weak to stand or if she was just tired. He lowered himself and sat next to her.

"They want us to say we're spies. Give them information,"

Bunny said. Her voice in contrast to Caroline's: hard and taut like leather.

"None of this makes sense," John said. His broken leg ached from the brief walk. He massaged the top of it.

"It doesn't matter," Teddy said.

"What doesn't?"

"What we do. What we say," Teddy said. "How much we beg them to tell us what they want to hear."

Caroline sniffed. "I just want to go home."

"I keep thinking of Gary, what he must be going through," John said. "And my parents."

"Mine, too," Caroline said.

"Do you think they're still looking for us?" Bunny asked.

"It's been months," Teddy said.

"Months?" Caroline whispered. She turned away from them.

Bunny looked to John and he didn't know what to say. He'd figured it had been a while, but months? Even he was surprised at the revelation.

"How do you know?" she asked.

"I started making nicks on the wall with a small stone I found," Teddy said. "No one's looking for us anymore. Remember Stephanie McAllister? She disappeared, and after a week they called off the search. Never found her body. They probably think we're all dead."

"Mine would keep looking," John said. Until his dad saw a body, John knew he'd never stop searching.

"I don't know why they haven't killed us already," Bunny said.

John had had the same thought. It was as though the creatures were watching and waiting for something. Maybe for one of them to break.

"From what I can tell," John said, "we've landed in the middle of some conflict. We're human, so we're the enemy."

"I keep telling them I don't know anything about the Resistance," Bunny said.

"We've got to stick together," Teddy said. "When they let us out of here—"

"If," Caroline said.

"*When*," Teddy repeated. "We stay together. No matter what."

"The question is, where are we," John said.

"We must have come through some window or portal, some thin space," Bunny said.

"What do you mean? What's a thin space?"

"The Celts believed there were these places that are thin that connect one world to another. It's usually a faerie realm. There's stories about them in other cultures too, but I remember reading about them last year in school in World Lit," Bunny said. "Same sky. Same landmarks, at least from what I could tell when they grabbed us. The same, but different. At first, I thought maybe we ended up on another planet. Our captors are certainly not human, but I think we are on Earth—a very different Earth. A different reality."

John tried to make sense of this. "Who do you think they are?" he asked.

"Aliens," said Bunny.

"Ugly aliens," Caroline said.

"And some of them can fly," Bunny said. "Which makes me wonder, are there multiple species of aliens? Or are they all the same?"

"I don't care how many species they are," Caroline said. "I hate them."

"How do we get back to our reality?" John asked.

"I don't know," Bunny said.

"So what you're saying is, we may be trapped here? Forever?" Caroline asked.

"Now, hold on a second," said Teddy.

"Look, I don't know anything for certain. But I've been thinking," said Bunny. "Since we crossed together, maybe our only chance at getting back is together as well. Maybe it was something about that space."

"What about that pilot?" Teddy asked.

"She's dead," John said.

The whole reason they were in this mess was because of her and her downed aircraft. John wished they'd never gone looking for that light in the woods, never touched the woman in the cockpit. He wished they'd let her bleed to death. In the end, she had died anyway. And now they were trapped.

The door opened then and a guard came for Teddy. He looked at them with resolve and courage.

"Be strong," he said. "We'll find a way out of this."

Then he was led out of the room, and the door closed again.

"I don't know if I can take this much longer," Caroline said.

"Listen to me," said John. "You can and you will. And when they let us out, we will work together to get home."

"You promise?"

"I do."

After Caroline, too, was led away, John sat quietly with Bunny.

"In those stories, you know, the ones that Frank and Oscar love so much, did the people ever return?" he asked.

But before Bunny could answer him, the door opened again, and the guard came for John.

38

TEDDY

Seven Years Later

TEDDY SPED ALONG THE COASTLINE, KEEPING HIS EYES PEELED FOR any sign of trouble. But he'd already been out for two hours and hadn't seen anything. He wondered if the intel had been trustworthy. He wouldn't put it past the insurgents to give them false information. They'd done it before.

Teddy veered away and flew out across the deep. The ocean a vast blue-gray. He'd never followed it to whatever lay on the other side. Had no idea if he could even make it in his craft. It wasn't made for long travel or deep space. That was next on his career path. He wanted to go to space. His Ruu friends who had come from it didn't seem to think it was such a big deal.

It was a journey that took thousands of years. Most of which they were in a deep sleep. Teddy doubted they even remembered what it had been like.

He'd studied their books, saw the pictures of a home planet that looked similar to Earth, which is why they'd come here to begin with. Their planet suffered a massive famine, spurring them to look for another home. Earth proved to be the place. Even though they looked very different, they were still bipeds and shared the same elemental needs. FI, his teacher, told him about how terrifying it had been to land and engage with the first batch of human hostiles some years ago. How the humans had attacked first. How the Ruu just wanted peace. But things escalated into the Thirteen-Day War, and unfortunately, both sides suffered many casualties.

Since then, though, things had changed drastically. Teddy now knew a world where the Ruu and humans lived in harmony, except for the small group of human insurgents who made life difficult from time to time. Teddy supposed that there was always a group that caused trouble. Even the Ruu had their share of political divisiveness, especially when they first set out to leave their home planet. Not everyone thought it was a good idea. Those Ruu were left behind. Now they were dead; their planet was too close to their sun.

Teddy only knew the Ruu to live up to their code: honor, trust, loyalty.

It was humanity that seemed to run against it.

Hovering over the water, Teddy followed a team of dolphins that swam beneath him. The water shimmered like a team of sardines twisted and thrived underneath. An image came to him—the feeling of being in a small boat, rocking back and forth, pulling a net. He touched the rough, gray scales of the fish.

Teddy turned back to the shore, confused by what he had seen and felt. He'd never been on the ocean before. According to his education, the ocean was unclean. It was a dangerous place.

A flier swooped alongside him, its wings sparkling like jewels in the sunlight.

"What's up, Mey?" Teddy said.

"Enjoying the view?"

"Nothing to report," Teddy said. "There's no one out here."

"Yeah. Quiet on my end, too."

"Drinks later?" Teddy asked.

"Can't. Got plans. But next time?"

Teddy nodded.

"See you back at base," Mey said, and veered off to the right.

Teddy brought the aircraft straight down and landed close to the shoreline. He stepped out, removed his helmet, and deeply breathed in the sea air. He held his gun out in front of him, checking the perimeter, but there was nothing there. No sign of human activity. Or life in general. The old buildings, either gutted by scavengers or destroyed in the conflict when the Ruu first arrived, now crumbling or falling over, like ancient men.

A loud cry sounded overhead and he aimed his gun above. But it was only a single white gull streaking across the sky. Teddy watched it for a few moments, in awe of its freedom.

He suddenly felt a prickling at the base of his neck. A knowing. Or déjà vu. A sense that he should know this place, or that there was something here he was missing. But that didn't make any sense. He was from the desert. He'd been found—abandoned as a baby, like the others. He shuddered. Who could leave their children to die like that? Thankfully a Ruu patrol found them, took them in, gave them a life.

But there was a tingling in the air. Something called to him. A memory pulled back in the deep recesses of his mind. Before he could grasp it, he saw a flash to the left, in his peripheral vision. The seagull again? No, this was a light traveling at high speed. He thought it might be another aircraft, but theirs were black and didn't have the same shape. This was round or like a sphere. Nothing they flew was that shape.

Teddy jumped back inside his craft, put on his helmet.

"I've got something," he said into his communications device.

He lifted off the ground, hovering at first as he tried to spot the object on his radar. He took off after it, but it was erratic, zigzagging across the sky, not following a typical pattern and there was no vapor trail.

The light headed out to sea. Teddy followed and then it disappeared.

"Pilot 521, please return to base."

Teddy wanted to ignore the order. He scanned the sky, hoping to see the light, but it was gone. So he turned and flew past the burnt forest, over the other side of the mountain, to the beautiful domed city he called home.

Teddy looked into the scanner, which would upload everything he saw. He knew his supervisors would have questions about the light. It was much easier to show them than to try to explain it.

Mey waited for him. With his wings off, he didn't look as menacing. He was the average height for a Ruu, about six-foot-five. And like all Ruu, he didn't try to make Teddy feel much shorter. The Ruu were homogenous in their kind, unlike humans.

"You really saw something out there?" Mey said.

He seemed tired. As if to verify Teddy's thought, a film rolled over his eyes, making them milky white, just for a moment, before the large irises became yellow again. Mey would be asleep in no time. And Teddy wouldn't see him for another day or two. That was a thing he envied about the Ruu. They didn't need much sleep. They could stay up for days with only eight hours of sleep, unlike humans who needed to sleep every night.

"Yeah. But it was . . . weird. Maybe they'll be able to tell what it was after viewing the footage."

Mey shrugged. "Maybe. Hey, have fun on your date," he said.

He smiled and Teddy's stomach lurched. He knew Mey was just trying to connect with a very human gesture, but seeing a Ruu smile was actually terrifying. Teddy never got used to it, even though he'd seen them do it countless times. The Ruu had tiny, razor-sharp teeth and that combined with their pencil thin lips made their smile look the opposite of warm and inviting. It looked like they wanted to devour.

"Who said it's a date?"

Mey held up his three-fingered hand in goodbye, and Teddy waved in response.

He didn't have much time to think about it because he had to get ready immediately if he didn't want to be late.

Teddy entered the restaurant. It was full of humans and Ruu sitting at tables and standing at the bar. He spied Bunny at a table for four next to the large screen that projected images of different kinds of animals in their natural habitat. A large cheetah stared out at him from the wall.

"Sorry," he said and bent to kiss her.

"It's okay. I just got here. Busy tonight."

"No John and Caroline?"

"Caroline's not coming."

"Oh."

Teddy knew Caroline was still in pain. Since losing her daughter, Emily, she spent all her time working at the hospital. John was no better. He took extra patrols. They were both still grieving, and Teddy couldn't blame them. He had no idea how he'd react if he had a child that was killed. And the betrayal of it—knowing a human was responsible—made it even tougher to bear.

"There's John," Bunny said and waved him over.

Teddy stood and the two shook hands. He noticed that John's grip seemed extra strong.

"You been working out?" Teddy asked.

John shrugged. "A little."

"I can tell."

"Yes, well, not all of us have a fancy craft to hide behind." John smirked.

The jab was in good humor, but Teddy could feel its bite just the same. It was true, Teddy relied on machinery, compared to John's hand-to-hand training, but that didn't mean he wasn't in good physical condition.

Bunny rolled her eyes.

"Please promise me we're not going to do that tonight, okay? Tally up the points between you two?"

John smiled, but it was the one he gave when he wanted to hide his true feelings. Teddy decided to give him a break.

"No one's counting anything," Teddy said. He waited for John to sit, then he sat. He thought a healthy competition ran between them. Bottom line, he knew that John had his back when it really mattered.

The waitress came, a girl with bright green eyes.

"Can I take your order?" she asked.

They ordered from the menu.

"How are those lenses working for you?" Bunny asked the waitress.

"Pretty good. The headaches stopped after about a week. But I can read, watch anything anywhere, and the best part is if I'm with someone boring, I can do it and they don't even know."

She left to put in the order.

There was an awkward silence among them. John broke it first. "How's work, Bunny?" he asked.

"It's fine."

Bunny spent her days trying to come up with ways to merge Ruu biotech with human anatomy.

"Actually, we had a bit of a setback this week. I'd rather not talk about it."

The last time she complained of a setback, as she called it, the human test subject had to have his right arm amputated. Teddy had to console her, remind her that they were volunteers, no one had forced the man to sign up. But still Bunny had cried as he held her.

"Anyway," Bunny asked John. "You have a good patrol?"

"Yes. A small skirmish with a group we had been tracking for about a week," John said. "But everyone made it back."

"Where?" Teddy asked.

Teddy envied John. He hadn't seen any Resistance activity along the coastline, which is where he'd been flying over most of the week. Their intel had been wrong. The Resistance must still be inland.

"About fifty miles north," John said.

"Casualties?" Teddy said.

"None of mine. But they lost four men, two women. They fought hard," John said. Teddy heard the respect in his voice. "Wouldn't be taken alive. My unit is trained, loyal, and any one of them would sacrifice their life for the greater good if need be, but these Resistance fighters . . . they're willing to do anything. It's not natural."

Teddy wanted to ask if he'd found any evidence that connected them to Emily's death, but he thought better of it.

"Caroline's leaving me," John said.

Bunny put her hand on John's.

"I'm so sorry," she said.

"She just can't . . . she blames me because I wasn't there to save Emily."

"You didn't know about the bomb. No one did."

John nodded, but it was an empty gesture. "When she's asleep, sometimes I hear her moaning about Emily. She cries and says something about how she should have saved her. How she shouldn't have let her drown. But that's what's so strange— Emily didn't drown. And Caroline knows that."

"I'll check in on her this weekend," Bunny said.

"Thanks. What about you, Teddy?" John was relieved to change the subject. "See anything interesting up there today?"

Teddy hesitated. "There was this light."

"What kind of light?" Bunny said.

"I don't know. It moved fast though, faster than me. It kind of jumped ahead. One moment it was there in the sky, the next it wasn't."

"Strange."

"Yeah. It's probably nothing."

He didn't tell them about the feeling he had when he was out over the ocean. The one where he felt like he'd been there before.

John got up, walked over to the piano in the corner of the room, and began to play. John had told him once that playing piano reminded him of home—and he didn't mean the domed city. Teddy had thought that was an odd statement. He couldn't remember anything prior to where he lived now. They were all practically babies when found.

"I feel so sad for them," Bunny said. "Remember their wedding? It was such a beautiful day."

"They're not over yet. Maybe you can talk to her?"

"You know Caroline. Once she gets an idea in her head, it's hard to remove it."

After dinner, Teddy walked Bunny home and kissed her goodnight. They'd been seeing each other for the past year now. And it was a good thing they had going. He didn't intend to mess it up by moving too fast.

That night Teddy dreamed of water and fish and a man with kind brown eyes. Strong hands that had showed him how to hold a fish and cut it open. The insides spilled out. Blood covered the wooden floor of the boat. The man patted him on the back, proud of him.

Teddy woke in the dark. Sweating.

He knew instantly upon waking that the man in the dream was his father, which was impossible because he'd never known his father.

His chest tightened.

A headache spread across the back of his skull. There was something there, unburrowing itself, trying to make its way to the surface.

The smell of the sea flooded Teddy's senses, and a strange thought popped into his mind: *home*.

39
BUNNY
....

BUNNY DIDN'T SLEEP WELL. SHE HADN'T FOR WEEKS. IT WAS because of the girl. The one who had to be strapped to the table. Normally Bunny only worked with people after they had been sedated, if she interacted with the person at all. Her expertise was on the internal implementation of technology. Sometimes it was a Ruu, but mostly it was humans.

Just as Bunny was about to make the incision, the woman woke. Her eyes slid open and widened as she took in her surroundings.

"It's all right," Bunny had said to her.

But the woman tried to get her hands free. Bunny patted her shoulder to try to calm her.

"How could you?" The woman spat in her face.

Bunny wiped the spit and said, "If you have changed your mind, I can call the office and we can start the paperwork to stop the procedure."

It was strictly a volunteer program because, as with any trial, there was the occasional problem. Bunny installed the small chips or she worked with them after and tested brain and physical function. At that point, the volunteer was happy to be doing such important work. The goal wasn't to become more like the Ruu, but to enhance humanity—to become the best version of themselves. Because the Ruu had augmented themselves thousands of years ago now, they were able to travel through time and space, see four dimensions, and do away with most forms of pain.

This woman was close to her age—in her twenties. She had a wild look to her, like she'd been a trapped animal.

"You're free to go at any time," Bunny had said.

"Free? Is that what you think? None of us are free. They're already in your head. Can you remember a time before them? What was your name? Who was your mother?"

"What are you—" Bunny had started to say when her Ruu assistant entered the room.

The woman began to scream and thrash on the table, trying to break out of the restraints. But that was impossible. They had been designed that way.

Bunny's assistant had a syringe in his hand. Just before he stabbed the woman in the arm with it, the woman had turned toward Bunny and yelled, "Run!"

Ever since, Bunny had the same nightmare. Sometimes she saw the woman on the table. Her eyes wide with terror. Blood dripping from her nose. Other times she was outside in some forest area. There was a downed plane and a woman pilot she'd never seen before yelling the same word at her.

Run!

In the dream, she experienced a fear so strong that she'd often wake from it disoriented, confused, and covered in sweat.

It was a physiological reaction. Her cortisol triggering a fight-or-flight response. In the dream she always chose flight.

In reality, Bunny had nothing to run from. She had an amazing job, good friends, and a boyfriend. She was doing important work. Already human intelligence had advanced with the chip inserted in the brain as the test subjects were able to perform complex mathematical equations in a matter of seconds.

But the woman had stayed with her. Haunted her. In and out of her dreamscape. When Bunny had gone to read her file, it was missing. It was a little strange, but not unheard of. Things went missing all the time.

Didn't they?

Like memories.

But the dream kept pestering her. Bunny hid the dream from her friends, even Teddy, because of a sense of shame. It was as if she was losing some kind of battle she didn't know she was in. She worried that her implant might be broken. It was the only explanation she could think of, because if her implant could enhance brain function, if there was a malfunction, it would make sense that she could potentially have all kinds of issues. Hallucinations. Projections. Even memories that were never hers to begin with.

Finally, when she'd had enough, Bunny went to her lab and took a small knife. She made an incision just behind her ear where the implant was. The one everyone had—human and Ruu. It was what allowed them to communicate, to enhance their vision, to increase strength, to study and read the whole canon of Ruu knowledge on the mainframe. According to Bunny's training, she understood the implants connected everyone on Earth.

Removing the implant had its risks. The headaches and physical discomfort could make a person lose their mind. In fact, she'd seen it happen to a Ruu. She had been part of the team that had to fix the technology within the implant and she had been allowed in the surgical room. Once his pain receptors were no longer blocked, his whole body went into shock. Since he'd had the chip since birth, he'd never experienced pain before. His tolerance was next to nothing.

Bunny knew the pain would be excruciating, but she needed the dreams to stop.

As soon as the implant left her, she bent over and threw up. The pain was sudden and intense. She focused on the bloody device on the table, trying to center her mind. She knew it would pass soon and she could get to work fixing whatever was broken.

Over the next hour, the pain gradually lessened, but it was replaced by a wave of understanding. The lie of her whole life was exposed and it knocked her to the floor. She crumpled into a fetal position. But she didn't stay there. No. She allowed herself to cry for only a few minutes. She had no idea if she was being watched. Maybe someone would come for her once they saw that she had removed her implant.

Her brain still throbbed, but she remembered that she wasn't from here. She was from another place. One where she was Bunny Stapleton and she had a father and a brother, and a mother who left her.

The horror of her situation made her want to throw up again.

She remembered being tortured when she first arrived. How

the Ruu kept asking where she was from. Oh, how terrified she'd been of them. They had seemed not just alien, but sinister in nature, especially when they smiled. She remembered being afraid and alone and wanting to go home. She'd been separated from the others. For some reason, possibly to break or shame her, her head had been shaved. She raised her hand and could almost feel the nicks on her scalp.

Then there was a big gap in her memories. She went from torture to what she had been brainwashed to believe had been her life all along. It was a good life, one that consisted of living in the city, studying technology. The story of her being rescued as a baby because she'd been abandoned had been fabricated. Somehow she had crossed into this world or dimension, she wasn't sure what to call it. How many years had she been gone? She looked in a mirror. She thought her age to be about twenty-five, but she wasn't sure. She had no idea how many years she'd been in captivity. She only knew she wasn't a teenager anymore. And this was not her home.

She had to get to Teddy. She'd tell him first. Together they would tell John and Caroline.

Bunny worked the rest of the night. As she dismantled her own implant, desperate to figure out what made it work, she discovered a memory inhibitor included that she hadn't known about. It made sense though. How else could the Ruu ensure that they had no memory of their life before? But why had the Ruu needed to keep them from remembering? What was so threatening about them?

Then she thought of the woman. The one who woke up during her procedure. She was clearly not a willing participant.

Then Bunny felt nauseated again. She actually made it to the toilet in time and threw up.

Bunny had been experimenting on people against their will. She'd been complicit in helping the Ruu invade and control the human mind. She understood. It wasn't about enhancing human beings, opening them to their full potential. It was about control. Every human that Bunny knew had one of their implants. She shuddered. She had believed the Ruu were benevolent, that after the Thirteen-Day War, a peace was negotiated. The Ruu shared their technology with humanity and now lived together, working toward a better life. Was it all a lie? The biggest trick was humans thought they were autonomous.

Instead, they were slaves.

Bunny removed the devices from John, Caroline, and Teddy. All three had the same reaction as Bunny had—physical pain, followed by the intense emotional pain of understanding the truth about who they really were, where they came from, and what they'd been through.

"Seven years?" Caroline said when Bunny told them what she'd discovered. Her face was carved with long, jagged shadows in the candle light.

"You're certain?" Teddy asked.

"Yes," Bunny said. "From what I could tell. There's a possibility it could be longer, but our ages would correspond with the time we left until now."

The number was staggering. For seven years they'd been under the Ruus' mind control without even knowing. The memory inhibitors had basically blocked their past memories and given them new ones beginning with their time in the domed city. It made sense, as the Ruu themselves also had memory inhibitors. When bad things happened and they didn't want to think about them, they erased the memories to end their suffering. But Bunny thought it was voluntary. Now she wasn't so sure.

She had originally thought the Ruu so forgiving because they seemed to be able to move past difficulties and past trauma in their lives. Bunny had no idea the price. A forced forgetting that wasn't forgiving at all. It was an annihilation of self.

"Our families must think we're—"

"Dead."

"My poor mother," Caroline said. "To lose both children. It's unbearable."

Bunny thought of her father, how he must have fallen apart when she disappeared. First his wife had left him, then his daughter. The pain she had inadvertently caused him made her worry for his well-being. She wondered if he had stayed in Monterey. Or had he moved again? What did her mother feel? Did she think of her still? Seven years was a long time.

"All of our parents . . ." Teddy said. He turned away from them. "I wanted to be a pilot." The recovery of the memory hit him like a force, and Bunny could see him wipe away a tear.

"They are cruel," Caroline said. "How could they do this? Do you think everyone here has been implanted like we were?"

"Probably, yes," Bunny said. "And for longer. The general population must have had these implants since birth. It makes sense. The Ruu operate on a caste system. From the elite down to the common workers. No one moves out of the caste they're born into. Everyone has a place, a job to fulfill. They don't pick their careers. It's chosen for them at a young age. There are no entre-preneurs. No free enterprise. Their government is an oligarchy, not a democracy. What better way to get a hostile native popu-lation under control than literally employing the same controls that you use on your own kind?"

"So it's all been a lie?" John said. "All of the indoctrination—the Ruu coming for a better future . . . There was no sun moving too close. No threat. Just an excuse to colonize and take over another planet?"

"I don't think it's all been a lie," Bunny said. "They did need to find another home. But I think that when humans resisted their arrival, the Ruu discovered we could not coexist. Or at least live together in the way they wanted. Humanity is too diverse, too individualistic. The human race would never agree to such a rigid caste system. They would never give up their free will. So they forced us into submission by wiping our memories—our will—clean."

"Those who understood what was happening broke away," Teddy said. "Formed the Resistance." He shook his head. "This whole time we've been fighting against humanity, not for it. They made us think—"

"We were the good guys," John said.

"When we first got here, they tortured us for weeks," Caroline said. "Why?"

"I think they were experimenting, trying to see what would break us. How long it would take," Bunny said. "They also genuinely seemed to be confused by us, even afraid. We couldn't explain anything. Who we were. How we got here."

"I remember asking my interrogator 'why' for the hundredth time," Caroline said. "I now recall that he gave me an answer."

"What?"

"Practice."

"Which might have been true," Bunny said. "When we were determined not to be a threat, they gave us the implants and we became part of their society like the other humans who have the devices."

"This is crazy," Caroline said. "We have to get out of here."

"What do we do?" John said.

"I have an idea," Bunny said.

Bunny pointed to the small devices she'd removed from them.

"With these."

It was dangerous. They would be behind enemy lines. And if the Ruu found out . . . Two fliers would be all they would need to send. Bunny had seen one rip a man in two before. Their bodies had been so augmented for strength and power that they were almost invincible. The only weakness was a spot in their armor right below the chin. John had excellent aim, but she knew even he'd have a tough time making that mark.

But Bunny figured that if they tried to leave in the exact place they arrived, they'd have better luck returning to their home and not jumping to another dimension altogether. She'd studied how the Ruu were able to travel from one galaxy to the next. They had actually bent time and space, folded it in on itself, so to speak, so that they could travel faster than light. Her understanding of physics had been rudimentary compared to the Ruus', but she knew they, in essence, created a shortcut in the fabric of space and time. Bunny figured she could apply it to interdimensional travel. They had already come through once. She just had to open the space again.

The four of them stood around the table while Bunny explained the plan. They would leave the following night. If anything happened, they would split up, contact each other through the altered implant that Bunny would give them.

"You think it'll work?" John asked.

"It'll work," Bunny said, though she couldn't know for certain.

What if they didn't return to their original dimension? What if there were an infinite number of parallel dimensions that spun out from one another? What if they got trapped in some sort of two-dimensional reality? Or what if they each went to a different dimension? There was no way of knowing with 100 percent certainty what they'd be getting themselves into, or where they would end up. But they had to try. The risk was worth it.

"If we don't go now," Caroline said, "we may die here."

The others were silent for a moment. Then John spoke. "There's something we haven't discussed." He paused. "What if they follow us through?"

"We can't let that happen," Bunny said.

The Ruu could easily conquer their world—if they

discovered its existence. As far as Bunny knew, they didn't know about it. She intended to keep it that way.

"If this is a parallel world, one that has splintered off from ours, that means there are Ruu in our world," Teddy said. "They are in their galaxy and just haven't arrived yet."

They were all silent. Bunny hadn't thought about that. What if they returned home to discover it already burned and taken? This world just a preview of what was to come in their own.

"Even more important that we get back then," Bunny said. She saw her dad and brother running, a Ruu swooping overhead. She even pictured her mother, terror in her eyes. Before Bunny would have cared about her family, but now she also felt a sense of responsibility for them, given what she knew. It was that responsibility that would ultimately carry them home.

"Do you think there's something to the light I saw in the sky?" Teddy said. "It may be nothing, but it's been bothering me. What do you think it was?"

"Was it like when we saw the UFO back home?"

"Kind of. Yeah. What if our world is pressed up against this one somehow?" Teddy held the palms of his hands together to illustrate. "And there's a bleeding-through that's starting to happen?"

"I'm not following," Caroline said.

"When we saw the UFO back home on our Skywatch duty, we followed the light to the woods and found that it was a plane from this side. Somehow it crossed over. What if the light I saw the other day came from a plane or something from our dimension, from back in Monterey?"

"Like the space between the worlds is getting thinner?" Bunny said. "Maybe it has something to do with the Ruus' arrival."

"Or maybe the atom bomb," John said. "Weren't there more flying saucer sightings after World War II?"

There was no way to test the theory, but Bunny thought it could be plausible. After all, they were dealing with parallel dimensions and aliens—something she would have only thought of as science fiction before.

"Let's say we do find a way through," said Caroline. "What's to stop them from coming, too, like John said?"

"*We* are," Teddy said.

He looked around the room, setting his eyes on each of them. When he stopped at Bunny, her heart melted. Teddy's love had been the biggest surprise of all. It had happened in spite of the Ruu.

"There's a chance we could have temporary memory loss with crossing over. I'm not one hundred percent sure that I've calibrated it so we won't. And our brains are fragile. We have compartments and the need to make meaning. Too much trauma on the mind can have negative consequences."

"We'll remember," Teddy said. "And if we don't," he placed his hand on top of Bunny's, "you'll figure out a way."

"All right then," Caroline said. She took out a pair of latex gloves from her bag and held up a small surgical knife. "Let's get these things back inside us."

40

FRANK

....

WHEN BUNNY STARTED TELLING THEIR STORY, FRANK HAD STOOD with his arms crossed, a defensive position. He didn't know what she was going to say, but he figured it was going to be a tall tale. In fact, when she got to the part where giant winged aliens swooped down and captured them, he even looked around at the others to see if they were all in on the joke. Maybe he was on an episode of *Candid Camera*. But there were no hidden cameras. The more she spoke, the more he realized she was telling the truth.

"And once we were through," Bunny said, "the memory inhibitor was released again. So that's why we didn't remember. It was as if we never left. Except . . ."

"Except Teddy didn't make it back," John said.

"I saw him," Caroline said. She had left her bedroom during Bunny's explanation and leaned against the wall, listening. "In the end, right before we left. I don't know how many the Ruu sent after us, but he ran toward them, while we entered the shimmering light. *He's* the reason the rest of us made it back."

Her shoulders sagged and Frank thought he saw a hint of the scar on her face that she'd suffered during her first hours of interrogation. Looking at her now, Caroline seemed so incredibly fragile. Almost a shell of the girl he knew.

"He's alive," Bunny said. "That much we know."

"So," Frank began, "what you're telling me is that you went into the woods that night, found a downed aircraft of some sort, were transported to another dimension or reality where creepy evil aliens had invaded the Earth, lived there for seven years under alien mind control, and Teddy became a pilot, John some kind of a platoon leader, Caroline a doctor, and Bunny a scientist?" He stared into their faces. "That's—"

"Impossible," Bunny started to say, "I know, but—"

Frank held up his hand, cutting her off.

"But I know you guys. Well, not you so much, Bunny. But I know him." Frank pointed to John. "And there is no way that he would ever lie like this, or get into a street fight with some random guy. Or look at me with the serious expression he has now. So there's only one explanation. You're telling the truth," Frank said.

"And that means that aliens are real. I knew it!" Oscar grinned.

Frank almost couldn't believe how similar their experience had been to the mirror universe idea he had pitched earlier. Very different from how Einstein imagined it, but still. He'd have to read up on the theory. Maybe even make it a subplot in the story he was writing.

"I got a question, though," said Oscar. "If what you're saying is true, how come you guys aren't older? If you lived over there all that time?"

"That's confusing to me too," Bunny said. "It must have something to do with crossing between the realities and dimensions and coming from this place to begin with."

Frank didn't think that made much scientific sense, but he wasn't about to argue. This was uncharted territory.

"How we experienced time there wasn't the same as it is here," Bunny said. "There were still twenty-four hours to a day and all of that, but here hardly any time passed."

"Which means that for Teddy, he could have been there another seven years," Frank said.

"Yes, I suppose that's true," Bunny said and looked away.

If someone had told him yesterday that Bunny and Teddy would be together, Frank wouldn't have believed it. Bunny was so stuck-up. She barely even spoke to anyone. But she had changed. This Bunny now had conviction. She wasn't judgmental and was obviously willing to give her life for someone else. This Bunny, he was almost certain, he had never known.

"What about the Mandarin? How come you guys all speak it?"

"Even though it's still Earth, it's like a parallel one. History is different on the other side. Here, much of the world was colonized by the British. So many places speak English because of it. Over there, the Chinese were the ones that sent out explorers. They were the colonizers. They had different wars, too. The Ruu adapted the two most common human languages: Mandarin and English. We learned it through our implants."

"So there isn't even an America?"

"Nope."

"No Russia?"

"Oh, there's a Russia, but it isn't like this one. No atomic bomb. No technology. It's mainly open land used by the Ruu for agricultural purposes."

"But if parallel dimensions exist, couldn't there be a lot more out there that you *didn't* go to? What makes you think that you can reach that specific dimension again?" Oscar asked.

"Teddy makes it possible," Bunny said. She held up one of the implants. "He's still got this. I think we can use this device to open the portal. Even though Teddy's on the other side, we're still on the same frequency. We're connected, so the dimensions are connected."

"I don't know, Bunny," Caroline said.

"Caroline, you don't have to go," John said.

She was quiet. Frank understood a little of her conflict. If everything they said was true, he imagined the idea of having to return there would be too painful—and terrifying. He wasn't completely sure he was ready for the nightmare they described.

"I'm not making any promises," Caroline said. "But I'll see you through the woods."

"Good. Now, are we done talking?" Bunny said. "Because time isn't slowing down. We have no idea how long Teddy's been stuck there," Bunny said.

"She's right," said John. "We just need to get a few things first. Then tonight, when it's dark, we'll go. Frank, you all right to drive?"

Frank nodded, but he was far from sure.

Later, after night had set in and everyone had sneaked out of their homes, they met near John's house. John collected the rope, flashlights and batteries, knives, a canister of chicken noodle soup, and water, and put them all into a duffle bag.

"Why the soup?" Oscar asked.

"We don't know what condition Teddy will be in when we find him. He may need food," John said. He held out his hand for the last item. "Frank?"

Frank slowly removed his dad's gun from his glove compartment and gave it to John. John opened it and checked for bullets. He handled it as if he'd been around guns his whole life. "I've got a case of bullets in there too."

"Good," John said. He put the gun in his back pocket.

"Let's go."

They piled into Frank's car and headed for the tower.

After just a few minutes, a pair of headlights shone on them from behind.

"Who is it? Police?" Caroline asked.

"Shit. My dad's gonna kill me," Frank said, thinking about what he would do to him when he found out he had his gun.

"It's probably the car that's been tailing us from my house," John said. "My guess—Miller."

"Seriously? He's like one of those suits from the movies," Frank said. "Always on the case."

"We gotta move. Now," John said. "How fast can this thing go?"

"Fast," said Frank and Oscar in unison. They had put in a new engine a couple of months ago.

"Great. Lose him."

Frank put his foot on the gas and took off.

"Turn right," John said.

Frank strained to turn the wheel all the way in time. He swore he could feel the car lunge to the side and almost lift off the ground. He expected the girls to scream, but they didn't make a sound. Instead, it was Oscar who let out a high-pitched yell. Out of the corner of his eye, Frank saw him gripping the dash as if his life depended on it. He'd give him hell about it later, especially in front of the girls. Right now there wasn't any time for it.

"Left," John said.

Frank almost missed the turn.

"A little more warning next time!" he yelled.

"Eyes ahead, Frank, you're doing great."

"He's still there," Caroline said.

"Damn."

"I thought you said this car was fast."

"She is," said Oscar. "It's Frank's driving. If I was behind the wheel—"

"Not helping!" Frank said.

"Okay, cut the lights," said John.

Frank did as he was told.

"Up ahead there's an alley on the right."

"Where?" said Frank.

"Here!" John yelled.

Frank heard the tires peeling out on the asphalt. He wondered if he'd have any tires left after this.

A side alley connected a short group of homes. He pulled in and slammed on his brakes. They all turned to look in the rear window.

Miller's car raced past.

"Now what?" said Frank.

"We wait," John said.

They sat in silence, afraid to make a sound.

Frank wiped the sweat from his forehead.

After what felt like forever, John gave the green light. "Let's go. But keep your headlights off."

Frank obeyed, mystified at John's demeanor. He glanced sideways at John in the passenger seat. Gone was the soft-spoken pushover Frank once knew. John had been replaced by someone who acted like he was used to being in charge, someone who expected others to follow.

Frank backed slowly out of the alley and continued driving in the direction of the tower. There was no other car in sight, but his heart still raced from the adrenaline of the chase.

Or maybe it was at the thought of what he was driving into.

41

CAROLINE

THE NIGHT SKY BORE DOWN ON CAROLINE. IT WAS AS IF SHE COULD feel it growing, swelling in all directions. If she could just reach her finger high enough, she might be able to pop it. Then the stuff of the universe would come pouring out over them and wash them all away into nothingness.

The stars above mocked her. If she could only make everything still, she would expose what lay beyond the facade. The unknowable would be known. For she knew that on the other side of their world was something real—she had seen it. She had *been* there, wherever *there* was.

And she never wanted to go back.

But here she was on the edge of that strange dream she'd woken from. The nightmare that she had lived for years. She ran her hands along her cheek, feeling where the scar should be. The scar was inside of her now. Something tugged, like she was still attached to the other side. It pulled her back, and here she was, not even putting up a fight. They were all allowing it to happen, being drawn back over to that terrible place.

She hated the Ruu. First they had tortured her. Marked her.

They took away her past. Then they'd given her everything—a sense of purpose, a home, a life. But it hadn't been real. It hadn't been her own choosing. Even John. True, they hadn't forced her and John to marry. What they had shared was real. She knew that. He had loved her even when they were kids. But would she and John have been together if they had stayed in their own time and world? Would they have had Emily? Probably not.

Anger filled her.

The Ruu should have left her in the cell to rot. She would have preferred any bodily pain and isolation over the bottomless sorrow of losing Emily. That pain was greater than any physical harm could ever be.

Caroline had a sense of déjà vu as she looked at the sky. How naive she'd been when she thought she could actually help defend their country. That she could actually protect anyone. First her brother and then . . . Caroline couldn't even say her name. She shivered.

She heard the sound of wings beating and checked to see if anyone else had heard, but no one flinched. It was only in her mind. The longer she was home, the more she tried to reconcile her two lives.

The fact that in this world, none of it had even happened.

She reached down and felt her stomach. No life had ever been there.

But the name was just behind her lips. The creatures, just behind her eyes. She caged them both. But they pulsed there, trying to escape.

● ● ●

When they pulled up to the observation tower, Caroline noticed the lights were off upstairs. No one was on duty tonight. They were alone.

Caroline wished she could travel back to that night when this all began. Back to when she wanted to do her duty, be part of the club so it would look good on her application when it came time to apply to college, anything to give her an edge. If she could, she would tell herself that she would be fine without the club. She would be better off without the pain and the knowing.

That girl seemed so distant now.

She saw the ends of the yellow frayed ribbons whipping around the wooden rails of the stairs. The tape clung to the crime scene, even though no crime had been committed in it. The crime was in the woods. The crime was in another place.

"Okay," John said. "Ready?"

One by one they exited the car and walked toward the woods.

An owl hooted suddenly, and Caroline saw each of them look up, afraid.

John put his hand on her shoulder. Caroline didn't know if it was meant to comfort or restrain her. She didn't like either intent so she moved slightly and he removed it. He may have known her, but that was before and she didn't want to think about that time. She didn't want to think about him and her and the three of them.

"This place gives me the creeps," Frank said.

"Me too," said Oscar. "It's like something's watching us."

"And you think it'll be better in the woods?" Caroline asked.

They had no idea what threats were really out there, past the stars. Maybe even heading toward them now.

"At least the clearing is out in the open," Frank said.

"That's where they strike," Caroline said.

"Come on," John said. "Don't scare them."

"They *should* be scared, John," Caroline said. "We should *all* be scared. Can't you feel it? It's like we never broke free and they're calling us back." Caroline pulled Bunny's arm, causing her to stop. "The signal you saw—are you sure it's Teddy?"

Bunny paused for a second. The others stopped, too. "Yes," she said.

Bunny had been the one to sit with Caroline during her grief. To brush Caroline's hair in the days after, when she didn't have the energy or desire to care for herself. Caroline knew Bunny like a sister. Could read Bunny as well as she could herself. The flicker of doubt flashed just for a second across her eyes. But Caroline saw it. Just like she had seen John's pain earlier.

The eyes never lied.

She hoped Bunny and John knew what they were doing.

"We should keep moving," John said.

Bunny nodded and they continued walking toward the clearing.

Caroline prayed they'd return safely. With Teddy.

But she wouldn't go back. Not ever.

42

JOHN

THE DEEPER JOHN WALKED INTO THE WOODS, THROUGH THE DARK, tangled branches and undergrowth, the more his senses sharpened and focused. The fog of walking in a dream, clearing slowly like it did every day in the natural world around him. When Bunny had removed his device, he had felt the gray clinging in his brain, like it lingered in the treetops, but now it was being blown out to sea. His whole body felt alive, as if every single cell were singing and stretching and growing.

Even though Caroline wasn't walking alongside him, he felt her presence. He was as familiar with her as he was with his own body. He felt her fear and uncertainty the closer they got to the clearing.

Caroline still hadn't forgiven him. He doubted she ever would. But she hadn't been the one to dig their daughter's body out from the debris. In his arms, he had felt her leave him. The moment she moved from life to death.

Caroline had tried to resuscitate Emily for over forty minutes until he had to pry her away. Maybe she blamed him for that, too. If she only had more time, she could have found the breath. She could have brought their daughter back to life.

Even though he had seen many miraculous things, he'd never seen anyone raised from the dead. The Ruu weren't God. Later, when Teddy was home and when time didn't heal but at least made the carrying more bearable, John would talk to Caroline's stepdad. He would ask him questions about faith that he hadn't known how to ask before.

John stopped just before the clearing.

"It's there." He pointed up ahead. He removed the gun from the belt of his jeans and checked the bullets, even though he knew it was fully loaded.

"Is that really necessary?" Oscar asked.

John closed it back up.

"It won't kill them, if that's what you're worried about. But it might startle them. Slow them down."

"Maybe you should leave it back with us then," Oscar said. "What if one of them gets through?"

"They won't," Bunny said, but John heard the uncertainty in her voice.

If he had to, John would give his life to prevent that. He could do that now. Before, when he'd signed up to be a Skywatcher, he was embarrassed to admit, but it had mainly been about a girl. He wanted Caroline. Sure, he watched all the films about the danger Americans faced, but he didn't really understand it. Now, after seeing what a real enemy could do, how a whole way of life—no, how much of humanity—could be wiped out, he believed that he could make a difference.

John led them through the tree line that ran right up to the edge. The clearing was empty except for yellow tape that now marked a spot on the ground.

"You should stand back," Bunny said to Oscar and Frank. "I can already feel a shift in the energy. Our implants are working, triggering the portal."

"What are you talking about? We're coming with you," Frank said.

"No," Bunny said. "We can't risk it. We could lose you without an implant. Besides, it's dangerous over there. It's better if you're waiting for us on this side. Help us when we come back through. We don't know what kind of state Teddy will be in."

John hoped Bunny was right; if the device was only a link between the two realities, then traveling between them would be a given. But if it opened up other dimensions, too . . . well, there was no telling where they'd end up. John supposed he would find out.

"Caroline?" John said.

She moved and stood next to Oscar and Frank.

"I'm sorry," she said. "I just can't."

"It's okay," John said.

"No, it's not. It's not. Don't you dare say that." She broke and started sobbing. "Nothing will ever be okay again."

John felt the thickness in the air. He was torn between wanting to stay and comfort Caroline and also the pleading in Bunny's eyes. She needed him. Teddy needed him.

Before, he would have gone back for Teddy out of a sense of obligation. Now he chose to go back because Teddy was his brother. They'd been through too much for John to just leave him alone.

John clasped Bunny's hand. "Whatever happens, don't let go," he said.

The air began to wobble.

"What's happening?" Frank said.

A bluish-green hue surrounded John and Bunny. He braced himself for what was next.

"John!" He heard Caroline yell.

A force pulled Bunny from him, but he held on tight, almost yanking his arm out of its socket.

And then they were out of the dark and into the light.

John dropped to his knees, drawing Bunny down with him. He steadied his heart rate and breathing, practicing the techniques that his superiors had taught him. He smirked. That was something he could leverage. He had trained with the Ruu. Knew their strengths and weaknesses. He was dangerous.

John held a finger up to his lips. Bunny nodded. He glanced around. They were alone in the forest on the other side. It was still charred and barren. No sign of Teddy. They were targets out in the open. For all he knew a squad of fliers was heading their way.

"I've got a signal," Bunny whispered.

"Where?"

Bunny pointed in the direction of the coast.

"Okay, stay low," John said. "Keep close to me."

They crept along the blackened forest floor. John noted the areas of green—new growth that had started breaking through. Had that been there the first time they had come through? He couldn't remember. He hadn't exactly been looking too closely when he first crossed over years ago. In fact, he had no idea how much time had actually passed. But the green unnerved him.

Now, with every step, John became even more and more wary. But they were alone except for the sounds of birds.

"Let's head for the coastline," John said. "Before I left the insurgents had supposedly gone underground close to the sea. We had reports of a bunker not too far from here."

"The sea? Smart. The Ruus' fear of water will keep them from it."

"Exactly."

When they came to the coastline, John's hope fell. There was a structure, but from his vantage point it looked as if it had been damaged. He also saw the small Ruu flag flapping in the wind.

"How long have we been gone?" John wondered aloud.

"I'm not sure," Bunny said. "Shit. I lost the signal."

He recalled Caroline's words, her worry that the device's reading could just be a trap.

"Let's get closer." John made his way to the Bunker. The walls were crumbling, and from the markings on the remaining structure and ground, he could tell there had been a skirmish here. He found a hatch and opened it. A ladder descended deep below.

"I wonder if anyone is here," said Bunny.

John ripped the Ruu flag off the stand. "See this? This means it's been given the all clear. There are no rebels here. But there may be Ruu."

John's already tense body tightened even more at the

thought. He studied the perimeter, but he could see no threat. Experience told him to stay alert.

"I doubt it," Bunny said. "The chances of them being down here in the dark so close to the ocean are next to none."

"You never know. We need to be careful. I'll go first," John said.

He climbed down and Bunny followed after.

There was a light switch at the bottom, so he turned it on. Luckily, a soft light glowed down a long corridor. Four rooms splintered off from the main hallway. Three were empty. The original use a mystery, as there weren't beds or desks or anything. The fourth had a couple of cots, blankets, and some medical equipment. John picked up a surgical knife. Caroline would know what it was used for. John pocketed it, just in case he might need it. He also gave one to Bunny. Three backpacks rested against the wall. He wasted no time investigating their content. Inside each were canned food, first aid supplies, water bottles, and a map. John took the water bottle and drank. He offered it to Bunny as he opened one of the maps. It showed a meandering maze of tunnels and rooms.

"They did it," John said.

"What?" Bunny looked over his shoulder.

"The rebels. They built their underground network."

"You think that's here?"

"Or maybe . . ." John pointed at the large metal door at the end of the corridor. "There."

John tried to open it, but it would not budge. He put his ear up against it. Nothing.

"The Ruu suspected the insurgents went underground.

Maybe they found where the rebels were hiding and that's why this has all been abandoned? The flag marking it sure seems like they did."

"This place is creeping me out. Let's go back up."

When they'd climbed back up, out of the bunker, John looked up and down the coast.

"I should never have left him," Bunny said. "You should have let me stay."

Had Bunny blamed him all along? She didn't realize—he'd had no choice. "I couldn't. Teddy wouldn't let me."

"Is that what he said to you? He told you to get me through?"

"Yes. He said no matter what happened that I was to make sure you got home."

"Home?" Bunny said, turning away from him. "Home was with Teddy. And why the two of you felt like you could make a decision about me—*my* life, and what *I* want—is beyond me."

"I'm sorry, Bunny," John said. "You know how Teddy was when he made up his mind. He wouldn't even want us back here now. He'd want us to live our lives."

A tingling sensation ran from the back of John's neck up to his head.

"Bunny, we've got to get out of here."

She wiped her eyes. "I know."

"No, *now*," he said.

"Is someone coming?"

John held up his hand as if she were one of his men. She stopped speaking. He tilted his head. That's when he heard it.

Wings.

43
BUNNY

BUNNY RAN EVEN THOUGH SHE KNEW IT WAS POINTLESS TO TRY.
They were completely exposed. The flier would capture her in
seconds. But it was in her nature to try to escape. To try to live.
She would be tortured, possibly killed this time. Or worse, they
would erase everything again. She would lose her friends, her
love. If there was a way she could take herself out before it got
her, she would.

A large shadow blocked the sun. She didn't look up as she
ran. She didn't want to freeze in terror. The shadow moved over
her and then it grew larger as the creature descended.

The winged alien landed right in front of them in combat
uniform, making both her and John stop. He stepped in front of
Bunny. He held the gun in front of him, taking aim at the only
vulnerable spot on a Ruu—his neck. He also held the knife from
the underground bunker in his other hand.

What did he think he would do? Bunny thought. Fight the
thing if he didn't get the shot?

She wanted to stop him, but she also wanted to live.

She pulled out the knife John had given her.

She would fight too. They took Teddy; they might as well take her.

But the Ruu didn't move. He cocked his head to the side. If she didn't know what was inside the uniform, she might have thought it was a bird.

"What do we do?" Bunny whispered.

"Just wait," John said.

The Ruu studied them. Instead of lunging for them, the creature retracted its beautiful, enormous wings. The sunlight made the tips sparkle; she had to shield her eyes.

Then it spoke.

"Took you long enough," it said and removed the helmet.

What?

But Bunny didn't wait to ask. She ran to him.

Teddy picked her up and kissed her. He then reached out his hand to John, but John embraced him instead.

"How——?" John began to ask.

"Did you make it?" Teddy said. "Tell me you made it home."

"Yes. We did."

Bunny ran her hand from his chest to his back. The wings were folded and clearly attached to him. Before she'd left, she'd been involved in augmentation research and human trials to make this kind of transformation possible. But she hadn't succeeded. Now . . .

Her heart sank. *How long had they been gone?*

She looked at his face—the small lines that hadn't been there before. The little gray in his temple.

"How do you have Ruu wings?" Bunny asked.

"I volunteered for the human trials."

Bunny just stared in shock.

"Don't look at me like that. They weren't painful. Well, uncomfortable at first. But now . . ." Teddy's wings expanded to their full width. "They're a part of me. Where's Caroline?"

"She's back home," John said.

"I can't believe it," said Teddy. "So you all made it. How did everyone react? Did you just appear out of thin air? After missing all those years?"

They heard a sound just then and Teddy changed the subject. "We'll talk later. For now, we have to go. The Ruu are probably on their way already. No one's been in this area for years."

"Years?" Bunny asked.

"Ten since you left," Teddy said.

They'd been gone ten years?

"Oh, Teddy. How did you—"

"No time," he said. "Come on." He took her hand.

The three of them ran from the beach back toward the woods. Even though Teddy had those wings on his back, he seemed to run without a problem. She would have thought them heavy. But he ran like they were a part of him now, like he'd been born with them.

The questions she wanted to ask flooded her mind.

Why are you wearing the wings? What happened to you when we left? Where are all the others? What did you do all that time? Did you find another love?

But she forced them down, focused on putting one foot in front of the other. They would have plenty of time for questions and answers once they were through to the other side. They would have more time for each other.

They were almost at the space in the clearing when she heard them. Coming in fast. This time she glanced back and counted three. There was no way they could fight them off.

She activated their devices.

"Where is it?" John yelled.

"There!" Bunny pointed to the spot that was already beginning to shimmer.

She ran as fast as she could, but she wasn't fast enough. John was almost there, just a little ahead of them.

"Go!" she yelled at Teddy.

Instead of leaving her, he picked her up, and suddenly she was hovering above the ground. He moved with tremendous speed, crashing into John and hurling them through the liquid air.

IF FRANK HADN'T SEEN IT, HE WOULDN'T HAVE BELIEVED IT TO BE true. One moment John and Bunny were standing there, the next they were gone. His heart raced and he felt a little sick to his stomach. It was one thing to have faith in the things not of this world, it was another thing to actually see something out of this world happen.

Frank waited to see if they would pop back out, but they didn't. He walked near the spot where they disappeared. Oscar followed him. The portal that Bunny had opened now seemed closed, but they didn't want to chance being sucked into it. He stopped short when he noticed the hairs on his arms stood up as if there was some kind of electrical current that now ran through the air. They did the same on Oscar's arm.

"They're really gone," Frank said.

"I should have gone with them," Caroline said. "John . . . if anything happens to him. I . . ." She looked at Frank and then away. He saw her wipe tears.

"He'll be okay," Frank said.

"You don't know that." She sat down on a stump.

Frank wanted to ask her about John and them getting married and her child, but he thought she might get more upset. Even with what he'd seen, he still had trouble wrapping his mind around parts of their story. How could they really have been gone for that long? And how was it possible that they'd had entirely different, full lives?

Caroline put her head on her arms. It looked to Frank like she was giving up.

"What're you doing?" he asked.

"We don't know how long they'll be gone," Caroline said.

"So we're just going to wait? Do nothing?"

"Unless you two have a better idea."

Frank kept walking around the area. It was impossible. People didn't just get swallowed up.

"We should have brought food."

"I have Oreos," Oscar said.

Caroline held out her hand for one. Oscar tossed her the box. Frank kept his eyes on the air where John and Bunny had disappeared. He heard her open the box, take out a cookie, and crunch it in her mouth.

"Where did they go?" Frank asked.

"You really weren't listening earlier, were you?"

"I was, but I—"

"What—you didn't believe us?"

"No," Frank said. "Yes. What I mean is, how do we know they went to the same place?"

"We don't. We can't really know anything until they get back," she said. "Want one?"

She held out a cookie. Frank walked over to her, grabbed

the Oreo, and sat down on Caroline's left. Oscar sat on the other side. The three of them ate cookies and watched the air. Gone was any indication that anything had ever happened. The air was just air. No color. No shimmer. No wobbling. It was just maybe a little thinner, as if it was a higher altitude.

Suddenly inspired, Frank removed a notebook from Oscar's bag that he had thrown in earlier and began to write. He didn't want to forget any of the details. In the end, if all he had from this was a great story that would finally get him published, that was still something.

"What're you writing?" Caroline asked.

"He's working on his stories," Oscar said.

"I didn't know you wrote."

Frank shrugged. "I just mess around."

"He's going to be published one day."

"Oscar. Cool it." He preferred his writing aspirations be kept under wraps.

"Can I read something?" Caroline asked.

Frank hesitated, but since she was asking so nicely, he turned to an early page, one where he'd written about a man waking up on a mysterious planet.

"This is good," she said, and handed him back the notebook. "Wow. I had no idea."

"I don't broadcast it or anything," Frank said. "But yeah, writing is awesome. The club has been cool, too, because studying astronomy helps gives me ideas for stories sometimes. I really want to be an astronomer."

Caroline nodded.

Whether she wanted to hear more or just longed for a

distraction from worrying about John, Frank wasn't sure, but he accepted the invitation and continued. "Did you know there's credible evidence that what's inside our atoms is what's inside the core of massive stars? They're elements heavier than hydrogen, and when they go through thermo-nuclear fusion, they explode, and their insides travel through the universe." Frank looked up at the stars. "It's crazy to believe, but we share an imprint that's traceable to the origins of the cosmos."

Caroline and Oscar followed his gaze.

"What makes you want to be an astronomer?" she asked.

Frank thought about it. He could give many answers, but the most simple was, "I want to know what's out there."

They sat and watched the sky in silence for a few moments.

"Listen," Caroline finally said. "I know we haven't always gotten along, but I really do appreciate you helping us. Thank you."

Frank marveled again at how different this Caroline seemed.

"You're welcome."

"You too, Oscar," Caroline said.

Oscar held out his hand and Caroline smirked, but she shook it.

Just then a change in the air made Frank turn to the spot where Bunny and John had disappeared earlier.

"Do you guys feel that?" he said.

They all rose to their feet as the air moved again. It rolled like liquid and started to change color.

"They're coming back!" Caroline said.

Frank heard them before he saw them. Yelling. Screaming.

And a deafening sound of something speeding toward them. Was that the whooshing of wings?

"Move!" John yelled as he tumbled through. Some winged thing had Bunny in its grasp at the same time it tackled John.

Frank didn't stand around to wait and see what was chasing them. He took off running along with Oscar and Caroline. They bolted out of the clearing, each hiding behind a tree, when, as if it had been cut off by a knife, the speeding sound instantly stopped and all was quiet again. Except for the heavy breathing.

"What have they done?" Caroline said, her voice a whisper. Frank heard Caroline but he couldn't see her from where he hid. "It's here!"

"Can you see anything?" Frank asked Oscar.

Oscar shook his head, unable to speak. Frank steeled himself and peeked around the tree. The three bodies were in a heap. The winged creature was on top of them. He heard groaning.

"It's going to eat them," Oscar said.

"The Ruu don't eat people," Caroline said. "But it will kill them."

"What do we do?"

She held a finger up to her lips.

Frank listened, waited for their screams. But none came.

"Something's off," she said, and she came out from her hiding place.

"Wait," Frank said. "We don't know—"

"John!" Caroline called.

"We're all right!" he shouted back.

Frank looked at Oscar and nodded. They stepped out at the

same time. Bunny and John were getting to their feet. So was the winged creature. Frank braced himself for what the creature might do, but Caroline ran up and hugged it.

"Teddy!" she cried.

Caroline, John, Teddy, and Bunny took turns embracing. For a moment, Frank felt shy, as if he were watching a family reunion that he wasn't a part of. He and Oscar stood a few paces away.

"Caroline, your face." Teddy pulled away.

"You didn't tell him?" Caroline said to Bunny.

"There wasn't much time to talk."

"Tell me what?" Teddy asked.

"Time. It works differently over there than it does here. While we were gone for years, it's only been days here."

"Really?" Teddy's face had a look of confusion and pain. "How is that possible?"

"I know, it's a lot. It's going to take some time to process. We just recently regained our own memories."

"So, you're saying I'm seventeen again?"

"We all are," John said.

"What does that mean?"

Frank only half listened to their conversation, he was too focused on the wings Teddy had sprouted.

"Welcome back, Teddy. But, umm, how do you have wings?" Frank asked.

"Hey, Frank. Oscar," Teddy said. "Man, it's good to see you guys again."

To Frank's surprise, he pulled both of them in for a hug. Teddy wore a type of red jumpsuit that was hard like armor.

Frank touched his wings—a kind of multicolored metal. He wondered if it was aluminum—the stuff that astronauts were using in space.

"Is this what the Ruu wear?" he asked.

"Only their fliers," Teddy said. "For years we thought it was genetic, but it's actually part of their biotechnology."

Biotechnology?

"Here, help me."

Teddy got down on his knees as he showed them how to remove the wings. They were surprisingly light for being so big. They slid out of two holes in Teddy's body, right at the top of his shoulder blades.

"How do you get them to move?"

"I control them with my mind," Teddy said. "It's like having another limb. I don't even have to think about it."

"I can't believe they did this to you," Bunny said.

Bunny stared at him and the air became charged again. This time, with something different. With possibility. Frank could feel the connection between Bunny and Teddy. And with Caroline and John, who were now holding each other.

"It'll be light soon," Frank said, uncomfortable again.

"What do we tell people? Now that Teddy's back," Caroline said.

"How about the truth?" Oscar said.

"And risk being experimented on by the government?" Bunny said. "Or worse, the technology gets in the wrong hands? Just imagine what the Russians would do if they could access other dimensions."

"Or what our own government would do," Teddy said.

They were quiet.

"Frank's the storyteller," Caroline said. "What do you think?"

At first he thought they were going to tease him, like they normally did. Teddy would make some joke or Bunny would brush him off. But they looked at him expectantly, like he would have a good idea. Like he was part of their group and they needed him.

"Give me a sec."

Frank thought about all of it. How this all started from watching the light in the sky. He thought about how they had been a group of strangers that were now friends. He thought about how there was so much in the universe that he didn't yet know. The thought made him excited about the future, not fearful. Whatever happened, he was part of something bigger than himself, and he wasn't alone.

"Okay," he said. "This is what I think we should say."

45
CAROLINE

BY THE TIME CAROLINE RETURNED HOME IT WAS EARLY MORNING.
Her mother was already out back, standing in front of a blank canvas. A faded quilt covered her shoulders against the cold. The mist seeped through the beams of the wooden fence, hovered on the ground, making it seem like she had floated out of a dream.

Caroline heated some water on the stove.

She heard Charlie's padded steps down the hallway before he entered the kitchen.

"Did I hear you come through the front door?"

Caroline appraised him—disheveled hair, dark robe, and slippers. He looked like he hadn't had a true sleep in ages.

"I was up early," she lied. "Went for a walk."

"Oh." He stood at the window, overlooking the backyard.

The kettle sounded and Caroline prepared tea for her and her mother. Charlie preferred coffee, so she didn't offer him a cup. But she did place her hand on his arm.

"You're going to be okay," she told him.

He looked at her funny. "Isn't that what I'm supposed to be saying to you?"

"Maybe." She shrugged. "But you need to hear it, too, sometimes."

She saw him then as he really was—a sad man, hopeful, but not happy. As long as he was looking to her mother's wellness as a source of his happiness, he'd never attain it. "You know, Charlie, maybe you should take a trip. Go on one of those retreats you used to take before. Listen to what God has to say to you." She didn't say before Jack, though that's what she meant. "You used to come home from those so inspired."

Charlie removed the coffee grinds from the cupboard. "Maybe I will."

Caroline left him in the kitchen to prepare his coffee and went outside.

"Hey, Mom," she said.

If her mother heard her, she didn't give any indication. She continued to paint in tiny strokes what Caroline knew would eventually turn into the right eye of her brother.

She set the tea down and pulled up a chair next to her mother. She reached out and pulled up some of the quilt that had fallen off one of her mother's shoulders. The quilt wasn't really soft anymore. Caroline wondered the last time it had been washed, probably more than a year ago. She remembered her mother making it. Working on it at night while they watched *I Love Lucy*. She was certain the baby was going to be a girl, so she chose pink and green and tan as the primary colors. When she had a boy, she kept it anyway.

"Mom, when's the last time you did your hair?"

"What?"

"Your hair?"

Her mother frowned. "I must have done it yesterday. Or maybe the day before? I don't know Caroline. I've been very focused on my work."

She continued to paint the eye. It was uncanny how she had perfected it over the past year. It could almost pass for the real thing.

"Let me do it for you?"

Her mom shrugged. It was the okay Caroline needed. She went in the house and came back out with a brush to tend to her mother's hair. Carefully, so as not to hurt her, Caroline undid the large bun her mother wore, allowing her light brown hair to fall past her shoulders. She hadn't done much with it in a while, so there wasn't much style. And it was a lot grayer than Caroline had remembered as well. Though there was a lot about her mother and her life before that she didn't fully remember—kind of like all she had to go on was an outline of an image. The rest was fuzzy; she was just now beginning to color it in.

Her mother continued to paint as Caroline brushed.

"You know, Mom," Caroline started, but she stopped herself. What was there, really, to say?

She thought of her own loss. Of how all she'd wanted to do was stay in bed, but she couldn't. Her patients had needed her. How she had never really properly grieved the death of her own child. Her Emily. Caroline could feel it, the moment she was taken from her. She'd been at the hospital, when she felt a sense of deep cold. Emily flashed in her mind. She ran from the building, there was smoke in the air from where the bomb had gone off. Ignoring any sense of danger, Caroline had run toward it. She ran toward her baby's death.

Caroline had held her and kissed her closed eyelids until, finally, John pried her hands free. He took Emily from her. She had screamed after him. Her clothes full of their baby's blood.

Caroline understood now why her mother had all but disappeared after Jack's death. Caroline had been on the edge herself, but her work at the hospital brought her back. If she didn't have that . . . she might have ended up stuck, lost in limbo like her mother. It wasn't natural for a parent to outlive their child.

Being back, she didn't know what was worse: living a life in which Emily never existed, or that fact that Emily had lived and was taken from her entirely too soon. Either way, Caroline was alone.

How could she go on? How could she survive without being able to talk about her? But in that moment, looking at her mother's newest portrait of Jack, breathing in the open air together, Caroline finally understood something. She wasn't the only one who'd lost something. John had, too. He was the only other person who could truly share her pain. She'd been such a fool, too selfish in her own anguish to even allow for his. Her pushing him away had made it worse for the two of them. She realized that now. She also knew that she still loved him because even here with her unknowable future, the one thing she was certain of was that she wanted John in it.

She only hoped it wasn't too late.

Her mother had needed to find a reason to live. Right now that reason was getting up and painting the same images every day. She might never fully make it back from the edge. So Caroline said the only thing she could.

"I love you, Mom."

Her mother stopped for a moment. Her brush extended in midair.

"I love you too, sweetie," she said, and resumed painting.

They both brushed—Caroline, hair, and her mother, the canvas. The light whooshing sound like a call-and-response. After a while, Caroline didn't know who was calling to who, but it didn't matter. She was in the answer.

46
TEDDY

FOR YEARS TEDDY HAD DREAMED OF COMING HOME. IMAGINED HOW his parents were getting along without him. How his life would be so different if only he had stayed. He had longed for home like a pilgrim, oftentimes praying to Saint Peter for the opportunity. He'd kiss the silver medal he wore around his neck. His nostalgia-laced dreams skewed his perception of what life would be like when he returned.

He had expected a hero's welcome. Or at least a man's.

Here, however, he was still a boy.

Nowhere was this more evident than at home. His parents, overjoyed at his return after two weeks, now hovered about him, even his dad. He couldn't blame them. Their son had returned from the dead. It was a miracle, especially considering he'd barely escaped with his life.

At first Frank's idea of him being kidnapped and tortured by a strange, black magic religious cult seemed a bit out there, but people bought it hook, line, and sinker. How else could the doctor explain the strange markings, the deep holes in his upper shoulder blades? The fact that Teddy had been missing longer than the others? The cult was gone now, back into the recesses of Los Angeles or the middle of the country or wherever cults go back to. They couldn't say. The members had worn balaclavas the whole time. Given them funny-smelling drugs that altered their memories and sense of time.

Teddy had to admit, Frank was a genius.

The sheriff didn't want word to get out that a cult had infiltrated his town and kidnapped its children, so he kept it all pretty hush. Nothing quite like saying the words *cult* and *Satan* to crush the tourism industry of a beachside town.

Dr. Miller was the only one who didn't seem to believe their tale.

"Teddy," he'd said the day he interviewed him. "Would you mind repeating the part for me about how the cult leader—" He looked at his notes. "Benjamin was his name? How did he let you go again?"

Teddy knew Miller was trying to break him. That he had his doubts. Dr. Miller was around the same age Teddy had been when he left the other side. But Teddy suspected he had seen and done more than Dr. Miller would ever experience. He had to keep his cool, though—act like a respectable seventeen-year-old boy—but he was getting tired of the pretense.

"Listen, Dr. Miller, right?" Teddy said, even though he obviously knew his name. If Miller was going to play a game, then he would, too. Teddy grabbed a cigarette from the pack of Lucky Strikes on the table. "I'm not going to repeat myself because no matter how many times I do, it's still not going to satisfy that nagging thought at the back of your brain."

Dr. Miller smirked and sat back.

"And what is that?"

"That in the end, you'll never know what happened. I could say cults. I could say Russians. I could say spheres and extra-terrestrials. I could even say time travel. But all of it is moot." Teddy put a cigarette in his mouth and lit it. "You weren't there. You didn't see. You only came after."

Teddy blew a long plume of smoke in the air between them.

Dr. Miller just looked at Teddy.

The guy was a bit uptight, but in another world, another time, maybe they could have been friends. Dr. Miller would have been useful on the other side. Here, his kind was just starting; over there, he was a relic. There, there were no men walking around in fancy suits, taking the time and care to ask questions. There was no slow, investigative process. There was only the now, the immediacy because it all came down to the fact that the world could end at any moment. In actuality, once the Ruu came, one could argue that it already had. Humanity's way of life had changed forever. Teddy wanted to make sure that didn't happen here.

Teddy would join the Air Force like he planned to after he graduated. It killed him a little that he'd have to go through basic training and all of the rudimentary flight school simulations and drills. Maybe he'd figure out a way to bypass some of it. But he'd have to be careful. He wouldn't want to stand out too much.

He wondered if he could convince Bunny to join him. He'd spent years without her, he didn't want to lose her again. But they didn't have to make any decisions yet. They had their whole senior year. It seemed frivolous to Teddy to become an

American high school student again and play basketball and go to prom when he felt the fate of the world on his shoulders. But Bunny reminded him that he wasn't alone. They had each other. They had their friends and they would face each day as it came.

Teddy knew she wanted to know about his life after he was left behind. He'd eventually have to tell her about what he did for the Ruu. He wasn't proud of it. Surviving had come with a cost. She didn't need to know everything. It would cause her unnecessary pain to know some of his history. But he didn't want to just yet. He'd rather focus on the future than the past.

After the interview Teddy's dad embraced him as soon as he got in the car. He did that now, more than before. Teddy leaned into it each time, knowing a lifetime without it. His dad's hands were large and rough from years of a life at sea. Wrinkles cushioned his eyes and mouth. He knew now that he looked like his dad. In a few years, he'd look even more like him.

"Ready to go home?"

"You bet," Teddy said.

47

JOHN

THE SUIT PROTECTED JOHN'S BODY AGAINST THE COLD WATER, BUT his hands, now red and stiff, bore the brunt of it. He worked steadily with his father in the early morning hours. They'd found a good harvest, rare for them. Even though abalone still fetched a great price, his father told him it was time to give up the business. He was meeting with someone later in the day. He didn't want to become like the other Japanese—leaving the central coast for the north. John knew the rugged coastline with the forest and the fog reminded both his parents of their home in Japan. John had overheard their discussion last night—his mother had been forced to leave once. She wouldn't go again.

Orchids was where the money was going to be, his father thought. There was a large interest in orchids among Americans, especially Caucasians. His plan was to start growing them like his second cousin did over in the valley.

John contended that he may be right, but John wouldn't follow his footsteps. He didn't want to work in a nursery. His father's hands, strong and calloused from years of water and shells and fish, would be perfectly suited for the work.

John looked at his hands, the tips of his fingers shriveled from being in the water. He knew what his hands were capable of now. And they were not for growing. They were for tearing down, making right. They were for protecting and fighting. They were not rough with wear like they would be in his future. Or like they had been in the past. It was too confusing to think about where and who he had been.

In a way, he'd been given a gift. They all had. They could start over. Create the lives they wanted here. Not one that had been forced upon them. Although . . . not all of it had been forced. John caught an image of Caroline—a bouquet of wildflowers in her hand, hair swept back, beautiful dress. Their wedding day. Next to the birth of Emily, it had been his favorite day. The Ruu may have erased the memories of who they were, but they didn't control who they had become. They didn't force John to fall in love with Caroline. They didn't force Bunny and Teddy or the friendship among the four of them either. Maybe it had been their subconscious drawing them together. Or maybe it was something more profound—something spiritual, like love.

John had seen love within the Ruu family units as well. How taking care of their children wasn't some innate animal instinct, but was motivated out of genuine affection and care, same as humans.

Love existed on both sides. It's what united them. It seemed to be the constant.

But so were fear and pain, even if the Ruu had found a way to avoid the latter. The Ruu may have felt that they were evolving in the most efficient way with their implants, becoming better without suffering. But John realized in coming back that as difficult as it was to endure pain of any kind, not doing so was the greater weakness. Because feeling pain was the only way to appreciate pure joy.

Over there, he'd had his own family. Even though, in this world, he had lost that, the love was still there. A love that had been real. And so the sense of loss he carried was something he couldn't ignore and didn't want to—to do that would be an erasure of not only who he had become, but the acknowledgment of the life he had built.

The night they rescued Teddy, they decided it would be the best to return to normal, to do the things they did before they left. Normal for John was baseball.

After finishing baseball practice one day, John drove his dad's truck past Caroline's house. He slowed it down, hoping she'd see him and come outside. They hadn't had a proper conversation alone since Teddy came home. A shyness wrapped itself around John now. He recognized it right away. It was the awkwardness he'd felt as a youth. One he shed in manhood. But it embraced him again now that he was home, and he couldn't shake it. It was the double consciousness, he supposed, for he was wholly John at seventeen and John at twenty-four at once.

In another place, in another time, he would stop the car, walk up to the door, and knock. When she answered, he'd kiss her like he'd done a thousand times before.

But now. In this place and time—his hands were weak. They didn't have the scars they would wear in the future.

He was only a boy.

John sped up when he was clear of her house. He drove home, greeted his mom who was giving piano lessons to a neighbor girl. Later he would play for her. It was interesting to him that he had turned to piano in the other place. He saw it as proof that he had missed home. That he had missed his family. Even though his memories had been suppressed, his subconscious had known.

Gary walked into the kitchen then, two paddles in his hands.

"Wanna play?" he asked John.

Gary had been obsessed with table tennis ever since earlier that year when the Japanese team had won the championship. He was working to become a great American player.

"Sure," said John.

John followed Gary to the garage. He wasn't very good at first, but little by little, he'd started to get the hang of it with Gary's coaching. He supposed this was how it would be for a while. He would relearn his place in the family. He'd try not to think about Caroline. They would find their way back to each other. He really believed that. Just as the loss of their child had torn them apart in their future, he knew that it would bind them together as well.

As they played, Gary watched the ball with complete concentration. And in a moment, John saw his daughter's face. Emily had made the same expression—furrowed brows, tip of the tongue out—when she was concentrating hard.

John missed the ball.

"Point," Gary called as he ran after it. "You okay?"

"Yeah," John said. "Don't think you have to go easy on me."

"You can tell?"

"I know you're not left-handed," said John.

Gary grinned and switched the paddle to his right hand.

"You asked for it."

Gary served the ball and John returned it. John kept his eyes on his brother's face, so much like his daughter's, and he did not lose.

48

BUNNY

....

BUNNY STOOD IN HER ROOM. SHE WALKED OVER TO HER BULLETIN board dedicated to Ada Lovelace and touched her face.

"You would have liked it over there. The things I've done and seen . . ."

Technology here was archaic compared to what she had been exposed to on the other side. She would have to figure out what role she would play in this world. Whatever she decided, she'd have to go slow, be careful not to "discover" too much at once. She would never want to draw suspicion her way.

After she graduated high school, Bunny still planned to go to the Jet Propulsion Laboratory in Pasadena. They were the only ones remotely close to space exploration. She could help them speed up their process. In no time, they'd be sending more than rockets into space.

She had started reading physics journals to see who would be the first to propose the idea of a parallel universe or realities in quantum physics. One article mentioned a scientist's lecture in Dublin that offered a theory of other realms, but the scientific community was still years away from accepting the theory as any kind of possibility. If they would even accept it at all.

If the wrong people discovered either side, or found their way through to this world, it could be disastrous. The amount of power and influence that having access to a parallel universe and its technology could bring, especially because of how advanced the other side was would be catastrophic. In the wrong hands, her world would be altered forever.

She removed the newspaper ad for a computer program-mer from the board, just under Ada's profile. It was an elementary job, basically a human calculator, but as a woman, this would be her entry point. It certainly wouldn't be where she ended up.

"But it's a start, Ada. It's a start."

She looked at the poster on her wall, then flopped onto her bed, and picked up the Agatha Christie book she'd pulled from the shelf. She opened to the first page.

"Oh, how I've missed you."

Later that night, Bunny stood with the others at the edge of the ocean, watching the surf crash on the rocks.

Tomorrow was the first day of school. Their senior year. Bunny was dreading it like the others. She struggled to imag-ine sitting in classes day after day given all that she now knew. The agony of having to listen to rudimentary material being explained over and over, watered down for the masses. It seemed so pointless. There was important work to be done.

"You think the Ruu will figure out what happened?"

Caroline asked. "This is twice now that they've seen humans disappear into thin air."

Bunny had been running the possibility in her mind. "I'm hoping they'll think we jumped to another galaxy. Since I used their same tech for that."

"Hopefully they'll focus on taking over the whole planet and won't have time to wonder how a couple of people vanished before their eyes."

"And if the Resistance is doing their job, they'll be busy," Teddy said. "They made a lot of progress in the years you were gone."

Bunny felt a tightness in her chest. Teddy had been trapped there another ten years after they'd left. They still hadn't talked through all that he had experienced. All that he suffered. Alone. She reached for his hand, hoping that he understood he wasn't alone now.

"Do you think they've done it by now? Wiped out all of humanity?"

"No," Teddy said. "There's whole underground communities now. Not just where we were, but supposedly they exist all over the globe."

"So humanity has a chance," John said.

They looked at one another and smiled.

"There's one thing that's still bothering me," Frank said. "I understand the concept of the thin space out in the woods, though that is usually reserved for myth and folklore, but seeing the UFO in the sky . . . it broke through to our world before landing. We all saw it. Of course, there have always been sightings of strange, unexplained things in the sky—due to all kinds of things—falling stars, birds, natural phenomena. But the frequency and type of UFO we saw didn't start until the 1940s. Do you think it could have something to do with the atomic bomb? What if that accidentally opened up a connection or a bleeding through between the dimensions?"

"Do you think that means the Ruu have already found a way through?" Caroline asked.

"If they did, I don't think they'd be quiet about it," Teddy said. "Or that they would just appear to random people out in a cornfield in the middle of nowhere. But the Ruu are out there. It's just a matter of time."

Bunny had come to think of what had happened to her as destiny. Something beyond her control had orchestrated it. Her journey to the other side had been full of pain, even torture in the beginning, but also the beautiful truth that she belonged to others and they to her. She had found love and acceptance. She could face anything with that truth.

Bunny extended her hands, one to Teddy and the other to Caroline until they all linked hands, even Frank and Oscar, becoming a semicircle.

Frank chuckled.

"What's funny?" Caroline asked him.

"We started off as Skywatchers, thinking Russians and the atomic bomb were the threat. Never thought the threat would be aliens."

"No, but you're right," Bunny said. "We're still Skywatchers. Now even more of a first line of defense."

"We can set up a rotation," John said.

"In the tower?" Caroline said.

"Sure. We can keep our eyes on this area, and we know the portal is accessible here."

"We should also listen," Bunny said. "Radio signals. That's how we'll find the Ruu and anything else coming from space."

"I'm in," Oscar said.

"Me too," said Frank.

John, Teddy, and Caroline didn't have to say anything. They were in it for good. Just like Bunny.

Strange how at first all she'd wanted to do was leave this place. Now she felt a calling to it. She was truly home.

They all tilted their heads toward the sky as if they could see it—the Ruu ship breaking through the atmosphere. But the black sky was thick with stars. The moon, however, only a sliver. Beyond that, it was hard to see.

Bunny stared at one of the stars long and hard until it began to expand and then explode in her mind's eye. She followed the light, as it traveled across time and space and dimensions, to where it eventually reached the six of them.

AUTHOR'S NOTE

I've always been fascinated with UFOs. As a little kid, I was mesmerized by *Close Encounters of the Third Kind*, often finding myself looking up into the night sky and wondering *what if?* Though I have seen strange lights in the sky, I don't think I have ever officially seen a UFO. It doesn't mean I'm not still looking.

The idea for this book came to me a few years ago. On a trip to a local bookstore, I found *The Close Encounters Man* by Mark O'Connell, which is about Dr. J. Allen Hynek, astronomer and ufologist and the U.S. Air Force's expert on UFOs for almost twenty years. While reading, I came across a chapter that mentioned the Ground Observer Corps.

The Ground Observer Corps, later called Operation Skywatch beginning in 1952, operated between the years 1950 and 1959. Because there was no radar to warn the country about hostile aircraft, the United States government called on its citizens to stand guard on towers and rooftops to watch the skies for possible enemies. President Harry S. Truman himself delivered an address appealing to the public, saying, "Every citizen who cooperates in Operation Skywatch, as well as in other defense activities, is helping prevent the war none of us wants to happen."

Volunteers of all ages, armed only with binoculars, scanned the skies and phoned in anything they saw to filter centers, mainly staffed by Women's Army Corps volunteers. Maybe because more eyes were skyward than usual, reports of silver discs, flying saucers, and blips flooded the centers.

Chalk it up to the growing fear and tension of the Cold War. Chalk it up to some great conspiracy that the government was hiding from that crash in Roswell, New Mexico. Chalk it up to the influence of the science-fiction movie boom on the collective American consciousness post-WWII. Whatever it was, the evidence was clear—people were seeing things that they could not explain. And this both scared and excited them.

The Cold War eventually ended. Technology advanced and there is now no longer a need for human volunteers to watch the skies. However, there are groups all over the country, amateur and professional ufologists who meet and debate and search for answers.

Have aliens been visiting our planet for years? Are there parallel universes bleeding into ours? I don't know. But I'm open to the possibility. I'm still asking—*what if*?

ACKNOWLEDGMENTS

Thank you to my high school drama class, who listened and helped me think through some of the story bits early on.

Thank you to Greg Kawai, not just for lending me your last name, but for your encouragement, friendship, and expertise.

Thank you to Kerry Sparks, who has always championed and believed.

Thank you to Eric Reid, who made new dreams happen.

Thank you to Liza Kaplan—you make me better.

Thank you to the whole team at Philomel, specifically Cheryl Eissing, Talia Benamy, Marinda Valenti, Maddy Newquist, Kristie Radwilowicz, Theresa Evangelista, Marie Bergeron, Felicity Vallence, and Kaitlin Kneafsey.

Thank you to my family, whose love and support means everything.

Thank you to my readers. I hope you enjoyed the ride!